DISPERSION

PART TWO OF THE SPECIOUS SERIES

ROBIN BERKSTRESSER

Book cover design by The Book Design House www.thebookdesignhouse.com

Dispersion/Robin Berkstresser–1st edition

For Printed Copies ISBN 10: 0692082417 13: 978-0692082416

Dedication

To my dad. He felt left out on the last one.

C O N T E N T S :

Acknowledgements

I probably should start out thanking everyone for waiting (some more patiently than others) for the second part of the story to come out. Hopefully this buys me a bit of time before ya'll start harassing me for the third book!

Once again, thank you to my mom for being the first and last eyes on this story. I also am extremely appreciative for all of the feedback from Emma and Jessica. The three of you saw an embarrassingly rough first version and somehow still stuck with me.

And, of course, thank goodness for everyone at KM Editorial. Katie McCoach, I'll never be able to put into words how grateful I am to have found you.

PART ONE

CHAPTER ONE

I flinch at the rotting smell lingering in the living room, waiting for it to get worse, and swallow down the pit of anxiety that refuses to leave. Down the hallway is the room where it all started. I sacrificed so much in the vain hope this might work.

The sheets I placed in front of the door remain in the same position. For the first time since we left Potentia, I address my older brother. "I don't know what state Matt's going to be in."

Dominic's eyes don't leave mine. "As long as he is still tied up like you said, it will be easy enough." He pulls out his medical bag and rummages through it.

Allison bites her nails, chest frantically heaving. When I catch her eye, she stops her nervous chewing. Beside her, Jess stares blankly at the sheets, nose still at an awkward angle. The bruising around her eyes somehow makes her appear even more haunted. Her sharp features are relaxed in a vague expression.

I was wrong. That room isn't where it all began. It's where everything fell apart.

Without thinking, I take a step forward. Jess flinches away and lowers her eyes. I bite my tongue. This is all my fault.

Dominic speaks calmly. "The two of us will go in first to make sure he is properly secured."

"I need to go in there with you," Allison says, pushing her unruly red hair out of her face.

Before Dominic can respond, I say, "As soon as we make sure it's safe for you to go in there, I'll let you know. We don't want you to put the baby in danger."

Allison looks down at her stomach, nodding reluctantly.

Dominic tests the feel of the syringe before returning his steady gaze to mine. "No time like the present, Joe. You take the lead."

I force myself not to react to his cruel nickname. We need him to cooperate. I take a big step forward to remove the sheets from the cracks and toss them away carelessly. I pull the door open, my sweaty palms forcing me to tighten my grip.

We lost so much for the possibility of getting Matt back. He has to get better. How else can I justify what's happened to us this past month? If this doesn't work, how could I ever look at Jess again?

Matt must come back to us. There's no other option.

Taking a deep breath, I push the door open and retch, eyes watering. No matter how much I'm exposed to the smell of rotting flesh, nothing can prepare me for it.

I look around...and don't see Matt in this bedroom.

My eyes close. It was all for nothing. He must have escaped.

"He is on the other side of the bed," my brother says. At the sound of his voice, a weak moan escapes from behind the bed.

A decomposing hand is tied to the bed with his arm at an awkward angle. I move to the other side of the room, and the rest of Matt comes into view. I suck in a breath.

When we left, he had turned only hours before. His body hadn't truly started to decompose yet and still had at least a little bit of life in it.

The isolation from a food source forced its body to turn on itself, and the result is horrifying. Its skin has turned an unhealthy gray as it's wasted away. An empty shell has replaced the once-solid frame. Its head turns and snaps menacingly, teeth shining through a ruined bottom lip.

It stumbles to its feet and lunges toward me. Even though it's no longer the person Matt was before, I can't help but feel bad for this creature. It must've been in agony this whole time we've been gone. Solitary isn't something I would wish on anyone...unless it were my older brother who put me there in the first place.

"If you're not going to do anything, get out of the way," Dominic says, pushing me to the side. He shoves the creature back on the bed. There's a small crack as he pops its shoulder out of its socket.

Before it can react, he stabs the syringe in its neck and takes a step back. Within seconds, the creature goes limp. Its yellowed eyes close to hide its insanity.

Matt's entire body is motionless.

"What did you do?" I ask.

"I gave him a sedative so we could administer the medicine properly." Each word Dominic speaks is measured and even. He pulls another syringe out of his pocket and twists off the cap. Methodically, he measures certain parts of Matt's decomposing body to insert medicine.

Dominic crinkles his nose in disgust as he touches him, but offers no other sign of emotion as he upholds his promise.

Even though I don't want to acknowledge him, I still ask, "Why are you doing it like that?"

"Why would I waste my time explaining something to you that you will not understand?"

I clench my jaw. "Why do you talk to me like that?" I spit back.

"Because I can." Before I can respond, he continues. "It is going to take several hours before we know if it is going to be successful. The cancer needs time to fight off the infection."

"Do you think it's going to work?" I ask.

"Honestly, Joe, I am not entirely sure. He has not been able to feed on anything but his own body since he turned. Even if he does make it back, it is not going to be for long. As soon as this is taken care of, I want to leave this place and find the group out in Acroisia. Don't forget your part of the deal."

"We're not leaving with Matt sick," I say. It's important that I make this clear now. "We need to give him as much time as we can."

"My word might not mean much to you, but I will help him stay alive as long as I can. I will fulfill my part of the arrangement," Dominic says. "But then you have to fulfill yours." He takes a seat in a chair.

I gently move Matt's body under the tan comforter to hide his appearance as much as possible from Allison. With only his head uncovered, I take a step back. It's still blatantly apparent he's lost way too much weight. His cheekbones accent his bony face, erasing the warmth his wide features used to bring.

I open the window to get some fresh air. The vehicle we used to travel here is visible through the corner of the window. During the drive, I was eager to get away from Dominic after being trapped in such a small space with him.

It appears I haven't been able to.

"Allison, the two of you can come in here now," I say. It's going to be a shock for them to see him like this, as it was for me, but at least his deteriorated body is somewhat hidden now.

I take a seat on the floor and wait to find out if our friend will come back to us. If there is a reason for all of our recent suffering—a reason for why Jess won't make eye contact with me anymore.

The memories of our captivity suddenly come flooding back. The seemingly endless passage of time stuck in my windowless cell. While Allison was treated fairly and I only had to endure some uncomfortable genetic tests, Jess was subjected to much worse. Neither she nor Dominic have disclosed what happened exactly, but I have my guesses.

Allison's unsure footsteps enter the room, followed by a desperate sob when she spots Matt.

"Dominic says it's going to take several hours before we'll know if it worked," I say. I look past her in the hope of seeing Jess. There's only Allison. "Where is she?"

"She wanted to take a shower," Allison says.

She glares angrily at Dominic, but he doesn't notice. He's too preoccupied with observing his experiment. Allison takes a few tentative steps toward the bed and stares down. She caresses some dark hair off of Matt's forehead and sits down on the bed beside him.

"So now we wait?" she asks, voice full of anticipation.

"Now we wait." I stare out of the open window. The fresh air helps hide the stench of death, but not enough to fully override the evidence of the disaster.

Out in the distance, I spot the creek where Jess and I shared our first kiss. That night was when Matt turned into one of the mindless beasts. There's never enough time.

Dominic clears his throat, reminding me why we're here in the first place. He's the reason this happened. If it weren't for him, Jess wouldn't be so broken. I want to hit him in his smug face and break his nose again.

My eyes tear away from him and fall onto Allison and Matt. We have to put up with Dominic for Matt's sake.

I sigh. "I'm going to walk around the property and make sure all of the fences are still in place." I need to get out of this room and away from Dominic.

"Be safe," Allison says. Even though she addresses me, her attention remains focused on Matt. Her hair has fallen over her face, hiding her expression.

I hesitate before I leave the room, watching my brother. He rubs his beard as he reads through his notes, eyes darting across the pages. Did he take the same copious notes when he ran his experiments on me? After he forced me into giving him some of my spinal fluid to run genetic tests on, I wonder if he had that same thoughtful expression while he recorded it all.

How about with Andrew, when he turned him into one of the Letum only to see if he could bring him back? Are those the notes he's going over now, or are they someone else's? He never admitted how many people he ran those experiments on. I'm not sure I even want to know.

And Jess? Did he write down everything he did to her in there? All of the beating and breaking her—both physically and mentally—does he think he has that down to a science? Does the answer to how far his abuse went lie in that notebook?

For all the importance placed on genetics, I don't understand how Dominic and I come from the same parents. We went to him for help because I was naïve enough to believe there was still some good left in him. I can't make that mistake again.

I close the door behind me, taking a deep breath of the—relatively—better air. The shower is still running.

I grab a machete and head outdoors with fresh determination. This is something I understand. I can go out there and kill the Letum. I may not be able to get Jess to look at me, but at least I can do this.

I sprint toward the fence and follow it clockwise around the cabin. With every step, I'm more desperate to find one of the Letum. Out of all the times I wanted to avoid them and they showed up anyway, none are here the one time I actually want them.

I exhale air. What's becoming of me if I'm almost begging to find the Letum? I push that thought away and start running, trying to escape its implication.

My side aches in protest at the physical exercise. A small voice in my head cautions me to slow down. It reminds me of my prolonged captivity. I ignore it.

If I can kill some of these creatures, maybe the balance will return.

I spot the awkward movement right past the fence and exclaim in relief. Without another thought, I jump over the fence and race toward it. The infected reacts to my noise and moans in excitement. It used to be a young woman. Its dress has been torn down its body. Its yellowed, dead eyes register my movement as it moans in its version of excitement.

I run toward it. In one fluid motion, I slam my arm down and the machete crushes its face inward. Its eyes split apart, revealing the gray mush inside its head.

It falls instantly. Its face is unrecognizable, and it's hard to believe it ever belonged to a person. The hair attached to the head is a shade of brown similar to Jess's. Its left boob hangs out of its dress. It's such a vulnerable, shocking sight that I automatically readjust the dress to cover it.

This used to be someone. If a cure is possible, did I rob this person of her potential to be saved?

I drop my head. So much is wrong, and I don't know the way to correct any of it. All I know is I need to be strong for Jess and Allison. I let the tears flow down my face but resolve that these will be the last.

I take a few deep breaths and get back to my feet. I leave the girl behind and cross back over the fence. While I made the first half of my walk in a fury, wishing to encounter some of the infected, I spend the remainder walking slowly, hoping for avoidance.

Luckily, I don't see any other Letum and complete the circle around the fence. The sun rises to its full height and sweat drips down my back. I make my way back up the patio. I set my weapon down, the darkened blood drying, and open the front door to go back inside.

The shower is still running. I frown. I must've been outside for over an hour. I take large steps toward the noise and pass by Matt's tomb. Allison and Dominic haven't changed positions.

Even though I know the answer, I still ask, "Is Jess still in the shower?" The unease raises my voice.

Allison's eyes widen. I run to the bathroom and bang on the door. "Jess? Are you okay?" I call out.

Her silence is deafening. Pain shoots through my hand while I continue my desperate pounding. I shouldn't have left her alone.

I slam my shoulder against the door again and again until I force it open.

Jess doesn't even turn her head at my loud entrance. She sits naked in the shower while the water slides down her body, weighing down her normally curly hair. Her lips have a bluish tinge and her teeth chatter.

The water heater wasn't built to last this long.

"Are you okay?" I repeat.

She doesn't react.

Bruises cover her entire body along with various cuts and scrapes.

I clench my fists and struggle to breathe. Dominic decided he could do that to someone else. He took something and hit her, bruising her all over. He must've held her down with a knife when he cut her. All she did was choose me, and he saw that as reason enough to ruin her life.

Someone like him doesn't deserve to live.

"Jess..." Allison's soft voice comes from behind.

Allison pushes past me and grabs a towel from under the sink. She turns the water off, and Jess finally notices we're in the room with her. Her eyes are blank.

"You're going to get through this," Allison says. She steps into the tub and drapes the towel around her. "You're strong enough for this." Allison's hands rest on Jess's shoulders. The two of them make eye contact.

Very slowly, Jess shakes her head.

Dominic joins us and says, "What is going on in here?"

Jess drops her head. Allison jerks up in fury. There's only one thing I can think to do. I push Dominic out of the room and close the door behind me.

"I don't know why you're trying to hide her. It's nothing I haven't seen before," he says.

My gut tells me he did much more than look at her. The obvious physical abuse is one thing, but if he did more...I can't accept that. It's all my fault.

He turns away and walks down the hallway. I shove him into the wall—hard. His arms rise to catch himself. When he turns to face me, our father's strong features etched across his face, there's an angry amusement in his expression.

I wish we were back in the territories so I could take the tools he used on Jess and punish him with them.

Dominic chuckles darkly and faces me. "There's nothing you can do to change the past. That must be eating you alive right now."

I tighten my jaw and struggle to remind myself that we need his help with Matt. My hands shake with tension.

"I bet you're overwhelmed imagining what I did to her." Dominic smiles smugly. "I hope you fall asleep at night wondering what I did when we were alone."

He steps even closer and his head is now inches away. I tilt my chin up to maintain eye contact.

"Whatever you think happened, whatever your worst fear is, I did *more*," he says quietly. "And you brought her to me so willingly."

He smiles again and walks away.

The moment he disappears into Matt's room, my body slumps as I sit on the floor. He takes pleasure in making me squirm, but what if he isn't talking it up? What if he did do more?

My hands won't stop shaking.

I don't care that we're brothers. I don't care that we need his help. If he hadn't walked away, I'm not confident I could keep control. I want him dead...and I want to be the one to do it.

Once Matt is back, there won't be anything to stop me.

My breathing hitches. Even if I kill Dominic, that won't be enough to reverse what happened to Jess. There's nothing I can do to take that back.

CHAPTER TWO

"It's almost time," Dominic says after checking Matt's pulse.

Color has returned to Matt's face; however, he still isn't healthy. The grayness that overtook his body has subdued but is not entirely gone. He tore through his lower lip in his desperate attempt to hurt Allison right after he turned. It's caked in his own blood, which has turned a rusty brown.

I stand up and unconsciously hold my breath. Allison's eyes widen and she shares an expectant look with me. The desperate longing in her face is unmistakable.

I feel it, too, but toward Jess. She should be here with me, at my side. Instead, she went to our old room.

"He's actually coming back?" Allison's voice shakes.

Dominic writes something in his notebook. "Yes."

Matt is just another experiment to him.

The minutes tick. Time is tedious. I'm painfully aware of every second of this wait. I study Matt for any signs of change. Nothing happens.

"Are you sure?" This could be one of his cruel jokes to give us false hope. Even if I don't always understand his motives, he's forever scheming to do something. This may all be part of one of his ploys.

Dominic glares at me. "Patience, Joe. He's coming back. I know what I'm talking about."

Matt's eyebrow twitches.

I freeze.

With a quick intake of breath, Allison caresses his face. "Matt, it's me. Can you hear me?"

Quietly, Matt responds with a groan. His eyes open and stare into nothingness. There's no sign of any recognition. My heart drops. It was all for nothing.

"It didn't work," I say, shoulders sagging.

"Give him a little more time," my brother says. His eyes rapidly scan Matt's body.

"Please come back to me." Allison's voice is full of emotion.

Matt's dulled eyes make their way to Allison. After a few seconds, they focus and he grunts. "Allison…"

Her hands shoot to her mouth and she cries out. Dominic shines a flashlight in Matt's dimmed, yellowed hazel eyes as he writes more notes down. Satisfied, he returns to his seat and observes.

"What happened?" Matt asks, his words slightly slurred from the damage done to his bottom lip. Pure confusion etches itself into his boney face.

Allison is still overwhelmed with emotion, so I say, "You turned, but we brought you back."

"I knew it," he says. He gathers his strength and responds. "How?"

"We can go over it later once you feel better. Right now, all that's important is that you're alive," I say.

Jess should be here to witness this—the reason we risked and lost so much.

He returns his gaze to Allison. "I've been gone for a long time. You're huge."

Allison chuckles and wipes away some tears. "You always were so romantic."

"I've been told I'm quite the Casanova," he says.

"And who told you that?" I ask.

"Myself," he says and weakly laughs at his own joke.

Matt takes his right arm out from under the covers and freezes when he spots it. Before he turned, he had a strong, healthy body. Now, his skin is pale, covered in sores, and shockingly thin.

Allison quickly grabs his hand and kisses it. She places it on her stomach with hers on top.

He lets out a deep breath. "You're beautiful."

Another tear rolls town Allison's face. "I love you so much. It's been so hard without you."

I can't help but allow a small smile at the two of them. "I'm going to let Jess know you're back."

Matt gestures around the room. "Speaking of her, why isn't she here for my homecoming?"

"She's resting. She'll come see you later," Allison says, so I don't have to.

Without another word, I leave the room and walk down the hallway. I knock gently on our old room's door. I'm surprised when I hear a response.

"Please don't come in," Jess says.

I rest my head against the door. "It's me, Elliot."

"Please don't come in," Jess repeats. Her voice is so soft it barely reaches me.

"I won't," I say, fighting the urge to ignore her request. "It worked. Matt is joking and back with us."

"It did?" Her voice is a little louder, the surprise evident in her tone.

"Yes, Dominic actually was able to do it," I say. I instantly regret saying his name.

She doesn't respond, so I say to myself, "Now I need you to come back to me."

I rest my head on the door for a little longer in the hope that she will reach out to me. When I accept that she's not going to say anything, I sigh and head back.

I reenter the room in time to hear Matt quietly ask, "How long do I have?"

I lean against the wall. How much time did we truly buy for Matt?

"I am not entirely sure," Dominic says.

Allison smiles down at Matt. "That's not important right now. You're alive and that's what we should focus on."

Matt shakes his head and sits up slightly higher in bed. "It's important. I need to know. You have to have some type of idea," he says to Dominic.

"I do not have a lot of data to support my theory, but this is what I suspect," Dominic says. His tone is all business. "Andrew turned and we got him back. I only let him continue in the infected state for forty-eight hours. When he returned, the cancerous cells were spread enough that we could not eliminate it from his body. I tried treatment, but after a couple of months, he was in enough pain that he was ready to pass on."

Allison pulls Matt's hand into her lap.

"How long?" Matt says.

"Is now the right time?" I don't want him to focus on how much time he has left and not be able to enjoy it.

As always, Dominic ignores me and says, "You were turned for about a month instead of two days. The cancer had to spread much more than it did in Andrew's body. I have some medication that will slow its growth, but it has some serious side effects."

Allison glances down at her stomach. "Will he live long enough to meet our child?"

Dominic's mask breaks, his eyes softening. Almost instantly, his expression returns to its typical confident look. I've never seen compassion in Dominic, not even after our mother died. I must've misinterpreted it.

"It depends on when the baby is born," my brother finally answers.

"How long?" Matt says again.

"Maybe a few days," Dominic says. A moan escapes Allison and he finishes, "but there is not a true precedent for this. I could be wrong."

My head whips to Dominic. I'm not sure I've ever heard that phrase come out of his mouth.

"But I am confident I am correct," he finishes.

"When are we due?" Matt asks helplessly.

Allison's shoulders slump in resignation. "In more than a few days."

Life is so cruel. Matt turned because of an unexpected play at genetics, and we were able to find a miracle and turn him back only to lose him again so quickly.

"There's nothing more you can do?" Allison asks Dominic. Silent tears run down her face.

"I can keep Matt comfortable as long as possible. That is about as much as I can do for him," he says.

Allison's face falls. Matt gathers his strength and pulls her in for an embrace. She cries into his frail body.

"We do have one option though," Dominic begins. Allison's head perks back up. "We can induce the baby early."

"You can do that?" I ask. I don't know a lot about pregnancies, but there are reasons why they're supposed to go until full term.

"I brought some supplies from our territory for the baby. It is not guaranteed, but we can try to have the baby be born early," Dominic says.

"Let's do it," Allison says. "A father should be able to hold his child."

My brother opens his mouth to respond, but Matt speaks first. "Hold on. What are the risks?"

Methodically, Dominic responds, "At this point in her pregnancy, the most likely challenge we would face would be if the child's lungs have not yet fully developed. Though, by thirty-seven weeks, it is a minimal risk. I have brought steroids that I can administer to the child before birth to reduce that."

"Is it safe? I'm not going to be selfish and jeopardize their life. Our child is more important."

Dominic hesitates before he responds. "It will be safe."

"Anything else?" Allison asks.

"In addition, the baby's immune system will not be as strong as one carried to full term. Once again, I have medication to fight off any infection—should it occur. I don't foresee any major complication arising from inducing the child early."

Matt's eyes narrow in suspicion. "Are you certain?"

"Yes."

"What are we waiting on? I can't wait to not be pregnant anymore. I'm a planet," Allison says. She wipes the tears off her face and smiles down at Matt. He easily returns her joy, and for a moment, it's easy to forget that he's dying. His happiness is, as it always has been, completely contagious.

"I have something I want to do first," Matt says. A smile plays on his ruined lips. "If I can smell myself, you all can, too. Can I shower and change clothes?"

We all chuckle and Allison says, "Let's get you up and clean." She gets off the bed clumsily. I walk over to help support Matt out of bed. The two of us move the covers off of his body and I grab one of his arms to support him. He cringes in pain. I let go immediately.

"What's wrong with my arm?" Matt's voice is raised in panic.

Without saying anything, Dominic moves toward him and grabs his arm. He pulls and Matt screams. A pop echoes through the room.

"Next time warn me, brother," Matt says while he rubs his shoulder.

I bite my tongue at his relatively easy nature with Dominic. Even if he doesn't yet know everything that Dominic has done and is capable of, it's still hard to see him view Dominic as anything less than the scum he is.

Dominic shrugs. "Let me know when you are ready to start her labor." He stalks out of the room and after a couple seconds, the sound of the front door opening and closing echoes throughout the house.

"Come on, Matt, let's get you over to the shower," I say.

The three of us slowly make our way to the bathroom. He stumbles awkwardly and quickly gets frustrated. "I can't believe I'm this weak." He grits his teeth.

Allison studies him. "I love you."

Matt laughs slightly. "Good response."

She smiles but doesn't say anything else.

Keeping one arm available for him to use as support, I grab the doorknob with my other hand and push the door open. We help him to the closed toilet and guide him down. Clearly out of breath, he closes his eyes.

If he's this tired from the walk over, there is no way he's going to be able to make it through a shower.

I decide to address the obvious. "Not to be a downer or anything..."

"I'll help him with the bath," Allison says.

"Does this mean I'll get to see you in all of your pregnant glory?" Matt grins wickedly.

"Don't push your luck," she says through a smile. She leans closer to me and says only loud enough for me to hear "Change all the bedding, please."

I slightly nod. "Now you two kids have fun. Don't do anything stupid."

She gestures to her stomach and raises her eyebrow. Chuckling as I leave the bathroom, I grab clean sheets and a bedspread from the closet. I pause by our old room and listen. Faintly, I hear Jess's sobs. Without a second thought, I drop everything and go into the bedroom.

She's lying in the middle of the bed in a fetal position. She jerks when I enter the room. I make my way over to her and place my hand on her shoulder. I want to end whatever is causing her pain.

"Please don't," Jess says. She flinches away and out of my reach.

Pity swells inside me. I'm at a loss for what to do. How can I comfort someone who can't stand for me to be in the same room as her?

"It kills me to have you look at me like that."

My eyebrows furrow. "Like what?"

"Like exactly how I feel about myself," she says.

I run my hands through my hair and try to erase whatever facial expression I had on my face. "What can I do to help you? Tell me what to do."

A fresh tear slowly runs down her face. "Let me go," she says.

I don't want to do this. I care so much about her.

"Is that what you want?"

Jess's eyes show her anguish, the same that I'm feeling, as she nods.

"But I love you," I say for the first time. I should have told her before instead of assuming she knew. I thought we had more time.

She shakes her head. "It doesn't matter."

"Of course it matters. Why wouldn't it?"

"Because it doesn't make a difference. I don't want to be with you," she says. "Let me go."

My breath hitches. All my life, I believed I was worth less than everyone else in the territories. I thought I'd gotten past that, but all those insecurities rush back. My voice cracks when I ask, "Why?"

"I'm not what you want anymore. I've been changed. The person you think you love is gone and has been replaced. She's not coming back. You're better off without me."

"What are you talking about?" My voice rises in frustration. I've never been more sure of anything in my life. "Of course you're who I want."

She cringes, and a fresh sob escapes her body. "Don't yell at me. Please leave me alone."

I slump over, my strength leaving. "I'm sorry." I get off of the bed and walk away. "I don't agree with you. I love you."

I thought I meant more to her than for her to discard what we had like this. Was it not the same for her as it was for me?

I reach the door and turn to her again.

"We're going to induce Allison and Matt's baby soon. I thought you would want to know and be there," I say. I don't wait for her response before closing the door behind me. I need to get away from that pain and rejection. I pick the bedding back up and continue with my original task.

She was my certainty. No matter what would happen, I knew she would always be at my side. She transformed me into the person I had the potential to become. She helped me gain the self-worth and confidence that had eluded me my entire life.

But now she wants nothing else to do with me. What else have I been wrong about?

CHAPTER THREE

Allison lies on top of the clean sheets and blankets, nervous excitement bounding off of her. Freshly bathed and looking marginally better, Matt sits next to her, holding her hand.

"This injection is going to start the process," Dominic says. "It is going to take awhile."

Matt says, "Hopefully not a few days."

I wince. The reminder of his impending death doesn't sit well with the situation. His time left isn't measured in years, months, weeks, or even days. He's down to his last hours.

"Are you ready?" Dominic asks.

"So ready," Allison says. Matt leans in and kisses her on the forehead through his mangled bottom lip.

My brother gently injects her with some medication and steps back. "I am going to be outside if you need me. Call out, and I will come back in if something happens."

"What?" Allison exclaims. Her eyes widen in fear.

"You're leaving now?" I ask.

"Like I said earlier," he says slowly, "it is going to take awhile. Frankly, this is going to be a bit of a waiting game for her, and there is nothing I can do. I would rather get out of the house and explore."

"You'll be close enough to hear us?" Matt asks, needing his reassurance.

His eyes flicker momentarily at Allison, and he returns his gaze to Matt. "I'll hear you," he promises. Before we can question him further, he leaves the room to go back outside.

"Well, he's a character, your brother," Matt says to break the silence that has overtaken the room. Allison and I automatically exchange glances. "What did I miss?"

"We went to him for help after you turned to see if we could bring you back," Allison says.

"I was able to put that together. I assumed that's why he was here," Matt says.

Allison bites her lip.

I continue our story. "When we got there, he drugged us and did their genetic experiments." Matt's mouth opens, but I ignore it and keep talking. "We were there for almost a month when my friend, Andrew, came and rescued us all. I went through a couple of uncomfortable tests but nothing extreme. He didn't do anything to Allison. I think he was waiting on her to have the baby."

"Is that true?" Matt eyes Allison.

"Besides being stuck in a room and not knowing what was going on, I wasn't mistreated at all," Allison says. He visibly relaxes.

"What did he do to Jess?" Matt furrows his eyebrows. "Is she actually here or are the two of you hiding the fact that she got killed? I don't understand why I haven't seen her yet." He scans my face for signs of the truth.

"She's...she's alive," I say. I almost said she was okay, but that would have been a lie.

"Oh, good," Matt says in obvious relief. "Where is she then?"

"Dominic didn't treat her kindly," Allison says.

"What did he do to her?" His tone is harsh and unforgiving, matching my own feelings.

I hold my breath. Does Allison know what happened?

She says, "I'm not sure exactly, but it did a lot of damage. Both physically and mentally."

"She told me to let her go," I admit. I hate how pathetic I sound.

"Jess needs time right now." Allison pats my knee. "She still cares about you."

I throw my arms up. "I want to help her, but I can't do that if she won't let me."

"However hard it is for you to understand, it's so much worse for her," Allison says. "If you truly care about her, you will give her whatever she wants right now."

How can she mean that? "Even if that means doing nothing?"

"If that's what she needs right now, then do nothing. You don't have to agree with her decisions, but you must support her."

"Women are tricky, brother," Matt says.

I ignore him and focus on Allison. "Will you reach out and help?"

She doesn't hesitate. "Of course."

"But he's your brother. I don't understand," Matt says.

"In blood, yes. He was jealous that Jess chose me and I had something he didn't. He had to correct that."

"I don't understand why he's here with us if he did something like that," Matt says, shifting his position to angle himself at me.

"For you," I say.

"Get rid of him. He shouldn't be here," Matt says.

"We need him," I say.

Matt shakes his head and takes a deep breath.

Allison winces and grabs her stomach. "What happened?" Matt asks in alarm.

His panicked expression elicits a laugh from Allison, and she says, "Our kid is actually on the way."

"Whoa," Matt says and looks in wonder at her stomach. I mimic his reaction. I can't believe a person is about to come out of her body. The three of us focus on her pregnant belly in awe.

A light knock at the door interrupts our musings. Jess stands at the doorway uncertainly. Her eyes are red, and she squints out of her blackened, swollen eye.

"Can I come in?" she asks. Her voice is barely audible.

"Of course," Allison says, her tone light.

"Welcome to the birth of our baby!" Matt says with joy. I admire him for his ability to ignore the elephant in the room. I wish I could do that.

Jess takes a couple of steps into the room.

"You can have my chair," I say. I jump up, and she flinches at my sudden movement. A frown crosses my face before I can hide the emotion away. Unfortunately, Jess notices—her pained expression says as much.

"I'm sorry," I say. All I want to do is make everything better, but I keep making it worse.

She wordlessly refuses my offer and leans against the opposite wall. Allison and Matt eye this awkward movement but don't say anything.

"I'm glad you're back," Jess says.

"I'm the picture of good health," Matt says.

"I can see that," Jess says. Her lips twitch in tentative amusement.

I don't understand how he can help control some of her pain when I can't. I should be able to do that.

"Knock, knock," Matt says.

Allison rolls her eyes with a grin. "Who's there?"

"Doris."

Allison goes along. "Doris, who?"

"Doris locked. That's why I'm knocking!" Matt delivers the punch line. His old booming laugh is replaced by a cheap imitation. Nonetheless, it's nice to hear again, and all four of us chuckle at the joke.

"Oh! There's another one," Allison exclaims and holds on to her stomach again.

"Come on! There's no way my joke was that bad," Matt teases. Even though he's seemingly carefree, there is a thin line of tension in his expression.

"It was pretty bad," Jess says. The two women share an amused glance that I want to be a part of. Because of our conversation, I keep my distance and don't say anything. For now, I'll do my best to follow Allison's advice and support Jess in any way that's possible—even if that means pretending to be invisible. I don't see how that's going to do any good, but whatever I try isn't helping. I can at least follow along with Allison's suggestions until I think of something better.

I sit back down in the chair. If Dominic is right, and I strongly suspect he will be, Allison has a long process to go through before the baby joins us. I might as well get comfortable.

Even though, historically, Dominic's guesses have almost always been accurate, I can't help but hope he's wrong about Matt's time frame. Maybe there is some other medication he can take to give him more time. If he was able to come back, that's almost a miracle. Surely we can get another one.

"Tell me," Matt says, breaking my train of thought and drawing my attention to him. He's staring directly at me. "What caused this infection?"

Allison rubs his arm. "Is now the best time?"

"I want to know why this is happening to me—why our family is going to be torn apart and so many people have died," Matt says.

He wants someone to blame right now. He's hoping this infection occurred for a good cause and there's a reason for his suffering. The truth isn't satisfying. It's not going to help. We did this to ourselves.

"We should wait until you're stronger," I say.

"According to your brother, I'm not going to be getting any stronger."

Matt continues to stare at me, demanding the answers that I don't want to give. It's worse once you know how avoidable everything was.

"It was the genetic engineering," Jess says from the other side of the room. "We caused all of this."

Allison carefully watches Matt's expression as he takes in the knowledge. She grabs his hand and holds it.

"Keep going," he finally says.

"For our generation, they isolated the gene that caused cancer and removed it from genetic possibility for the Planned," Jess continues.

His eyes dart to Allison, who, like myself, is Unplanned. "So you're safe then, right? This won't happen to you...or our child?"

"I don't think so," Allison says and looks down at her swollen stomach. "We should be safe."

"Thank goodness." Matt lets out a deep breath and visibly relaxes. "How are the two related?"

With Dominic's explanation echoing through my mind, I respond. "It turns out, all along, cancer was an evolutionary defense mechanism against turning into the Letum. When the infection would occur, a person developed cancer to protect themselves. The cancerous cells took over the infected cells."

"And that's why he injected me with cancer—to fight off the infection." Matt shakes his head in disgust. "I remember one class when my educator was going on and on about how important genetic engineering was and how fortunate we were to be born in the territories..." He tapers off and glances toward Allison. "This was right after our parents found out about us and we started sneaking off together, I think."

Despite everything, Allison smiles at the memories. "And look where that got us," she says and gestures toward her stomach as she cringes at another contraction.

Matt chuckles that same weak noise that's a terrible alternative to the booming laughter he used to have and holds her hand until the pain passes.

"Anyway, they mentioned how we couldn't get cancer anymore and what a great accomplishment that was because there was no cure for cancer," Matt says.

Allison's face falls, and Matt immediately cups her chin.

"There has to be a way or something we can do," Allison says.

"Maybe," Matt says.

We look at each other, and there is a dull acceptance in his expression. He's already accepted his fate.

CHAPTER FOUR

Sweat pours down Allison's face while she shakes her head in defeat. "I can't do this anymore. Something's wrong."

Matt kisses her on the forehead, ignoring the film of moisture. "You're doing so well. Just a little bit more."

She narrows her eyes as she breathes heavily. "You don't know what you're talking about. What if something is wrong?"

She's been in labor for almost thirty hours and pushing for the last two hours or so. It's ticking away at the time Matt has left. It's so limited.

For once, I'm thankful to have my brother with us. "Allison, I can see the progress. You are almost there. We are so incredibly close to meeting your child. Can you fight a little longer?" Fresh resolve takes over as she hastily wipes away her sweat and tears. "Okay, gather your strength. We are almost there."

Dominic's attention refocuses. I hold my breath in anticipation of the new arrival. Even Jess is showing a small twinge of excitement, the first emotion outside of her pain that she's hinted at since we left the territories.

"Okay," Allison grunts. "Okay."

"Almost there," Dominic says again.

Allison screams out, knuckles white as she squeezes down on Matt's hand. He leans in and mutters in her ear.

"The baby is crowning. I can see the head," Dominic says. "One more push should do it."

Jess peeks and immediately snaps her head back. "Don't look," she mouths at me.

She doesn't need to tell me twice.

With one final triumphant, guttural gasp from Allison, Dominic guides the baby the rest of the way out…along with a bunch of blood and other stuff I don't even want to think about.

"Is the baby okay?" Allison gasps.

"A towel, Joe," Dominic says as he cuts the umbilical cord.

I quickly hand it over in wonder. He gently wipes the child off. She clenches her pink fists up by her head, which is covered with thick, dark hair.

"The baby," Allison calls out again, this time much louder.

"She's beautiful," Jess says as a large cry echoes across the room.

Matt leans forward. "Healthy?"

"As far as I can tell." Dominic smiles as he hands the infant off to Allison. "Congratulations, you are now parents to a baby girl."

"A daughter?" Allison carefully takes her, and the two of them stare in amazement.

"Yes," Dominic confirms.

Matt's eyes break away from his child and make contact with mine. His lips spread in a broad smile, somehow accentuating his newly narrowed face even more. "Incredible," he says.

With Dominic in the corner making notes, Jess and I stand next to the bed.

Jess steps closer and stares down at the child in amazement. She looks up, as if to share this miracle, and we make eye contact. Her body tenses as she returns her attention down toward the family.

I continue watching Jess. As incredible as this is, with all that we paid to make it happen, was all of the pain to get here worth it? Will a couple more days with Matt justify the suffering? If I could take it back, I would without hesitation.

"You did so well." Matt leans down and kisses Allison on her forehead. "I love you so much."

With sweat still dripping down her forehead, she smiles with such unfiltered joy that it leaves me breathless. If she had given birth before the territories collapsed from the infection, this event would have been treated with embarrassment and disgust because the child was Unplanned.

"She's perfect," Allison says and examines her even closer. "And so small! Her fingers are tiny."

Matt spreads the baby's fingers and stares down in awe. "She's us, Allison," he says so simply.

Allison laughs and wipes the tears off of her face. "She has your ears."

"Well, luckily, Josie is going to have excellent hearing."

Allison's eyebrows rise. "Josie?"

Matt places his arm across her shoulder, smiling down at the daughter they created together. "She's a Josie."

"She is." Allison leans down and kisses her daughter.

"Josie is a beautiful name," Jess says.

Allison gazes up in confusion, as if she forgot we were here. Then, that expression goes away and in its place, her joy returns.

Jess squeezes her shoulder and, probably sensing the same private nature of this moment, says, "I'll be back later to check in on how you're doing."

"I'm going to go outside and check around," I say and turn to follow Jess out of the room. They have such little time left. I don't want to interrupt it.

I hesitate and turn back around to try to freeze the image of them huddled together as a family. Circumstance may be taking her father away from her much sooner than is fair, but it's impossible for Josie to be more loved right now. This has to be worth it. I need to remember this later when it's all over.

I leave the room and walk slowly down the hallway, still stunned at what I witnessed. It's one thing to hear about the birthing process, but another to be there for it. There were some moments in there I probably could have been okay with not ever seeing.

There has been so much death lately, but she's a new life and should be able to do whatever she wants. That has to mean something. We need to create a life for her that gives her the potential she deserves, something I never had growing up as an Unplanned in Potentia.

Even though the Letum killed the only family I had who cared about me, they at least also destroyed the ideals of a society that were inherently wrong.

I hate that sometimes the infection can almost seem like a good thing.

Crisp air chills my skin as I open the patio door. The seasons are changing. I almost go back inside to grab a light jacket, but decide against it.

My machete is still leaning up against the door. I grab it and test the feel of it. With this in my hand, I feel powerful and in control. I can use this to prevent the Letum from hurting me or anyone else I care about. They are much easier to navigate than those who are still alive.

I'm about twenty feet in front of the house when my brother calls out, "Wait up."

I close my eyes in preparation for whatever he plans on doing and stop. "What do you want?" He catches up, placing his arm around my shoulder.

I brush it off and scowl.

"I would have thought you would have been in a better mood. You got to witness a family moment that would not have been possible without me," he says. His smugness is overwhelming sometimes.

I take a step forward, ignoring him.

I test the feel of the machete in my hand again, feeling that same sense of power. What does he want? Anything that he ever does is self-serving, no matter the consequences to anyone else. Now that Matt is back, the baby is born, why do we need him anymore? Who would care if he were gone?

He catches up and grabs my arm that is holding my weapon. I turn around and glare at him, tugging my arm back. It would be so satisfying to punish him for everything he did to Jess.

"I am going to walk the line with you," he announces, his eyes marginally narrowed.

I could tell everyone else Dominic left. They probably wouldn't question me. Though, even if they did, who cares? He would deserve it. People like him shouldn't have a place in our world.

I clench my fist to get a stronger grip on the machete. My arm inches upward as Dominic takes a step toward the fence. With his back to me, I relax my grip slightly. I want to see his expression when he realizes he's about to die, that the life that he holds so precious is coming to an end, and that his manipulative plans failed him.

I kick a rock out toward him to get his attention again.

When he notices it, he looks back at me.

"I hate everything about you," I say.

He laughs and walks out of the way to kick that same rock. It goes a little farther. "We both know that isn't true."

"And why is that?" I ask. I take a deep breath to compose my thoughts. "At every opportunity you've ever had, you've consistently been horrible."

A steady gaze replaces his arrogant amusement. "That's not true."

I use my free hand to gesture toward the cabin. "Are you seriously going to argue that when Jess is in there traumatized by what you did to her?"

His eyebrow jerks upward. "And what about Matt?"

My voice shakes through my clenched teeth. "It doesn't matter. That doesn't erase what you did to her."

"So you would prefer to view it all in black and white?" Dominic's voice is sharp and inquisitive.

"You can't erase what you've done. You can't argue yourself out of that. It's not up for debate."

"You may not be able to forgive what I've done, but I can justify my actions," he replies.

Despite everything, I want to hear what he has to say. How could he possibly talk himself out of this?

"I brought Matt back and sped up Allison's delivery so they could be a family and Matt could meet his daughter. You consider that something good that I did, right?"

I roll my eyes at his statement. "Obviously that had a positive impact," I say.

"So in your black-and-white world, that was a white moment for me?"

I'm not sure exactly where he's going with this.

"And when I captured Andrew and performed those experiments on him, that was bad and, therefore, a black moment?"

"You killed my two best friends," I say through clenched teeth, flexing my grip on my weapon.

I push him out of the way with my free hand. He quickly rebounds and gets in front of me.

"If I had not run those tests and understood this infection better, I would not have been able to cure Matt and let him meet his daughter."

Our blue eyes meet. "The world is not black and white just as I am not. We are all shades of gray. If you are going to be thankful that

I provided this opportunity for Matt and Allison, then you have to realize what I did to Andrew was necessary."

"So now you're trying to pretend like you did this for the greater good? That you knew that would happen?" Before he can respond, I spit out, "Give me a break. You did that to them because deep down, you are inherently a bad person."

"As much as you want to believe that, I'm not. You should be grateful for me, yet you act like I'm beneath you," he says.

I scoff and shake my head. For the first time in this conversation, he seems confused.

Dominic finally looks away. "I'm tired of everyone glaring at me like I'm undeserving of being part of your little group or even of being alive," he says. "The simple fact is that the world needs people like me to make the decisions that may not be pretty but are necessary."

I should prove his point and end things, once and for all. I'll show him what doing things for the greater good looks like.

Once more, I tighten my grip and...

...I can't make myself raise my arm. My mind screams at my body to do something—to take control and power back. The two of us maintain steady eye contact. There's no telling what he's thinking.

Frustrated, I push past him, and this time, he allows me to walk away. The tension of his presence follows me, as does the sound of his footsteps, crushing the brittle grass below.

I climb over the fence easily and hit the ground determined to ignore him. The sounds of his footsteps are a constant reminder of his world of gray. I don't care what the end results are. There are some things you can't rationalize.

The familiar smell of rotting flesh comes through the air, revealing a large group stumbling through the woods. The seven of them react to our movement and moan in the world's ugliest melody. Their clothes are varying shades of the attire from the territories. The hunger and disease have torn away any individuality. All of them look at us in a similar madness, devoid of any human elements.

Scientific achievement led to this. How far we've fallen.

If I were by myself, I would head back over the fence for help. Seven is too risky for one person. But I'm not alone. I reluctantly turn to my brother and address him. "Are you going to be overwhelmed or can we take them out?"

He smirks. "The question is not whether I will be overwhelmed, Joe. If you feel confident, let's get a little exercise and smash their heads in." He tosses his knife between his hands. Without warning, he yells and sprints to face them head-on.

I could walk away right now and hope he gets bitten. He could be gone from my life and I would never have to worry about him or his intentions again. I wouldn't even have to actively do anything; I could passively let things happen.

The idea is so appealing that I take a step backward.

My mother invades my mind along with all of her dreams of us being a family. This isn't who she would have wanted me to become.

Dammit.

I rush forward to join my brother. No other thoughts. My only job is to take these creatures out as efficiently as possible.

I swing down hard on the nearest one and its brains explode out of its head. In one fluid motion, I bring the weapon down on the female next to it—she must have been working at the hospital judging by her outfit, like Jess—and take another one out. Blood drips down my extended arm and I slam down on yet another one. I pull it out to get my next target, but the weapon is caught on something. The blood on my hands loosens my grip and I drop the machete.

I exhale and turn toward the creature closest to me. It lunges at my throat, but I sidestep to avoid it. It stumbles past me and before it can react, I push it hard into the ground. I slam my boot down on its head, ending its attempts to spread its infection further.

After a moment of inspiration, I yank at its arm. There's a slight hesitation before it pops out. I swing it around and slam another infected to the ground and smash the arm into its head. The first hit doesn't finish the job, so I bring it down three more times before I'm convinced it's actually dead.

Before we went back to Potentia, Jess voiced a theory that's holding up so far. With every day that passes, the Letum seem to get weaker as they decompose. Maybe one day, they will cease to exist.

That's way too easy, though.

"Behind you," Dominic says, interrupting my thoughts. I turn around in time to see him bring his knife down on the creature inches away from me. Its momentum causes the corpse to fall into me, knocking my breath out.

I regain control and push it off to sit up, taking deep breaths to slow my heart rate.

"Thanks," I say once I've regained my composure. My hands shake while the adrenaline leaves my system.

He wipes his weapon against some of the dirty clothes of one of the dead. "Another one of my shades, little brother," he says.

I wipe my boot off harshly in the grass. The dark red mix of blood and decomposing flesh covers the green. I keep wiping the boot, waiting for it to become clean, to erase what happened. When I can't get it completely clean, I keep trying, getting angrier after each swipe.

"Use your words," Dominic says. I look up to see him watching me intently.

"You rationalize that all of the bad things you've done have led to good. But you can't stand there and tell me what you did to Jess was justified."

He drops his gaze. "Jealousy is a powerful emotion that can cause you to forget the bigger picture and indulge in temporary pleasures."

I walk back to my weapon and force it out of one of the dead's head. "As much as you like to think you have your different shades, you're wrong."

His arrogant look returns. "If you truly believed that, you would have left and hoped I would have been overtaken by the Letum."

I turn around and make my way back to the fence. "That had nothing to do with my thoughts of you."

He follows me. "Of course it did. You'd like to pretend otherwise, but you understand my reasoning. Every time you are thankful that Matt is here, know that it is because of Andrew's death."

I hop back over the fence and walk toward the house. "Piss off."

He laughs darkly. "Enjoy your time with Matt. You are welcome for it."

Does it make me a bad person if I'm happy for Matt and Allison even if this moment was a direct result of the pain and misery of my childhood friend? Is it fair for me to wish they were still here if it meant Matt wouldn't be?

I don't want to live in Dominic's world of gray.

I toss my weapon down and pass Jess on the patio. Her knife is in her left hand. I want to talk about what Dominic rationalized.

But I don't.

"Dominic went to the east," I say. I get out of the way so she can pass. She races off in the other direction. I watch her until she's gone from my sight.

I go back inside.

I poke my head in to check on how the new family is doing. Matt holds their daughter with an expression full of joy. He sits in the chair in awe while Allison sleeps off some of the struggle of her labor.

Matt glances up briefly enough to recognize it's me in the doorway before returning his attention to Josie in his arms. "Do you want to hold her?"

"Yes, but let me go shower first. I don't want to expose her to anything," I reply and gesture toward the blood on my arms.

His eyes widen. "Probably a good idea, brother."

"I'll be back," I say, quietly enough to avoid disturbing Allison. "I want to hold your daughter."

He smiles, his bottom lip still damaged in a horrifying reminder of what happened to him, and returns his attention to Josie.

I gently close the door. After grabbing clean clothes, I go into the bathroom. With its pink, flowery designs, this room is where Jess and I initially found Matt. At that time, watching his broad, still healthy body hunched over the toilet throwing up, I thought he had a normal, temporary virus. I didn't believe he could turn without even being bitten.

I turn on the water and undress, feeling relief as the bloodied clothes fall to the floor. Once the water is hot enough, I step in and savor the feel of the water flowing down my skin. I turn the water even hotter and close my eyes.

Hours before Matt turned, Jess and I kissed for the first time, which seemed long overdue. For months, we had been each other's support, but it took a near-death experience for Jess to finally take the leap of faith that moved us to where it was meant to go.

That night, she surprised me again by wanting to push our relationship further. Using the contraception she had gotten from Allison earlier that day, we sealed our relationship.

Thinking about it now, I hope they didn't consistently use it. Otherwise, how else did Josie get here? I better double-check with Allison on that, even if it might be awkward to bring up. Though, from the way Jess is treating me now, it's irrelevant. I doubt she's ever going to let me in again.

That night, she became my absolute certainty. In a world where everything was taken from me—my grandparents, mother, and childhood friends—I was positive she would be with me. Together, we would make it. How naïve I was.

My eyes shoot open at the image of Jess's naked, abused body sitting in this shower as the water kept cascading down on her. Did she start off by standing here, like I am, but instead of the positive memories I'm reliving, did Dominic haunt her?

Even though I've always used showers as a relaxing place to decompress and collect myself, I want out—now. My thoughts offer me no solace or comfort. They're a nagging reminder of how far we've come.

As quickly as I can while still being thorough, I use the berry-scented shampoo and soap to clean the blood and gore off my body. Once I'm satisfied it's all gone, I turn off the water. The new silence spreads across the room so that the only noises are the drips of the water off my body.

After drying off, I rush and put my clean clothes on. I want out of this room. The sound of coughing greets me when I open the door.

It's started.

CHAPTER FIVE

I run back to their room, though there's nothing I can do to help. Allison's eyes are wide as she looks at Matt. I hurriedly make my way to him to take Josie out of his arms. Matt hunches over as he fights through his coughing fit.

Allison sits closer and motions for him to join her on the bed. "Come here. It'll be okay."

Matt complies and crawls up the bed, his weak frame shaking. His eyes water as he struggles to regain control of his body. Besides his coughing, the only sound in the room is the baby's crying. I soothe Josie as Allison comforts her father.

In a startling realization, I stare down at the baby in my arms. I haven't held a baby since Carly was born, but that was so long ago. I must have been around ten at the time. Andrew and Chris handed her to me—so proud—and made sure I supported her neck enough.

I readjust to make sure I'm holding her securely. Once she settles down, Josie is happy enough to lie in my arms.

Matt's coughing continues, and Allison's soft voice murmurs encouragement. Josie keeps most of my attention, though, and I can't believe how she feels in my arms as a steady, warm weight, though she's so small.

In Potentia, everyone treated me with open contempt and wouldn't dream of letting an Unplanned have anything to do with his or her seemingly perfect genetically engineered babies. They would have never let me hold their Planned babies, let alone encourage me to have kids of my own someday.

Matt, finally recovering, takes a deep breath and says, "That was horrible. Is that going to happen until the end?"

I look away from Josie to answer his question honestly. "I assume so. Andrew coughed a lot before…"

"Let me hold my daughter again while I can," he says.

My attention returns to her. She looks so fragile. "Are you sure?"

"Of course. I wouldn't risk hurting her," he says. I gently hand her off and he holds her close to his chest. Allison snuggles into him, and the family recovers from the recent progression of Matt's illness.

Even with this new life, death is the unrelenting threat in our lives.

I quietly leave the room and pause outside the door. What should I do now? Matt and Allison are preoccupied, Jess can't stand me, and I'm sure as hell not going to spend time with Dominic.

While I long for my grandparents' lake to go fishing, there's something else that can be soothing and remind me of my grandfather. I head out to the garage area. A cool breeze hits my skin, so I lock my arms together.

In an old storage shed, which I doubt Matt's high-ranking parents ever set foot in, is an ax and pile of wood. They probably had hired help to make sure they could continue to live their sheltered, perfect lives.

It's amazing that Matt came out of that household as down-to-earth as he is. Allison probably had a lot to do with that.

I stand one of the giant logs on the ground and test how the ax feels in my hands. Once I'm comfortable in my grip, I slam it down. It doesn't split the wood as I had hoped, and I struggle to pull it out of its new sheath. In no time, a film of sweat covers my body as I warm up.

I can almost hear my grandfather's voice cautioning me to be careful and not miss the log.

I let out a deep breath to expel some of the negative energy from earlier in the shower. I can't change what's happened. I can only focus on the future and on making it right again.

But what's there to do? Any chance of keeping Matt alive would need to be done at the territories where there is a higher likelihood of the right technology. Though, Dominic brought the medicine that he needed to bring him back. Should I be thankful for that, even though he killed both Andrew and Chris in front of me?

Dominic shot Chris in reaction to me shooting at the Letum closing in behind him. If only I had let the creature get my brother, they would still be with us. He would never have had a chance to touch Jess and tear her away from me.

Knowing what I do now, would I have lowered my weapon and let the Letum attack him? I could have stopped all of this from happening. Would the trade-off have been worth it?

I make short work of the available pile, despite how exhausting and tiring it is. It's another reminder of my captivity and weakened physical stamina.

The sun goes down, and the temperature drops as a result. I wipe my brow and set the ax back in the aging shed.

A dog barks excitedly and I jerk my head up. I haven't heard that sound since my grandparents' dog...and he died a few years ago. Jess's outline appears as she walks back toward the house with a large dog running around her.

Even though I think that's what I'm seeing, I've got to ask to clarify. "Is that a dog?" My voice rises to make sure she can hear me.

The dog's ears perk up and it runs toward me without hesitation. The closer it gets, the bigger it seems. It looks like this monstrous beast is going to pummel right into me. I put my hands up in preparation for the impending impact. Two feet away, the dog sits happily. The way it pants makes it look like the dog is smiling at me.

I laugh. "Well hey there, buddy. Where did you come from?"

In response, the dog licks my hand. I scratch behind its ears and it immediately rolls over so I can scratch its stomach. I get on my knees and comply with her demands. Her black, thick hair is surprisingly soft.

"I know she looks intimidating, but she's sweet," Jess says. I look up with a grin still on my face and am shocked she looks almost happy.

"Where did you find her?" The dog is massive and hairy. I can't tell what breed she must be, so I assume she's a mix of many.

"I think she found me," she says. I wait for her to elaborate. She doesn't.

"I wonder what her story is," I muse. The dog flops back on her feet and takes advantage of my lowered height to give me a big slobbery kiss.

Jess shrugs. "She's home now."

"Have you thought of a name yet?"

Jess says, "Callie."

I pat the dog one more time on her head and get back to my feet. "I chopped up most of the wood out here."

"I see that," she says. "Are you afraid of an upcoming snowstorm?"

My eyes shoot up to hers at her almost joking tone. It seemed almost normal. When our eyes meet, the sadness returns and she drops her gaze.

"Do you mind helping me pile the wood against the shed?" I ask in desperation to try to keep her here with me.

She surprises me when she says, "Okay."

"Okay." My delight is evident in my tone and she frowns. Sometimes I wish I had as good a mask as Dominic.

We work together as we move the split wood and organize it. I bite my tongue the whole time, so we don't exchange any words during the movement. It's nice to pretend, even for a little bit, that everything is okay and we're a team.

The dog joyfully follows Jess. It's a little amusing. If I didn't know any better, I would have assumed they had been together their whole lives.

While walking, I accidentally kick one of the smaller pieces of wood that we missed. Callie barks in excitement and chases after it.

"Drop it," Jess says. The dog obediently walks over to her and drops the stick at her feet. "Good girl." Jess rewards her with a kiss on her forehead. The dog happily barks in response.

"Let her have it," I say with a chuckle. I'm going to do anything I can to keep the dog safe. I may not be able to help Jess the way I want to, but I can at least support those who can.

Jess snatches the stick away from Callie's jaws and throws it away. Tail wagging in ecstasy, Callie bounds after it.

"Where do you think she came from?" I ask as the two of us watch her run.

"She must have been at someone's house around here. She's too well trained to have been wild her whole life." She pauses and brushes her hair behind her ears. "You know, I've never actually seen a dog in person before. I've seen old pictures, and there would be dogs with almost every family."

Callie drops the stick off at Jess's feet, and she tosses it again.

"At Potentia, there weren't any dogs in the territory. My grandparents had a dog when I was growing up, though he died a long time ago."

"I didn't think I'd ever have one, but now that she's here, I can't imagine not keeping her with me," Jess says.

"I guess it's never too late for anything then," I whisper.

She drops her eyes. "Sometimes it is, Elliot."

Without another word, she turns and walks back to the cabin. Callie's giant head darts between her new toy and Jess before taking one last chew and chasing after her new owner.

I sit down and run my hands through my hair. I need to learn to keep my mouth shut. All I want to do is bring her in, yet I keep managing to push her away even further.

I sigh and get back to my feet, following Jess's trail that she created about five minutes earlier, and go inside the house.

The hairs on my neck prickle, though I'm not sure why. I look around the living room in alarm, trying to figure out what feels off. Nothing stands out and everything is in place, but my gut screams that something is wrong.

Finally, it hits me. It's the silence. There's always at least some noise, whether it be conversation, weak attempts at laughter, Josie crying, or even Matt's coughing. Now, there's nothing but the steady ticking of the grandfather clock in the corner.

"Hello?" I call out, heart banging in my chest.

Dominic's head peeks out of Matt and Allison's room. When he spots me, he closes the door behind him and walks over.

"What's going on? Why is it so quiet?" I ask, though I can sense the dread as to what's coming.

"It is time. Matt is dying," Dominic says.

"There's nothing else you can do? You're not saying this because you want to move on as soon as possible and Matt is preventing that from happening?" I ask in desperation. It's not fair.

Dominic narrows his eyes. "Despite what you may think of me, Joe, I'm being truthful. Do you not think that if there were a way to cure the cancer, I would still be in Potentia planning on how to save everyone?"

I open my mouth to protest but close it again as I see the truth in his words. He left Potentia because he no longer saw hope. If he could have saved everyone, he would have stayed. Not because he cares about anyone other than himself, but in a selfish desire to be the hero and get the recognition that came with it.

His tone softens as he runs his hand through the beard he grew after the infection started. "It will not be much longer now. Go spend what time is left with your friend."

I turn back around and reopen the door. Allison stares at me with a fierce desperation. I shake my head, and she closes her eyes. When she reopens them, that desperation is gone and in its place, an acceptance is there. She readjusts her grip on Matt's hands and leans her head against his thin chest.

Matt stirs in his uneasy sleep but stills again.

"Matt?" Allison asks and rubs his face with her free hand. "Come back."

Resting in the crook of his arms, Josie continues to sleep peacefully, not knowing what's going on. Jess stands in the corner, watching the scene unravel, seemingly showing no emotion—though I know that's not the case. Callie sits by her feet.

"I need to say goodbye," Allison says as her voice cracks with emotion. "Please."

Roused by her voice, Matt is able to break back into consciousness. His eyes briefly open to see Allison and close again.

"Since you said 'please'…" he mutters.

"Matt!" Allison exclaims, fresh tears falling down her face.

"I'm still here," he says, though all of the strength is gone from his voice.

Dominic was, once again, right. Matt's not going to be with us much longer.

"How do you feel?" Allison asks and cringes at his pained expression. She doesn't wait for him to answer. "Thank you for being my life and loving me—through it all. I wish more than anything we had more time, but I wouldn't change one second of our lives together."

"Even the…jokes?" he asks.

A choked laughter escapes as Allison responds, "Yes, especially those."

Matt fights to open his eyes again. "You…and now our daughter… are the best parts about me." He struggles to lift his head but is unable to. "I can feel Josie, but I can't see her."

"She's sleeping in your arms," I tell him. "She looks happy."

"Elliot…" Matt's croak barely reaches me across the room. It's so weak and pitiful.

"I'm right here, brother," I repeat his own saying back to him once I kneel closer to him on the bed.

He attempts a smile, but his broken bottom lip turns it into a terrifying grimace.

"Protect and care for them in my stead. Promise me," he whispers.

"I promise," I say as I gently touch his hand. I'm not even sure if he registers the touch. He's so far gone.

We watch, hopeless, as Matt's weakened body fights its way through another coughing fit. Once he finally recovers, his chest struggles to breathe, rising and dropping rapidly as he wheezes in an attempt to get enough oxygen. Barely open, his eyes scan the room.

"Here," Allison tells him and wipes her face.

She leans down, careful not to disturb Josie, and kisses him on his ruined lips.

"I...love you...so much," Matt says. The effort of speaking causes him to gasp for breath, his fallen chest rising less and less each time.

Allison's hands cradle his face. "You can go now. I love you. I love you. I love you." Her tears land on Matt's closing eyes.

His breathing continues to hitch, as his newborn daughter lies in the crook of his elbow—perfectly content and oblivious that she's about to experience the moment when she loses her father.

Matt's chest rises one last time before stilling. His exhale of breath echoes throughout the room.

We all look expectantly at Dominic while he listens for a heartbeat. He makes eye contact with Allison and nods his head slightly.

I lean back on the floor. I want to be out of this room and away from all this pain. I thought I had prepared myself for this, but there is no way I could have.

After all we sacrificed to make this happen, it's over.

I focus on my breathing. I have to be strong enough to handle this. Allison drops her head and falls back into the chair. Her tears fall silently down her face.

Jess reaches down and takes Josie, who fusses at the sudden movement.

My brother makes his way to leave the room. When he passes Allison, he lightly touches her shoulder in a surprising display of compassion. I don't think she even notices his touch. The only thing she's aware of is her sorrow.

The door closes and Jess's shoulders relax. With one arm holding Josie, she uses the other to pull Allison into an embrace. The two women hold each other for support with Josie in the middle.

I make my way closer to Matt and look down. What a difference from the first time we met when he rescued the two of us. His last words to me echo in my mind. I vowed to protect his family; they're already a part of me.

I say my last words to his unhearing ears. "Thank you for showing me how a man and father should act. I'll forever be grateful for that."

I squeeze his hand and drop my head.

CHAPTER SIX

The grief of losing Matt permanently shadows our every move, yet somehow, time still passes. Without Josie, I'm not sure how Allison would have reacted. During Matt's makeshift funeral, Allison clutched her with a desperate longing. Jess was faithfully by her side, offering whatever support she could.

Josie is now a couple weeks old. Though I agree with Allison whenever she asks if she looks like Matt, I don't see it yet. She still looks like a standard newborn baby.

I sit on the patio and look out in the distance. Jess has been gone for a few hours with Callie.

Finally, an exultant bark announces their arrival. I exhale.

"Hey, girl," I say, greeting Callie with a smile as she sprints toward me. Although no one would consider this hairy beast to be a lap dog, she hops up to share my chair. I tilt my head away to avoid her attempt to lick my face.

"Down." Jess's voice is stern. Callie complies immediately and jumps off the chair.

"I don't mind," I say, watching Callie, careful to avoid Jess's eyes.

"She needs to learn her size," Jess replies. Darkened blood covers her body. She continues inside, leaving Callie outside with me.

Since she's gradually recovered physically, she's been going out more and more to kill the Letum. Each time she comes back, she walks with more confidence and her head slightly higher, keeping it an unspoken agreement not to discuss her pain. Jess won't let anyone come with her, so I'm thankful for whatever limited protection Callie can offer her.

Once the door closes, I pat on my lap and Callie jumps back up. She sighs in contentment and rests her head against my shoulder. Listening to the sound of her, I allow my breathing to relax. With so many horrible things happening, her warmth is reassuring.

"Thank you for finding Jess," I say to Callie. "You've helped her in ways that I haven't been able to."

Callie tilts her head. She looks like she understands what I'm saying, but then she barks, licks my face, and jumps off my lap. She runs forward and looks back at me, barking until I join her in the grass to chase her around the front yard.

I wish we'd had a dog when I was growing up in Potentia. It would have been nice not to have felt so alone all the time.

Dominic's voice interrupts my distraction. "Who is playing with who?"

Callie lowers her ears. I pet her head while I turn to glare at my brother. "Why do you always have to do that?"

His eyes light up as he smirks. "What did I do now?"

I clench my jaw. "Every time I start to enjoy myself, you come around and do something to remind me how much I despise you."

"I'm a man of many talents," he says, still smiling.

I take a deep breath. "What do you want?"

He walks closer, and Callie approaches him. He puts his hand out for her to smell, but she's disinterested. Her hackles rise in anticipation. Dominic's grin widens further.

"I want to discuss moving on," he says.

I examine him closely, waiting for the catch. "I agree. It's time that you moved on."

"Oh, Joe, don't act like this. You remember our deal, I assume?" He quickly continues before I can answer. "We agreed that I would accompany you and bring Matt back to consciousness. I went beyond the call of duty and added a family union to the mix. Allison has had time to recover after the birth. Now you all have to go with me to join Acroisia."

"I still don't understand why you need us to get back there," I say. "You realize we're going to slow you down, right?"

"If they have any inkling as to what the real cause of the infection is, they will not allow a Planned to join them. If I go with you, I will rely on the fact that we are brothers to help shield me from exposing myself as Planned."

"I'm not as confident as you are this will work. You and I are built differently, Dominic. I'm quite a bit smaller. My hair is darker," I say.

"I am starting to believe we share more similarities than either of us would care to admit." Dominic smirks. "Besides, it is obvious that you and Allison are Unplanned. It will help me assimilate into their group—as long as everyone remembers our story."

"And why would I want to lie for you? After all that you did to Jess..."

He looks down at me. "Joe, I am not the only one you are going to have to lie for. They are going to suspect Jess as well. If you do not lie for me, I may be forced to throw her under also."

"She's never said if she's Planned or not, she may not be—" I start.

Dominic throws his head back and laughs. "Wake up. Just because you do not want her to be Planned, does not change the fact that she so obviously is."

If she's Planned, that means she could turn at any time, like Dominic. What if that happened? I may have lost her already, but at least I know she's alive.

I sigh and gesture toward the road. "When do you want to go?"

"Let's gather all of our supplies and leave tomorrow. We will take the vehicle far east to Acroisia." He stares me down. "You better make sure you remember the story."

I ignore his threat and turn my attention away from him. There's only so much of my brother I can take. Luckily, he takes the hint and walks away, probably to check the barriers again.

Allison steps through the patio door, yawning.

"Still not sleeping?" I ask.

With her free hand, she rubs her face. "Not exactly."

I hold out my arms. "Why don't you give her to me for a bit?" She opens her mouth to object, but I continue before she can argue. "We'll be fine."

She looks down at Josie as she bites her bottom lip. "You'll wake me if you need anything?"

"Yes."

She carefully hands Josie to me. Freshly accused of being difficult, Josie lies innocently in my arms. She's not sleeping but stares up at me contentedly. I wonder how much she can comprehend.

Callie sniffs Josie and touches her face with her cool nose. Josie's tiny hand reaches out and touches the dog, who licks her face. Josie closes her eyes, but doesn't cry out.

Callie sits back and stares out in the distance as if she's keeping watch for us.

Freshly showered and in a clean, white shirt, Jess sits down on the other side of Callie. "Where's Dominic?"

"He walked past the trees to the west last I saw him," I say. "This place is a lot smaller than before."

"You're telling me..." she murmurs.

"Dominic wants to leave for Acroisia soon now that Allison has had some time to recover," I say.

Her eyes light up. "He's leaving?"

"We all are. That was part of the agreement, remember? He would bring Matt back and in return we would travel to Acroisia with him to help cover up the fact that he's Planned."

"I'm sorry, Elliot. I'm not going with you," Jess says while looking at her feet.

I look away from Josie, eyes wide. "What do you mean? Of course you're coming with us."

"I'm not," Jess repeats. Her voice is even, devoid of any emotion.

I rub my forehead, trying to think of what to do. It seemed like Callie was helping her heal. I thought things would be getting better by now.

"Yes, you are," I repeat and shake my head.

Jess continues to stare down at her feet, her bruised face finally starting to heal, though her nose was never set right so it's slightly crooked. She wouldn't let any of us touch her to fix it—even Allison—and didn't address it herself.

"Why are you so determined to leave us, to"—my voice breaks—"to leave me?"

"I've already left," Jess whispers.

I've never known Jess to lie or be anything but honest. That statement is no exception. It's hard to believe this is the same person who captivated me. What the hell did Dominic do to her?

"Come back," I beg. "I promise I'll protect you."

Jess finally looks at me. Her eyebrows are furrowed, trying to hold in her emotions, making her sharp features even more prominent.

"Elliot, I can't. Okay? I can't be the person you want me to be. I can't even look at you. I can't." She tears her eyes away and back to the ground.

I try to blink back my emotion, ignoring the fat tear falling down my cheek. "Why?" I whisper.

"Whenever I look at your eyes, all I see is Dominic. Did you know the two of you have the exact same shade of blue? In my nightmares, it's those eyes that break through and wake me up, frozen in fear. I can't look at you and see those same eyes looking at me when I'm awake. It's too painful."

"I'm not my brother, Jess. I would never hurt you."

Josie cries lightly before settling back down.

"You're hurting me now. You may not mean to, but you are. When you look at me, all I see is your pity. I can't stand it," Jess says.

I admit my biggest fear. "I don't know how to be the person you need. All I want is to help and give you strength, but you're blocking me."

She briefly looks back up before turning away. "Maybe you're not what I need anymore."

Before I can respond, she whistles at Callie and the two of them walk into the shadows of the forest.

Careful not to disturb Josie, I sit down.

I gently rub Josie's face and her eyes close tighter in reaction. She doesn't yet understand the terrible world she was born into.

Overwhelmed, I watch the sun as it slowly sets.

Behind me, the door creaks open.

"Thanks for watching her. How was she?" Allison says, though her voice is still slurred from sleep.

"Fine," I respond, still staring out to the trees where Jess walked away.

"What happened?" Allison's voice is now more alert as she scans the surroundings for any hint. When she doesn't see anything, she asks, "Jess or Dominic?"

It almost hurts to say her name. "Jess."

"Oh, Elliot," Allison starts as she gingerly sits down and puts an arm around my shoulder. Her touch is comforting but doesn't have the same effect Jess's used to. "What happened?"

"She's not coming with us."

Allison takes a quick intake of breath. "What do you mean?"

"She doesn't want anything to do with me. I…" I struggle to find the right words. It's all so helpless. "I love her so much, Allison. I don't understand how she doesn't feel that way about me anymore. How am I so off base?"

Allison squeezes my shoulder to bring me closer. With her other hand, she holds Josie's tiny foot.

"I don't know how to put this delicately, so I'm going to go out and say it." She pauses. "As hard as this is for you right now, it's a hundred times worse for Jess."

"Allison—" I start.

"No, let me finish."

Josie stirs and cries out in reaction to the change in her mother's tone. Allison takes her to bring to her chest, calming her instantly. My arms fall on my thighs.

"What happened to her—what your brother did to her—is so terrible. No one should ever have to go through it. She's drowning in her pain, trying to claw her way back to"—Allison takes a breath—"not even to happiness, but to a point where she can tolerate everything."

I drop my head. It's what my brother did to her. I brought her to him. I'm the reason this happened.

Allison shifts Josie and grabs my hand with her newly freed hand.

"I don't mean to discount your own pain, Elliot. This is hard for you as well. It's hard to lose the one you love. Believe me, I know."

I cringe. At least Jess is alive, no matter her emotional state. Maybe if I knew exactly what happened, I could understand how to better help her.

"Allison, tell me what he did to her. I need to know." My voice drops at the end. I sound so desperate and pathetic.

Her tone is sharp, biting into me. "You don't need to know anything, Elliot. You may think you do, but you don't. Stop making her pain all about you. You can't take it in for her. That's not what she needs."

"What does she need?" I ask.

Allison laughs bitterly. "I wish I knew that too, buddy. But I can tell you what she doesn't need: someone looking at her like she's the victim."

"I don't look at her like..." I trail off at her raised brow. Is that what Jess meant when she said she couldn't stand my pity? How can I not look at her and feel sorry for all the things that have happened to her—all because of a situation I put her in?

Maybe both of them are right. I'm not strong enough for Jess anymore. I'm not the type of person she needs to get better. I'm only going to slow down her healing.

I draw in a deep breath, finally understanding the new role I need to have in her life. "If I'm not strong enough for her and not who she needs, can you be that person?"

She takes my hand again and squeezes. "I can try."

I have to have faith that Allison can support her in the ways I can't. I have to.

"None of this matters if she won't come with us, though. She can't be alone and expect to be safe." I bite my tongue as I almost suggest Allison stay behind with Jess. We can't get separated.

"Let me talk to her and see what I can do," she says.

Dominic, finishing up his route along the fence, is barely visible. I clench my free fist.

"If only there were a way we could get rid of Dominic. We don't need him anymore..." I taper off, finally voicing my desire and letting it hang in the air.

"That's not who you are."

I pull my hand away and stare intently at Allison, begging her to make the decision for me. "It could be."

She smiles ruefully as she pushes my growing hair off my forehead. "No, it couldn't."

I dart my eyes away to watch Dominic's arrogant strut across the field as he gets closer and closer to us.

I remember the feeling of my hands tightening around his neck when we were back in Potentia, the power of finally having control over him. I could do that again and finish the job this time. Allison doesn't know everything about me and what I'm capable of. I may not be strong enough for Jess, but if I need to, I won't let him go again.

Though, Jess said she couldn't look at me because Dominic and I share our eye color. Killing Dominic won't change my genetics or what happened. She still won't be able to look at me. She still won't come back.

No matter how hard I will it, I can't change the past. I can't right the wrongs my brother caused. But…what if I can control the future? Do I at least get a say in that?

"We are leaving in the morning. Make sure you all are ready. There is no point in delaying further," Dominic commands as he walks back after his barrier check. His weapon is still clean.

He walks out toward the vehicle and checks under the hood again for the third time today.

"I'm not leaving tomorrow morning unless we're all together," I say.

Allison sighs. "I know you won't. I'm going to look for Jess. Why don't you go inside and start packing?"

"Allison, you recently had a baby. Don't go looking for her. She'll be back soon. She doesn't even have her weapon." As soon as I say this, I get nervous. What if she runs into one of the Letum?

"If there's anything she can't handle, she'll be fast enough to run back," Allison says, obviously on a similar train of thought. "Josie and I will stay here and wait for her to get back. She may be more likely to come back if you're not here. Go inside."

Will her rejection ever stop feeling like a punch to the stomach every time I'm reminded of it?

"Call out if you need anything," I say as I stand.

"Will do," Allison replies.

As I go inside, I'm surprised by the sense of nostalgia this place brings. I've only lived here for a couple of months, a small fraction of my life, yet it quickly became a home. Before Matt turned and everything fell apart, this is where I truly was the happiest I've ever been.

I rub my hands on the back of their overstuffed couch. There's no going back now. Matt is dead, and Jess couldn't be further from me. Even though I've been sleeping out in the living room since we returned, I enter Dominic's room to rummage through the closet for the clothes I can bring. It shouldn't be too long of a journey. Dominic thinks only a couple of days' worth of driving, but I want to make sure I have something to change into—especially if we run into a group of the Letum.

I hate having their blood on me. Every time it happens, I think of the first Letum I killed—the one that got to Carly. I smashed a tree branch into it so many times I was slimed in its blood...and Carly's.

Everything I'm packing used to be Matt's. While he ended up being much bigger than me, in both height and muscle, he had old clothes that I've been wearing ever since they rescued us.

And then, Matt turned and I exposed us to my brother. I should never have believed that after an entire life of enduring his cruelty, I could trust my brother to change.

Why does he want us to go out to Acroisia so badly? He claims it's because they don't practice genetic engineering as we have in the territories. Logically, it makes sense that that's where we would go, as it should be safer. But, we grew up being told—over and over again— that the people in Acroisia were a backward population and extremely violent. They caused the Civil War because of their fear of science.

Then again, that same society also spouted all the propaganda about how pathetic Unplanned were, and look how they were wrong about that.

I'm not sure what to believe anymore.

After all the damage we've caused amongst ourselves in the territories with this virus, it can't be worse over there. Maybe they were right all along and we can find somewhere safe.

"It's going to work out, I promise. We'll find a way, but you need to come with us," Allison calls out from the hallway as the two of them walk into Jess's room, not closing the door all the way.

I freeze and hold my breath, listening to their conversation from Dominic's room next to hers.

"No, it's better if I leave," Jess says. "It's already a bad situation, and it's only going to get worse."

Josie cries briefly before settling back down.

"This isn't something you can get through on your own. You're going to need help."

Jess's pitch is higher when she responds in a rush. "Stay here with me. I can keep watch on the barrier and keep us safe."

Unable to hold my breath any longer, I let it out. There's a long pause without any talking. Do they know I'm listening? Sure, I'm ashamed that I'm eavesdropping...but I'll take any insight I can get.

"No, that won't work," Allison finally says, letting my heart resume its beating.

"Why not?"

"Elliot's not going to leave without us, and Dominic won't leave without him. Besides, how long do you think it would be sustainable, just us? If there is a large enough group, we could be overwhelmed."

"I still think our chances would be better," Jess says quietly enough that I almost don't hear her.

"Once we get there, we'll be at a much bigger place. There will be another community for us to integrate into. You won't have to see either of them nearly as much."

"I don't know..." Jess mumbles.

"Please, come. If not for yourself, do it for me. I can't stand to lose anyone else. We can be in this together."

I hold my breath again, waiting for her response.

"Okay," Jess says.

"You'll come?" The relief in Allison's voice is almost tangible.

"Yes, but I'm not happy about it. I don't think it's a good idea with—"

Allison cuts her off. "You may not see it now as the right choice, but it is. One day, you'll be grateful you did."

"I wish I could close my eyes and wake up a year from now with everything behind us and past all this pain. I don't know how much longer I can live like this," Jess says.

Allison laughs resentfully. "You want to race ahead away from this whole mess, and I want to go back to a time when Matt was still here with us. We're a great team."

"When we get to Acroisia, you'll stay with me?" Jess asks, her vulnerability showing how afraid she is of being alone.

"Every step of the way. I promise," Allison says.

Jess sighs. "I couldn't think of a worse situation."

"I know." Allison pauses. "Come help me pack up our things, though Josie doesn't have that much—only what Matt and I scavenged on various trips."

There are approaching footsteps, and I gently shut my door, so they won't suspect I heard them.

CHAPTER SEVEN

"Get in the vehicle, Joe. We are waiting on you," Dominic calls from the driveway, his voice bored and impatient.

With my bag slung over my shoulder, I take one last look at the house. Surely where we're going has to be better than what this place has been like lately.

"Let's go, Elliot." Allison's voice sounds pained.

I turn my back on the house and close the final distance between the vehicle and myself, jogging by the time I get to the vehicle.

I sit in the front with Dominic; Jess and Allison are already in the back with Josie. Callie's head rests on the floor.

Dominic starts the vehicle and it purrs to life. The last time we were all in this vehicle together, it was when we left Potentia to come back to Matt. Though the ride took almost five hours, not a single word was said. That seems like a lifetime ago.

Using the rearview mirror, I sneak a peek at the back seat. Jess's eyes are closed and her hands are shaking. When Allison notices this, she covers Jess's hands with the free hand that isn't holding Josie.

Jess's eyes open and something passes between them, almost a kind of strength. I look away.

Dominic is staring at me, his expression calculating.

All he's going to do is be a constant reminder to Jess of everything he has put her through—whatever that all may be. No matter what Allison thinks, I could do this—and I will.

He smirks as if he can read my thoughts and raises an eyebrow in question.

I look away. "Drive," I say.

"As you command, Joe," Dominic replies. "Fortunately, the vehicle that I took from Potentia allows free travel and has an excellent battery supply. It should be able to store enough solar energy throughout the day to last us through each night."

He plugs some information into the front console. "I do not have an exact destination to key in, so I am directing it out east. I suspect that once we get closer to Acroisia, there should be indications as to where to go. Based on an old map I saw, it looks like this road may take us straight to them. It used to be a major highway, but now all we can hope is that it's been kept up enough to get us where we need to go."

He finishes entering the codes, and the vehicle starts down the driveway. He's already opened the gate and we drive past it.

"Wait, let's close the gate," I say as I open the door.

"We are not coming back," Dominic says as he punches the code in to stop the vehicle.

"It doesn't matter."

I jog over to securely close the gate. Matt is buried here. We shouldn't let it be overrun with the Letum. He deserves a better resting place.

When I get back in the car, Allison mouths, "Thank you."

The vehicle quickly gains speed as it races down the street.

"How long will it take us to get there?" Allison asks.

"With the speed this can go, probably about three days of driving," Dominic says, his eyes alert on the road.

"What then?" I ask.

"We tell them our story, or rather, an altered version of it. We are all from the territories—that fact we cannot hide. The two societies have been separated for about a hundred years. There are going to be several cultural changes and mannerisms that will make it obvious we're not from there."

"How different do you think they'll be?" I ask. They used to tell us that they would hunt down the Planned and kill whoever they could get their hands on. There was no reasoning with them. They were vicious and uneducated.

"Your guess is as good as mine, Joe." I freeze. "Well, on second thought, it probably is not."

"Do you ever stop being an ass?" Allison asks.

Dominic's shoulders tense. "Going back to our story, this is important, so everyone pay attention. We are all Unplanned and managed to escape due to an overheard conversation on public transportation."

I eye his apparent height and strength. "Do you think anyone will believe you're Unplanned?"

For once, he looks unsure of himself and grimaces. "Let me do most of the speaking. Whatever you do, do not admit to having any sort of relationship with anyone who is Planned...even Matt. If anyone asks, he was Unplanned and was bitten."

"Is this necessary? What if the stories aren't true? We could have demonized them after the Civil War," Allison says as she shifts Josie in her arms.

Dominic strums his fingers on his thigh. "Of course the stories have been exaggerated. They still will stem from some seed of truth. Do you want to tell the truth and risk your daughter's life needlessly?"

His words echo through the vehicle, and no one responds to him. Even with the risk in going out to Acroisia, all of us prefer the unknown evil as opposed to what we know from the territories.

The ride passes by without any of us saying anything. There's nothing left to discuss. As time passes, with the sun's movement in the sky the only indication that the day is moving forward, the space feels more and more claustrophobic. Everyone must sense it because the random twitching inside the vehicle increases as time goes on—especially with Allison.

"Can you please pull over?" Allison asks, breaking the long silence.

"For what?" Dominic asks, his voice hoarse after some disuse.

"I need to go to the bathroom."

Dominic looks back. "Can you not hold it for a little bit longer? I would like as much distance between the territories and us as quickly as possible. The longer we are on the road, the more likely we are to run into someone else who might want to take what we have."

Allison raises her voice. "Dominic, after being pregnant for over eight months and giving birth to my child, I have to tell you, my bladder isn't what it used to be. If you don't pull over soon, we're going to have a problem."

I cough to try to hide my laughter, but Dominic still glares at me.

He types in some codes and the car gradually slows down until it comes to a smooth stop. Allison, leaving Josie on the seat, runs out of the car and past the trees to get some cover.

"Two minutes, Allison," Dominic calls out as she fades into the distance.

All of us, including Callie, get out of the vehicle. I stretch my legs and jog in place. After sitting for so long, it feels amazing to be able to move.

Callie sniffs the leaves off the side of the road.

"While we're stopped..." I say. I don't want to have to ask Dominic to stop again.

"Yeah, me, too," Jess says. "Come on, Callie."

Callie jerks her head up at the mention of her name but stays close to the vehicle.

Jess shrugs and walks out in the direction Allison went. I angle in another direction, far enough that I won't run into them, and walk out. I take long strides, appreciating the ability to stretch.

Though the sun is still out, it isn't warm enough to take the chill out of the air. I should have put on my jacket. The benefit to the season, though, is the changing leaves. Because they're still in the process of dying, they're a nice orange, reddish color. I take a deep breath of the fresh air.

I've finished readjusting my pants when Callie barks for the first time. It's not a bark that I've heard from her before. It's much more high-pitched than what I'm used to. She chirps it again and I run back toward the vehicle. Something is wrong. It wasn't her playful bark; it sounded like a warning.

I don't duck in time and a small branch hits my cheek. It stings as blood trickles down my face.

I break through the trees. While all of the doors are open, there's no one in or around the vehicle. With her hackles raised, Callie is in a defensive stance as one of the Letum comes closer toward the vehicle. Its clothes are in ruins, showing its rib cage and rotting flesh. As is characteristic of many Letum, its bottom lip has been torn in half, with each side flopping out as it moans and moves its tongue.

Josie wails, and I push myself to run even faster.

The Letum, attracted to her cries, changes course and reaches into the vehicle. I'm still about five feet away and can't stop it.

This can't be happening. Not after everything else.

Callie jumps through the air and pushes it on the ground. She tears out the flesh of the Letum's neck as it snaps its teeth, centimeters away from her own neck.

I push Callie out from its broken teeth and slam my boot on the Letum's head, stilling its murderous efforts instantly.

I grab Josie and hold her to my chest, her cries seeping through my shirt. I sit down on the ground, inches away from the Letum's dead body, and use my free arm to pet Callie.

"Good girl," I say as the adrenaline exits my body, leaving me shaking. "Good girl."

Callie looks at me intently, as if she's trying to say something, and licks Josie's exposed arm, leaving a small trace of blood from where she tore out the Letum's throat.

"Yes, you saved her," I say and hold Josie even closer to my chest. She starts to settle down her crying. Callie sniffs the Letum and growls.

I'm still breathing heavily when Allison calls out, "Hello?"

"Over here," I say, my voice gravelly.

She rounds the vehicle, with Jess directly behind her, and her mouth turns into a perfect circle. Her eyes dart between my gore-covered boots, the Letum, and her daughter in my arms.

"Oh, her arm," Allison exclaims and rushes forward.

"Not her blood," I say while her hand blurs as she wipes the blood away.

Callie barks happily and runs—so proud of herself—toward Jess, who kneels down and feels through her fur. Callie tries to lick her face, but Jess jerks her head away from her bloodied muzzle.

"I can't believe I left her. I wasn't thinking. I had to go to the bathroom so badly," Allison says.

"I wasn't going to make it back in time," I say through a daze. "It was heading right toward Josie. Callie took care of it."

"Elliot, I don't know how to thank you," Allison says, her expression alight with emotion.

I shake my head. "If I hadn't heard Callie bark..." I taper off, too afraid to even voice what almost happened. "Why did it take the two of you so long to get back?"

"I didn't hear her. We were talking and must've been farther away than you were," Jess says, staring at the creature.

Next to me, the Letum is lying there, its head ruined beyond any recognition. It looks like it used to have long, blonde hair. The infection and madness that followed has caused it to tear its hair out in random chunks, as if the hair got caught in something and it kept pulling. Its decaying smell is nauseating. I stand and throw up on the other side of the car. After a couple of deep breaths, I steady myself.

I look up at Dominic strutting back through the trees, confusion shining through his features at the sight of me throwing up.

He gets closer and peers over my shoulder. "What happened?"

"You bastard," I say and throw my arm back to punch him. Unfortunately, because of the gore on my boot, my foot slips and my punch bounces off of his jaw.

He grabs my wrist and twists me down onto the vehicle's hood, my face painfully hitting the metal and causing me to bite my lip.

"What happened?" he repeats.

When I don't respond, he twists my wrist again—harder. This pain is easier to feel than the horror of what almost happened.

"Let him go, you brute," Jess says and flexes her hand on the knife at her waist.

Dominic's grip loosens and I squirm out from his hold. I wipe the blood off of my lip.

"What happened, brother, is you left Josie alone and she almost got killed," I spit at him.

All of the anger leaves his face. "I was going to do a quick look around to stretch my legs."

"Why did you leave her with all of the doors open?" I ask.

"I...I..." he drifts off. "She was sleeping. I completely forgot she was back there."

I shake my head in disgust, though it's directed at all of us. We were so careless.

"Let's keep moving. The sooner this ride is over, the sooner I'm done with you," I say.

Dominic enters his opened door and slides into his seat, not saying anything.

"Come on, girl," Jess says, and Callie jumps into the vehicle. She's definitely earned her spot with us.

We start driving down the road again, picking up speed, with Allison fiercely holding Josie to her chest.

"I wasn't thinking," Dominic mumbles.

"Shut up," I say. "I don't want to hear it."

Though, Josie isn't his responsibility. He didn't swear to Matt to protect her as his own. Dominic was just the last one of us to leave.

I reach back and pet the top of Callie's head again.

The next stops we make, no one ventures out far, and we stay in groups of two, which pairs me with my brother. Being trapped in such a small space with all of us makes the ride go by even slower than I thought possible.

On the third day of driving straight through each day and night, we can tell we're getting closer to Acroisia when the road starts to get better again. There was a stretch throughout the second night where the vehicle automatically slowed down due to the road conditions. The ride was so bumpy, we had to stop twice to let Jess throw up. Each time, Allison held her hand afterward as she recovered from her burst of sickness. She used to be the tough one, but now she's not as strong as she used to be.

When Acroisia finally looms in the distance, I'm so ready to get out of the vehicle, I welcome any danger that may come along with it. It has to be better than where we've been.

PART TWO

CHAPTER EIGHT

While the territory buildings were known for their height—our living quarters had almost one hundred floors—Acroisia is spread out horizontally with everyone connected inside one enormous central building. The windows are few and far between.

Do they want to keep people from looking in...or looking out?

There are no trees within a hundred yards or so of the massive building. After spending all of the time out in the cabin, this feels wrong and developed. Compared to the territories, it's so much less advanced.

The concrete walls of the building are unwelcoming...but not as much as the men with their guns pointed at us.

"Stop your car and get out with your hands up," the tallest man calls out, though his accent cheapens the use of the "r" so it sounds more like, "Stop yah cah and get out with yah hands up."

We don't seem to have much choice, so I open my door and do as they wish. Behind me, the others do the same.

The man that addressed us walks closer, his gun still raised. I blink as I take in his appearance. We're about the same height, even though he looked so much taller than the other two. His wide features are set in a blank stare. He's probably around the same age as my father would be.

"I'm Elliot," I start, not knowing what else to say. Allison steps up next to me, with Josie in her arms.

"I'm Joseph," he says in a tense greeting. "What are you here for?" His gun lowers at the sight of the baby.

"We've come to join your society," Dominic says.

"Where are you from?" Joseph asks, still speaking quickly in this unfamiliar accent.

"We're from the territories," Allison responds.

While Joseph remains calm, his two companions twitch their guns. He holds his hands up to steady them. "We'll take you to Jonah."

"Jonah?" I ask.

"He's the second in command here at Veritas." Joseph gestures for us to follow him. "Don't worry about your bags right now. We'll take care of them for you."

Dominic ignores him and reaches into the vehicle. When he leans out, he hands Allison her bag.

"You're going to have to leave that here, ma'am," Joseph says, almost regretfully.

"She is a new mother and has diapers and wipes in it, along with extra pacifiers," Dominic responds evenly.

"I'm going to have to at least search it or else I'll get in trouble. Do I have your permission?" he asks.

I raise my eyebrows. Does that mean we could say no or is he simply pretending to be nice? Either way, he's at least acting a lot more pleasant than the guards at Potentia.

Allison nods, keeping a close eye on him as he rummages through the bag. Once satisfied, he says, "If you have any weapons on your person, please drop them on the ground at this time."

I left my knife in the vehicle, so I don't have anything to drop. Dominic, however, lays down his gun. Allison and Jess each set a knife on the ground.

"Thank you for your cooperation. We're also going to have to pat you all down to make sure you don't have any weapons that you're hiding," he says as he holds the bag out to Allison. I take it instead and throw it over my shoulder.

Jess takes a step back. "Is this necessary?"

"Ma'am, we don't know anything about you other than your ancestors were on the opposing side back in the Civil War. I can't allow you to enter our compound if I deem you as a threat."

Joseph comes to me first, while his two companions keep their guard up.

"Hands above your head and spread your legs," he instructs.

I set the bag down and comply as his hands pat down each arm and go down my body, until finishing around my ankles.

He does the same thing to Allison and gets it done as quickly as possible.

"That was odd," Allison murmurs next to me, quietly enough so no one else can hear us.

My smile diminishes once he begins patting down Jess. With her eyes closed she clenches her jaw as he makes his way down her body. When he passes her waist, her arms visibly shake. Callie whines at her side.

I glare at Dominic, who doesn't even seem to notice his handiwork. His focus is on the massive building we're about to enter.

"I'm sorry," Joseph says, jerking my attention back to them. "You may join the others."

Jess wipes her face and stands on the other side of Allison, who puts one arm around Jess's waist while she holds on to Josie with the other. Callie sits in front of her, not willing to leave her side.

"It's over now," Allison whispers.

Jess's breath hitches. "It's never over."

I instinctively take a step toward Jess, wanting to comfort her. Allison shoots me a warning glance and I freeze.

"You're next," Joseph says to my brother.

I glare at Dominic. This is all his fault, and I somehow keep letting him stick around. Who is worse—the person doing the action, or the one who allows it to happen?

Dominic gets in the stance as instructed. Joseph struggles to check his wrists, but eventually works his way down his body. When he gets to his right foot, he cusses and grabs a knife out from his sock.

"What's this?" he asks, the kindness immediately leaving.

"I forgot that was there. My mistake," Dominic responds.

Joseph's eyes narrow in mistrust. He looks toward the three of us and they soften again.

"I'll take you to Jonah now. After that, it's up to him if you get to stay here or not."

"What's going to happen to our vehicle?" Dominic asks.

"It's no longer your concern," Joseph says. His two shorter companions lower their weapons and open the door for us as we pass on into their compound.

The fluorescent lights are dimmed. The concrete theme from the outside continues throughout the long hallway. Our footsteps, and Callie's, echo across the stark walls. Since it's windowless, it's all extremely claustrophobic.

"Sorry about the low lighting. This section of the compound doesn't get a lot of traffic. We try to conserve energy," Joseph says as we turn a corner.

"Why do we have to speak to Jonah?" Allison asks.

He considers her as he takes us down another indistinguishable hallway. "Honestly, culture is a big thing for Jonah. He wants to make sure everyone is going to support it so we can continue to thrive as we've been. Don't be alarmed at his poker face though—he does it to everyone."

Joseph chuckles good-naturedly, though his humor rings flat. It's like he's trying to warn us.

We turn a series of corners, all of them as bleak and dim as the last, more confusing than the genetic engineering building in Potentia, until he finally stops in front of a black door.

He knocks and waits for a response.

"What do you need?" a hurried voice asks. "I'm in the middle of an important project."

"Sir, we have people here wishing to join us."

There's a rustle as papers are set down. "Bring them in," he says.

Joseph gestures for us to enter the room and we do so, piling in one by one, with Callie last.

In the room is a middle-aged man with hints of white in his stubble. His calculating dark eyes watch every motion and interaction as we get settled into the small, bare room.

The people here seem to decorate based on necessity, not design. In the middle of his desk is an outdated computer. He continues to type at something, though it appears like he's doing it for show.

"What are you doing here?" he asks in the same hurried accent as the guard. He tilts his head, causing his thinning, dark hair to fall to the side.

Dominic steps forward and the man in control turns his chair to face him head-on.

"We have come to join you," my brother replies. "Who am I speaking with? What is your role here?"

The man sits up straighter in his chair. "I'm Jonah. I'm in control of the operations of Veritas."

"Veritas?" I ask for clarification.

"That's the name of our compound here," Jonah responds. His eyes narrow again. "You're from the territories."

Dominic opens his mouth to respond, but Jonah cuts him off with his hand. I suppress an urge to laugh. Dominic isn't going to get along well with him.

"Don't pretend otherwise. Your accent gives you away." He cuts his attention back to his computer and keeps typing.

"Yes, we come from the territories, but we're Unplanned," Allison says, following the script.

Jonah looks away from the computer to her. "I can believe that with you. And looking at the other man"—he nods at me—"he is potentially as well, though he's still taller than a lot of the men here. But the other two?" He shakes his head.

"If someone is Unplanned, that does not mean he or she will not still receive certain physical attributes. When everything is left to chance, anything can happen—however unlikely it may be. For example, my brother and I, while we share the same parents, the only attribute we share is our eye color."

Jonah silently stares at our group. His eyes flicker between my brother and me. His comparison brings me back to one day in Potentia when Dominic compared the two of us in front of my classmates in a cruel example of how genetically superior he was.

Now, he's relying on my apparent Unplanned status for something different. He's trying to blend in and pass for the status of something he passionately disagreed with his whole life.

"While the two of you don't look like siblings, I can't deny the truth to what you said. My own sons look quite different."

Jonah leans back in his chair and crosses his arms around his bulging stomach.

"What's your why?" he asks suddenly.

Dominic tilts his head. "What do you mean?"

Jonah smirks and repeats himself. "What's your why?"

Completely sure of himself and his purpose, he responds, "I believe I was born to better society."

Jonah inclines his toward Allison. "What's yours?"

She looks down at her sleeping daughter. "I want to provide the best life possible for my child." She returns her attention toward Jonah. "It may not be super exciting, but that's what it is. I want the best for her."

"And you?" he asks Jess.

She shrugs. "To get through each day."

One of Jonah's eyebrows shoots up to his receding hairline as he studies her. Callie, sensing her distress, nudges Jess's hand with her nose. Jess absentmindedly pets her.

Finally, he breaks his attention away from Jess and stares at me intently.

"You?"

My heart races as I try to decide what my answer should be. We're in a sensitive position right now, and if he detects any lie in my voice, he may call us out on it. We seemed to get away with the deception regarding Dominic—and potentially Jess's—status of Planned, but we can't push our luck too much.

I let out a deep breath and admit, "I don't know."

From the corner of my vision, Dominic rolls his eyes.

"You're still so young, but that's no excuse not to know yet. I suspect you will discover your why soon enough," he says, not unkindly.

"Did we pass your test?" Dominic asks.

Jonah barks out a laugh. "It's not my test you have to pass. I'm merely here chatting with you before our leader has time to meet with you. He's busy and travels frequently. Whenever he's gone, I take control of the compound for him."

"Why did you ask us that question?" Allison asks.

"Just because you ultimately need to get through our leader, don't discount my opinion and the power I have here," Jonah responds.

I furrow my eyebrows at his tone. I'm not sure if he's trying to give us some advice and insight into the dynamics of Veritas or if he's threatening us. Dominic's tense body language tells me he's taking it as a subtle threat.

"How many people are at Veritas?" Allison asks.

Jonah narrows his eyes. "Who's asking? Someone who is looking to join our compound or someone sent to spy on us from the territories?"

Appearing affronted, Allison shifts her body away from him. "What use would we have to spy on you for the territories? They're gone."

Very still, Jonah asks, "What do you mean by that?"

"There's nothing left of the territories but the destruction the infection left behind," Allison responds.

Despite his tough persona, some surprise filters through. "Is that what happened?"

"Do you not know what's happened?" I ask. "How have you been protecting your people from the Letum?" He looks confused at my word choice, so I try again. "From the creatures?"

"We knew that they came from the territories based on their overall physical appearance. Well, from their assumed past physical appearance. Their clothing suggested the product of the territories." He lets out a deep breath. "We didn't know the extent of the damage."

The entire atmosphere of the room shifts completely. Instead of trying to intimidate and impress us with the power he has over here, his shock tears down the power play.

He rubs his right hand on the back of his neck. "Are all three of the territories gone?"

"I suspect that the infection took out ninety percent of the population within the first month of exposure and since then, has only left about two to three percent of the territories' citizens alive," Dominic says in an even tone, somehow managing to keep any emotion out of his response even though he's discussing the deaths of the society we grew up in.

Jonah stands up and gestures toward the door, revealing a gun holster on his belt. "I'll take you to Silas."

"I thought he was busy?" Allison asks, head tilted.

"He needs to hear this," Jonah says.

CHAPTER NINE

When we're led into Silas's office down the hallway, I hide my surprise at his appearance. Slightly older than Jonah, he looks like his complete opposite. While Jonah is dark, short, and rounded, Silas still has a thick head of blond hair. With his broad shoulders and blue eyes, he has more of the recessive genes that the territories placed in high regard.

Silas listens intently to Jonah as he recaps our conversation and what we've already told him. After he finishes speaking, Jonah is silent. Silas studies each of us with a piercing gaze, his expression softening slightly at the sight of Josie in Allison's protective arms.

When he finally speaks, his voice is quiet and controlled. "If the infection that caused the population to change originated from the territories, why did you bring it here?"

"It is not an airborne illness. Though your people have been fortunate enough to not have much exposure to it, it is transferred through a special enzyme that the infected produce in their saliva. Only if someone is bitten will they turn," Dominic says.

Jonah raises his eyebrows and looks nervously toward Dominic.

Silas rubs his strong chin and asks, "What caused the infection in the first place?"

"It was a result of genetic engineering," Dominic replies, keeping his shoulders squared.

Something flickers across Silas's eyes. It's almost like satisfaction.

"You seem fairly knowledgeable on this subject, boy," Silas starts. "Why is that?"

Dominic shrugs. "To be honest, I wish I knew more about it and what caused the infection to take place. Before my brother and I got out of Potentia, I overheard genetic engineers speaking amongst each other on the public transportation. That is when I knew we had to leave," he lies.

I hold my breath, waiting to see if they're going to accept this part of our story.

Silas asks, "Why are you here?"

Still acting as the leader and spokesman for our group, Dominic responds, "For safety. The territories and outer regions are overrun with the Letum. We have all lost someone, most recently the child's father, and we want a place where we can feel secure enough to start over."

"All I'm hearing right now is why you all need us. Why do we need you?" Jonah asks, shifting when Silas's gaze focuses on him.

"You don't know what it's truly like out there and what you're up against." I answer. "I've lost my grandparents, mother, childhood friends, and a very dear friend." I pause and look down toward Josie. "The Letum are only going to explore farther and farther out as time goes on. We know that the walls of Vis got opened and let all of the infected out. That may happen with the other two territories at any moment."

I let out a deep breath and finish. "When that happens and they get here, you're going to need all the help you can get to protect your people. This relative peace that you've been experiencing isn't going to last. If your people don't know how to properly defend themselves because you wouldn't let us in, that blood is going to be on your hands."

"If I let you in, you'll spread panic and fear throughout the compound. That won't benefit us," Silas replies.

Carly died because her brothers didn't want to burden her with the knowledge of what had happened. I can't let someone else make the same mistake. "Keeping your people oblivious to the danger out there isn't going to make it any less real."

Silas stands, moves away from his chair, and turns his back to us, looking out his tall window. From the way the outside looked, this is probably one of the few windows they built in. The scene it reveals isn't special, only the empty grounds beyond the compound.

"When my grandfather founded Veritas, he dreamed of providing a community where everyone could heal from the Civil War in a safe environment. He knew there had to be a better way. He didn't want a group of strangers living and working together, but rather, wanted a culture where we would all be family."

Silas turns back around and places his hands on his desk. "After he passed, my dad led us until his heart attack took him from us three years ago. Since then, I've sworn my life to the betterment of Veritas and devotion to God. One day, when my son leads Veritas, I want to leave a legacy for him that he can be proud of."

God was never a significant part of life at Potentia. In all of the territories, religion took a heavy back seat to science and what that could offer. I sneak a glance at Dominic. His expression betrays none of his thoughts, which, to me at least, tells me he has a reason to hide them.

Silas focuses his attention on Josie. "I don't want to create an environment where we don't help people most in need of it. You will be permitted to enter our compound on a probationary basis."

"We don't have to leave?" Allison asks, the relief in her voice apparent.

Silas smiles warmly at her. "Your child will have a safe home." His eyes shift to Callie, who is sitting loyally next to Jess. "As for the dog..."

Jess jerks her head up. "She won't cause any trouble, and she can hunt for herself."

In reaction to hearing Jess's voice, Callie licks her hand in acknowledgment.

"Very well. Jonah, take them through onboarding. It's only midafternoon, so you have plenty of time to help get them settled. I expect them to become functioning members of Veritas by tomorrow morning."

Dominic nods while a small alarm echoes through my body at his words. It's so similar to what my educator had told everyone in class. In the territories, there's a belief that everyone must serve a purpose.

Silas shifts his gaze between all of us. "Please, don't hesitate to reach out if there's anything I can do to ease you into this transition."

"Thank you so much—for everything," Allison says.

"Of course," Silas says and smiles down at Josie one more time.

Jonah exits the doorway and motions for us all to follow him. We file out of Silas's office, one by one, with Dominic taking up the rear.

He leads us down the hallway into a room with a large table that looks as if it was meant for a much grander audience. Jonah sits at the head of the table and we all sit with him, Callie faithfully standing behind Jess.

"I imagine you all are tired after your journey on the road, so I'll try to be as brief as possible. Once we get done here, Isaac, who helps me out on the operations side of Veritas, will go through the logistics of everything, such as where you will live and what your work will be."

Jonah's entire demeanor from earlier has changed. He smiles at us with a charm that doesn't meet his eyes. Even Dominic seems thrown off by this change in his attitude and taps his fingers on his thigh.

"What do we need to know?" Dominic asks.

"Let's get started with our history. From your skewed education, there will be some areas we need to clear up. Your whole life you have called our compound Acroisia, which if my memory serves me correctly, is Latin for blindness, right?"

Dominic says, "That is correct."

Jonah continues, "Here, we refer to our compound as Veritas, which stands for truth. The Civil War began as a result of the territories pushing technology and science, which eventually led to the desire for ungodly genetic manipulation. Which, as you shared with us, was the destruction of the territories, so we were clearly justified in starting the Civil War to escape the scientists' pursuit to surpass what God intended for us to know."

The educators of Potentia periodically would mention that back when we were a unified country, we were founded on a religious system. It was presented as a justification people used when they were afraid of scientific advancement.

I shift in my chair. I was still raised to value science above any form of religious thought. In Potentia, there was no true organized religion. While some people would meet on occasion, it was always on a small scale and the understanding was always perfectly clear: the society came above all.

Jonah, seeming to enjoy listening to himself speak, continues his spiel. "In the past, we've had some territory members join us and they've spoken about how abortion is used as population control against Unplanned." He shakes his head in disgust. "Here, we understand that every person is created in God's image and, therefore, sacred and must be honored. God has a plan for every person and that's why everyone is created so differently—and naturally. Children are meant to be blessings, not a scientific achievement. Do you all understand that?"

He makes eye contact and waits for us all to mutter in agreement. I sneak a glance at Josie and feel at ease for the first time since getting here. This is a place where they will value people as people, not only if their parents Planned them or not. My life would have been so different if I had been born here.

"Myself," he continues, "I've been fortunate enough that my wife has given me two wonderful sons. It's one of life's greatest joys to watch them grow up."

Jonah's eyes glaze over as he stares past us. After a few seconds of silence, Dominic clears his throat, bringing Jonah back to the present.

"And as we place such high value on all human life," he continues, "we have a zero-tolerance policy for any acts of violence. If you become a threat to someone else's life, we have the power to quickly rectify that situation."

"What exactly do you mean by that?" Allison asks.

"We must ensure the protection of the greater population. If we deem banishing you will protect another's life, we won't hesitate," Jonah answers, his tone low and harsh. "By joining Veritas, you will be subjected to all of our laws and beliefs. Knowing this, do you still wish to stay?"

"Who upholds it all?" Jess's quiet voice calls out.

Jonah, looking surprised that Jess spoke, answers immediately. "Silas of course, though I'm here to guide him on many decisions."

Dominic scratches the back of his head. "To make sure I understood you properly," he says, "residents of Veritas believe that every life is so valuable that if anyone threatens another human being, you will banish and disregard them completely from your compound?"

Jonah smiles. "That's correct. It's all for the best, don't you understand?"

His rhetorical question, or at least I hope it's rhetorical because none of us respond, lingers through the air. He's said everything confidently and seems so sure of himself and its assumed truth. But, how can he claim to value life so much when he's willing to get rid of it so easily? What if his truth isn't the same as mine?

"Do you all agree to uphold our beliefs and laws to the best of your ability?" he asks again.

Dominic turns his head, and the two of us look at each other. There's a sense of indecision on his face and I sense it as well. What other option do we have? Though, one more glance at Allison and Josie and I know this is what we have to do. I promised Matt I would protect them, and this is their best chance at safety. We no longer will have to live watching over our backs. Josie can grow up—safely.

Dominic shifts his attention back toward Jonah and seals our fate. "Yes, we do."

Jonah clasps his hands together in excitement that, once again, doesn't seem to reach his eyes. "Excellent. There is more that we'll eventually need to discuss, but I have another important meeting I must attend. I'll walk you over to Isaac, so he can get you settled and entered into our system."

Jonah smiles unnaturally at us again. "And, of course, let me know if you ever need anything."

Without even waiting for us to respond, he walks out of the room. We all scurry to our feet to follow in the direction he went.

Once again, he guides us through a maze of hallways that he is obviously familiar with. He passes through a set of double doors into a room with excessively bright lights.

There's a large wooden desk in the middle of the room with papers scattered all over it. It's much messier than the two offices we've been to so far.

"Isaac, you need to finish the logistical side of onboarding this group into our compound. Silas wants them to be fully functional by tomorrow morning," Jonah commands and walks out without any words of farewell.

A young, good-natured face peers out from a computer screen. He moves his chair to give us his full attention. "Welcome to Veritas. We're glad to have you here. Where are you from?" Isaac asks.

I automatically return his broad smile. He's already a lot more genuine than Jonah.

"We came from the territories," Dominic replies, still focused on the hallway where Jonah disappeared.

Isaac's eyebrows shoot up and disappear beneath his shaggy, dark hair. "Wow, I'm glad you were able to get out of there and join us."

Allison shifts Josie over to her other arm, catching Isaac's attention.

"I'll hold her for a bit, Allison. Your arms must be getting tired," I say. She smiles gratefully and gives her to me.

The solid, healthy weight of Josie in my arms is reassuring. No matter what else we can do to each other, she's innocent. Who knows what she could do with her life. That's still open.

"Oh, how old is your baby?" Isaac asks, his enthusiasm causing Josie to cry out tiredly until she settles back down.

Allison looks down at Josie in my arms, with such love and tenderness in her expression. "She's four weeks old today, actually."

"Well, congratulations! That's awesome. My older sister had a son about three months ago. The two of you should meet."

"That'd be great," Allison says and smiles at Isaac, who happily returns the gesture.

"What do you need from us right now?" Dominic asks.

Isaac chuckles, showing off his dimples. "Of course. You all look like you've been on the road for a while. I bet you're pretty tired. Let's get you settled, so you can clean up and rest before tomorrow."

Isaac rolls his chair over to his big monitor and clicks his mouse, waiting for it to turn on. Though his computer is similar enough to what we used at Potentia, it's still different. It looks clunky.

Isaac rolls his fingers on his desk as we all wait for his computer to start up.

"Sorry." He looks up. "I've been waiting on an update for the last few months, but it hasn't come through yet..." he tapers off and continues to beat on the desk.

Luckily, Isaac's back is to Dominic, so he doesn't see my brother smirk and shake his head.

Still hidden from Isaac's view, I nudge Dominic and mouth, "Don't."

"Okay, here we go. First of all, we need to get you into our system so we can assign your living suites, get a meal card, and sign up for work assignments."

"That soon?" I ask, unable to hide the surprise in my voice. Without even getting to know me, he's about to decide my future here, like they did back in the territories.

Isaac reacts with such a genuine grin, I relax. "I want you all to be comfortable and happy here as quickly as possible. This is to get you started. If you're unhappy with anything, all you need to do is come tell me and we'll work something out."

"If I don't like my work assignment, it can change?" I ask.

He chuckles at my expression. "Of course. Why couldn't it?"

Allison and I make eye contact, the wonder in her expression apparent. As an Unplanned in the territories, our fates were sealed with our birth. I never thought I'd actually have a choice.

I tentatively return his smile, happy to be away from the oppressive territories and their preconceived notions of the value they thought I could add.

"Let's start with you," Isaac tilts his head toward Dominic. "What's your full name?"

"Dominic Greer," my brother replies.

Typing into his computer, Isaac asks, "Age and birthday?"

"Twenty-eight. My birthday is January twenty-fifth."

"Room preference? Is there anyone you'd like to be with?"

Dominic shakes his head. "No, I would prefer to be alone."

Isaac looks toward Jess before returning his attention to his computer. "Work preference?"

"I would like to assist in security or the military," Dominic answers.

I'm surprised he doesn't want to get involved in their science department, though judging by Jonah's earlier comments, I doubt science is valued much over here. Dominic probably didn't want to raise any suspicion or stand out by requesting that work assignment.

"Okay, next," Isaac says and looks at me briefly.

"Elliot Greer, twenty-two, and my birthday is October eleventh."

"That's coming up pretty soon. Happy early birthday," Isaac says as he enters in my information. "And you'll be wanting a two-room suite with your wife and daughter," he says to himself as he keeps typing away.

Allison laughs as I say, "She's not my wife. We're not married."

Isaac flips his hair out of his dark eyes and turns to face us. "I've heard that people have children out of wedlock a lot in the territories. I thought that was a rumor. You'll probably want to get married soon. Some people may be uncomfortable with the two of you living together before marriage, even though you already have a child." As he finishes, his cheeks are red with embarrassment.

Marriage was an archaic symbol of the past. People in the territories would sign legal contracts to get approval for shared living quarters and permission for genetic engineering, but that was paperwork. From the history lessons, the educators always made it seem like it was unnecessary.

Allison chuckles again. "Honey, that's not what's going on. The two of us aren't together romantically. The two of us together...can you imagine?" Her smile somehow widens as we make exchange glances.

"I mean, no offense to Elliot, but that's not at all what's going on here. He's not the father of my daughter." Her smile fades slowly. "He died."

"I'm so sorry to hear that. I thought..." He tapers off and gestures toward me holding Josie.

"Forget about it," Allison mutters. "Elliot, I can take her back now."

Taking care not to disturb Josie any more than necessary, I give her back to her mother. Allison stares down at her intently. Jess puts her arm around Allison.

Isaac coughs and tries to get us back on subject, though he's much more subdued now. "Do you want a separate suite as well? You don't want to room with Dominic?"

Dominic and I look at each other, a smirk playing on his lips. Though it would help with our new image with Veritas, it wouldn't go over well.

"Individual, please," I say.

"Work assignment?"

I never thought I'd have a say in this. In the territories, everything was always decided for us. Given the choice though, there's only one thing I can think of.

"Is there anything in food distribution or something like that?"

Dominic's head jerks toward me as he watches my expression.

"It's what my mother did," I finish weakly.

"Hmmm," Isaac mumbles. "I can work with that. We have a small team that organizes food and other various supplies. I believe someone requested a transfer so this might work out well." He continues typing away to input all of our information.

"How about you?" he asks as he gestures toward Allison and Josie.

"Allison Lauren, and this is Josie."

More clicks fill the room as Isaac inputs this new information "Age and birthday?"

"I'm twenty-four, born February twenty-fifth."

"Do you want to live alone as well?" Isaac asks, his attention not leaving the monitor.

With Jess's hands still over her shoulders, Allison says, "Can I have a two-room suite with Jess?"

Allison looks hopefully up toward Jess, who nods her head in agreement.

At least the two of them will be together if I can't be. Allison seems to be following through on her promise to be there for Jess.

"I can do that...how about work assignment?" Isaac asks.

"I've always wanted to be an educator," she mutters, almost embarrassed to admit it.

Isaac clicks his tongue. "I doubt they will let you teach right off the bat, but I can put you in to be a teacher's aide."

"That would be great." Allison looks back down toward Josie. "What will I do with her?"

"We have a great daycare system in place," he responds. "My sister loves the caregivers there. They're great with my nephew."

Allison's eyes widen. "I've never had to leave her yet..."

He chuckles good-naturedly. "No worries. That's how my sister felt too, but she's comfortable with it now."

Allison clenches her jaw but doesn't respond.

"Last but not least," Isaac says as he turns back to his computer. "Name?"

"Jessica Borum. Twenty-six. August twenty-second. I'd prefer the medical field. I already have some training there."

"We could always use more doctors and nurses. That's great news," Isaac says absentmindedly while he finishes putting in all the information. "Let me print this."

He walks to the corner of the room where an ancient machine has come to life and is making a loud noise.

"Waiting on an upgrade for that as well, I presume?" Dominic asks, unable to keep the condescending tone of out his voice.

Fortunately, Isaac is oblivious. "I've been waiting on that one for a while," he replies. When it finishes printing, he gathers everything together and puts it in a large manilla folder. "I need to go get your keys. I'll be right back."

He goes into the small closet behind him and sorts through a large box.

Allison scans through her papers and looks across to scan Jess's.

"What time do you get off work, Elliot?"

I scan my page, slightly uneasy about adhering to a strict schedule after months of not even knowing what time it was. This is what I'm choosing, though. At least I have a say in this. "A little after four. Why?"

"I won't get back until about 5:30 and Jess has to report in around 4:30. Can you watch Josie until I get back?"

"Of course," I say and make eye contact with Jess. She quickly breaks her gaze, but not before I see the same concern I'm feeling in her expression. Allison's awfully protective of Josie, which makes sense, but she's going to need to trust other people with her. At least she has us.

Dominic sighs in impatience and taps his fingers on his thigh.

"Take it easy," I mutter, keeping my voice low enough so Isaac can't hear me. He's happy enough. There's no need for Dominic to ruin it for him.

Allison shifts Josie in her arms. I don't offer to hold her this time.

Finally, Isaac walks back toward us and hands us each a packet of papers. "In these, you will find a map of the compound that will help you navigate everything as you get accustomed to life here. In addition, there is information on where your living suites are. Here are the keys for each of you," he says as he hands them out. "Take care not to lose them, though if you do, come find me and I can help you out."

I start flipping through my packet while he continues speaking. "There are also first-day details for your job assignments starting in the morning, such as where to go, who you will be reporting to, and what to expect. It's not detailed, but they'll be able to sort you out tomorrow morning. I'll make sure they know you're all coming."

I freeze flipping through the papers as a title catches my eye. In bold, at the top of a page, are the words Worship Hours. Before I can read too much more, Dominic speaks.

"What time do I report in the morning?"

"After our morning worship, of course," Isaac responds. "Everyone is required to attend the worship after breakfast. Then our typical work hours begin, except for those in fields that require varying hours."

"For how long?" Allison has found her Worship Hours page and is reading it with her eyebrows furrowed.

"We meet every morning, normally for about thirty minutes, but sometimes, if the pastor is feeling especially passionate, he may go a little bit over. There's also evening worship before dinner, but that isn't mandatory. It's only there if you need to hear His word again. I like to go on the days that are stressful. It helps me put my problems into perspective."

"And what problems are those?" Dominic asks.

Isaac shrugs and smiles. "There'd be a lot more without Him."

CHAPTER TEN

Isaac's chipper voice continues our onboarding.

"We all live in the compound and work together to keep everyone functioning at their best. It's better to strive to improve Veritas as a community and from there, as individuals, we'll do better," our loyal escort, Isaac, says as he leads us down yet another monotonous hallway.

"We're all pretty centrally located around the Mess and Worship Halls. The farther away you get from those, the more work assignments take place. In each of your packets, I've included a detailed map to help you get around. If you get lost though, feel free to ask anyone for help. We're a big family here. Remember that," Isaac finishes.

"How many people live here?" Dominic asks.

Isaac blows some air through his lips as he thinks. "We're over two hundred, I believe."

"Wow," Allison says. "That's it?"

Isaac tenses before relaxing again. "After the Civil War, there were only about twenty at the compound when it started. The territories were ruthless..." he tapers off as he turns another corner. "We've had a lot of great growth lately that has allowed us to expand and spread His message even further."

"What do you contribute to your growth?" Dominic asks as he continues to eye the bare surroundings.

"There's obviously been natural growth as families have grown, but we've accepted a lot of new people into our community as well. As word got out about our reputation and culture, people started to come."

"They always made it seem like there were a lot more of you out here," I say.

"The territories almost took us out entirely. Only small pockets of people remained. We're having some growing pains. People who have always been used to being individual contributors are now expected to become leaders. To be honest, our culture and environment aren't for everyone—and that's okay."

"What happens if someone wants to leave?" Jess asks.

"Then they can leave, of course," Isaac says and laughs. "Geez, you guys are suspicious."

"Should we be?" Dominic asks.

Isaac blinks at his hostile tone. "Of course not."

Dominic's face breaks out in his charming smile. "Sorry for the question. It is quite an adjustment after all we have been through to hear about your culture and compound. It is like a breath of fresh air."

Isaac's grin returns and his easygoing attitude comes back. "That's what I like to hear."

We all pass through two more corners, with Isaac whistling happily until he speaks again. "These rooms are typically more of the family suites, so they're on the opposite side of the Mess Hall as the single suites. It's quieter over here. It'll be a nice place for your baby to live. My sister is across the hall from your room."

I frown at being so far away from the three of them. We haven't been so far from each other since we were captured in the territories. I let out a deep breath to get rid of some anxiety.

Isaac clears his throat. "Okay, the room to the left is the two-room suite. The keys that I gave the two of you will work for the room. Your belongings from the car will be dropped off as soon as they're screened. Do you need anything else while I'm here?"

"We should be good," Jess says.

"Thank you so much for guiding us through the compound." Allison smiles. "I'll be sure to let Jonah know how helpful you were."

Isaac blushes and looks away.

The door closes before I get a chance to say goodbye. After so long in a vehicle with them—and all the time we spent together before this—it's uncomfortable to leave them. I'm not sure if I'm ready to live a separate life from them.

"You coming, Joe?" Dominic asks.

I take two deep breaths to steady myself. Even though we won't be crammed into a small house together anymore, I'll still see them often enough. It'll be fine.

"Yeah, let's keep going," I say.

Isaac brushes some of his hair away from his face and keeps talking. "There weren't two rooms next to each other, but I got you two only a hallway apart."

"That's fine," I say, though I would have been happier if there were more space between us.

"The two hallways that you're on are designated as the male hallways, while the females have the hallways closer to the Mess Hall. There's a bathroom at the end of each that the community shares."

"We do not each get our own?" Dominic asks, his eyebrows raised.

Isaac shakes his head. "The family suites do, but not the singles over here. These were the first rooms that were built back when Veritas was founded. They were made with efficiency in mind, not luxury. Plus, with the population being so low, they thought it would be a good way to encourage people to get married and start families by offering a step up in living arrangements."

"Lucky for Jess and Allison that you placed them over there," Dominic mutters.

"I hope I don't get in trouble for that. I figured, with the baby and loss of the father, I could make an exception. I want everyone to be as comfortable as possible when they're with us—especially after having to live in the territories for so long. No one should make a fuss about it."

"I appreciate the exception. It will make the transition a lot easier on all of them to be together," I say and hope he can gauge the sincerity in my voice. Even though I'd rather be the one with Jess, I'm grateful she's not alone. She can lean on Allison.

"Of course," he replies and turns one last corner through the maze.

Each hallway looks the same as the others without any distinguishing characteristics. I see no future where I won't get lost at least a few times.

"Here's your room, Elliot, to the right."

I take my key out and place it in the lock. Nothing happens. "Is it not working?"

Isaac chuckles. "You have to turn it."

"I'm used to something else," I say, trying to regain some ground. Back in Potentia, all of our locks were based on our fingerprints. Even my grandparents had better technology than this.

Feeling silly, I turn the key and open my door to my new room. Its style is similar to the rest of the compound with its simplistic nature, but a bright rug in the middle of the floor makes it a little warmer. The room itself is probably about ten feet by ten feet with a bed against the back wall. It's bigger than the single bed I had in Potentia but smaller than the bed Jess and I shared. After sleeping on a couch for weeks and then in the vehicle, it looks tempting.

On the opposite wall of the bed is a six-drawer dresser with plenty of room to place objects. If I had any, that would be nice. There's also a modest corner desk in the far corner and an end table next to the bed. All of the furniture is unstained and looks solid.

As we're in the middle of the building, there are no windows in here. With the light off, it will be completely dark, regardless of the time of day. Back in Potentia, the massive living quarters obstructed the view from my room. Only a dim gray could go through. Is it better or worse not to see?

I ache for my grandparents' cabin where the windows looked over the lake and nature.

"Looks great. Thanks again for your help," I call out to Isaac.

He peeks his head in and looks around. "Your layout is the flipped version of my room. My bed is on the other side."

"Oh." I'm not sure how else to respond. The gray comforter on my bed is calling for me to lie on it.

"An alarm spreads through the compound to wake everyone up at 6:30 a.m. every morning. Breakfast is served from 6:45 a.m. until worship at 8 a.m. Dinner will start in about an hour. Let me know if you need anything. I need to show your brother to his room and get back to work."

I shut the door behind Isaac and fumble against the wall until I find the light switch. It comes on and I blink back as I adjust to it.

Once I'm satisfied I can find my bed without running into anything else, I turn the light back off. Walking over to it, I take my shirt and pants off, leaving me in my underwear.

Slowly, I climb into the bed and fall asleep within seconds of my head touching the pillow.

When the alarm goes off, I jerk my head up and try to figure out where I am. There's no light in the room outside of a small sliver under the door. I use that as a guiding point to get back to the light switch.

As the light assaults me, I blink and piece together what must've happened. I was so tired, I slept all the way through the evening and night until the compound alarm went off. My bag is in my room. A stranger came into my room and I slept through it.

The alarm silences and I let out a sigh of relief. Is it going to be like that every morning? That's going to be something to get used to after waking up with the sunrise every day for the last few months. Though I grew accustomed to not having a schedule in place, it's a small sacrifice for the stability and safety in Veritas. I can adjust.

All of my clothes have been taken out of my bag, and nothing remains. What could they possibly have against those? They were old leisure outfits from the territories.

I'm forced to put on the same clothes I've been wearing to go outside. When I open the door, an older man, probably in his sixties or so, is coming out of his room. What's left of his white hair is standing out in every direction.

I blink as I take in his hair loss. With genetic engineering, one of the first things they removed from the gene pool was baldness because it was such an easy gene to isolate. Between him and Jonah, this must be a fairly common occurrence.

"You're new. I'm Jerry," he says as he sticks his hand out. His flabby arm is covered in brown spots.

I shake his hand. "Elliot."

Jerry walks toward the bathroom and I follow him. "It's a good idea to get a jump start on the bathroom before everyone else comes out. That way you make sure you get all the hot water you want."

"I'll be honest," I say through a large yawn, "I'm not used to being up so early."

He nods. "I was out on my own before joining here forty years ago. It is a bit of an adjustment, so let me know if there's anything I can do."

I blink at how genuine his offer appears. Why would he be so kind to a stranger he just met? He doesn't owe me anything.

Jerry holds the door open for me. There are two stalls, four urinals, and four showers in the back corner. After I relieve myself, I grab a clean towel from the rack and get in the shower. The knobs are different from what I'm used to. When the water comes on, I jump back. It's still cold.

I keep out of the water's pathway as I wait for it to warm up.

The sound of my stomach rumbling makes me speed through my shower. None of their soap or shampoo is scented. It smells vaguely of clean laundry. I sniff my skin and shrug.

I wrap the towel around my waist and grab my dirty clothes. Jerry is still in the shower, but there are two other men by the urinals. When I open the door, I almost run into Isaac, whose head only comes up to my shoulders. He eyes my scar stretching across my chest—the great memento my brother gave me when we were children.

"Excuse me," I say.

He drops his eyes. "Sorry," Isaac mutters and backs up so I can get past him.

I pass more strangers in the hallway and almost all of them stare at my chest. Their attention is unnerving. I have to actively focus on not covering it up.

I let out a sigh of relief when I get to my room. I should be past all my insecurities surrounding my scar. I know this; Jess helped me find that confidence. Though, with her gone, nothing is certain.

I drop my clothes on the floor and stare at them in disgust. Some of the blood from the Letum that almost killed Josie is still visible. I run my hands through my hair, wondering why they had to take away the clothes. Do they expect me to wear the same, dirty outfit every day?

With nothing else to do, I open the top drawer in the dresser. There are identical boxer briefs and white socks. In the second drawer, shirts in almost every color are neatly folded. They all look a little small. The third drawer has black shorts made with loose, dark material. They feel comfortable enough to sleep in. The fourth drawer has this blue coarse material.

I pick up a pair and unfold it. They look like pants but have pockets in the front and back with a zipper and button in the front. I frown as I study them. They're shorter than I would like. They probably won't fit well and don't seem as comfortable as the pants we had in the territories. I fold them back up and close that drawer. Finally, at the bottom of the dresser are light, casual jackets in either black or gray.

At least I'll be able to put some clean clothes on. They must have kept the room stocked with standard sizes. I'll have to ask if they have any larger ones.

I open the drawers again and grab everything I'll need to wear today. Because the pants seem too short, I grab a pair of the loose shorts and put them on. They fall above my knees. I initially choose a purple shirt but put it back and exchange it for a gray one. The purple is way too outlandish.

I run my hands through my wet hair, trying to tame it, and rub my chin. I haven't shaved since we left four days ago. This is probably the longest I've ever let my facial hair grow. I scratch it, trying to decide if I should shave it or let it keep growing.

My stomach rumbles again. I'd rather go find something to eat than search for a razor—even though with my longer hair and stubble, I probably look a little wild. After years of always having to be meticulously groomed in Potentia, leaving the room slightly unkempt feels like a small act of rebellion, however ridiculous that may seem.

The clock on my nightstand tells me it's 6:47 a.m. I want to get to the start of the line in the Mess Hall. I haven't had any food since yesterday's small lunch of leftover food packets from the territories. All we ever had available in the territories was food packets. I'm not sure if that method of food distribution started before or after they broke away.

Not seeing any other shoe options, I put on my dirty boots. Even though they come up past my ankles, the mud and blood from the Letum make them clash with how clean I am everywhere else.

I lock my room as I'm leaving and put the key in the pocket of my shorts along with the folded map and work assignment instructions. I've never worn anything like them. The material is flexible. They're a definite improvement.

On my way to the Mess Hall, which I luckily remember from when Isaac showed me to my room yesterday, I pass Jerry. He waves cheerfully as he walks past me. I return his smile and focus on recreating the route backward from yesterday.

Luckily, it's almost a straight shot down the hallway. When I do need to turn, it's obvious because of the chatter coming from a big room. I follow the noise and let out my breath when I step into the Mess Hall. Large, brown tables fill the room with benches on each side of them. In the front of the room, is an elevated stage with a large pole and microphone attached. Though it looks like that space can be used for important events, it's empty right now.

In the corner is a short line of people—at least for the moment—waiting to go into an open doorway that leads out to another side, presumably where people go after they've received their meals.

I stand in line behind a couple, probably around Dominic's age. The father holds a young baby in his arms. His hair is even messier than mine and the mother's is casually put up in a bun. Both have dark brown hair, though hers is slightly lighter.

The woman, whose wide, long features look oddly familiar, turns her head to him. "Don't forget to tell her that he didn't sleep at all last night, so he'll probably be fussy today," she says.

"I know, babe." He yawns loudly, exposing his crooked teeth. "Trust me, I won't forget that he was up."

She leans up on her tiptoes and kisses him. "Thanks."

I shift my feet. My movement catches her attention and she looks up at me, her brown, tired eyes alight with interest.

"You must be one of the new folks. My brother was talking about you last night at dinner. I'm Catherine," she says.

"Elliot."

"Adam," the man next to her says in a deep voice that doesn't quite match his shorter height. He gestures with his head toward the now sleeping baby in his arms. "And this little guy here is Jeremiah."

"It's nice to meet all of you. Who is your brother?" I ask, though I'm fairly sure what she's going to say.

"Oh, I guess I should have started with that. Isaac is my younger brother. He works in onboarding and administration," she says needlessly.

"He mentioned he had a sister. Have you met Allison yet?"

Catherine and Adam shake their heads.

"Allison came with me, along with my brother and…" I hesitate, not knowing how to refer to her, "and Jess. Allison has a young baby, too—a daughter."

"Oh, that's wonderful news. I'll have to meet her. We can talk about all the joys of motherhood." Catherine covers her mouth as she yawns. "Case in point—like the lack of sleep."

"We could use more couple friends right now," Adam says. "There haven't been a lot of new parents lately."

Another painful reminder of Matt's death. I close my eyes to try to erase the image of his broken body taking its last breath as his chest stilled.

"The father died almost a month ago," I mutter. I don't want their pity, even if it isn't directed at me.

"I'm so sorry. I thought with your brother here…" Adam fumbles and shifts uncomfortably.

I let out a deep breath and look back at them. "No, they aren't together." I let out a brief chuckle at the image.

"Nonetheless, I'd like to meet Allison," Catherine says with such genuine kindness in her expression. "Isaac mentioned that you didn't come here with much. I'll talk to some of the ladies today after church about getting supplies for the baby together."

"That would be great," I say. "Thank you so much."

Adam clasps my shoulder. "If there's anything else, don't feel uncomfortable asking."

My eyes narrow, trying to figure out what his ulterior motive is. What does he want from me in return?

Both of them look at me openly, though slightly confused by my expression. I relax my face as the line starts moving. We all take a step forward.

"I think they're staying across the hall from you. At least, that's what Isaac mentioned last night."

"Oh, excellent. I'm sure I'll run into her soon then," she says as she refocuses her attention in front of her to follow the line. It's moving quickly now.

Right before I'm about to grab a tray, someone clasps my back.

"Oh good, Joe. You got us a spot in line," Dominic says as he cuts in front of the annoyed people behind me.

I brush his arm off.

"What would you like, dear?" an older lady in a white suit asks me from behind the glass on a long, metal serving station.

"Um…" I look at all the choices. I've never had so many options before. I'm not sure where to even start. Nothing looks familiar.

She smiles through her yellowed teeth. "You're new, right?"

"I am."

"How about this. I'll give you a meal and tomorrow when you come back, you let me know if you like it or not. Sound good?"

"That sounds great," I say and return her smile easily. She's about the age my grandmother was.

She plops some fluffy, tan, circular food on a plate, two brown meat links, and smothers it all with a brown thick liquid. In a separate section on the plate, she puts down something I recognize: eggs.

"This is a fairly standard breakfast. You have some pancakes and sausage, drizzled with some syrup, and some scrambled eggs to keep you nice and full between now and lunch," she says as she hands me my plate.

I take the plate from her. It's heavier than it looks. "Thanks."

"Of course, dear." She takes the time to smile warmly at me again before redirecting her attention toward Dominic. "And you?"

I walk past the hallway and sit at the table in the far corner, hoping my brother doesn't see me and sits elsewhere. Of course, I should have known better.

Thirty seconds later, he sits down next to me—somehow impossible to get rid of.

CHAPTER ELEVEN

I'm forced to accept Dominic's company when we walk through the giant archway to get into the church. Two giant, stained glass windows cover the opposite wall letting in the light from the sun. Between them, there's a T-shaped wooden spike with a shirtless, longhaired, bearded man hanging from it.

"What…" I whisper, not exactly sure what I'm seeing.

His hands are nailed into the wood and there's some sort of headband he's wearing that looks like it's covered in spikes. Blood drips down his emaciated body.

Dominic is staring at the figure in confusion as well.

"What could they possibly believe in?" he mutters, low enough so only I can hear him.

No one else in the room seems put off by the violent image at the front of the room. They accept the centerpiece without a second thought.

"Let's go find a seat," I say. We're already gathering enough attention by being unfamiliar faces and gaping stupidly at their religious figure. It isn't going to help this situation.

"Is this everyone at the compound?" Dominic whispers. "Surely they still must have some guards out…"

While I obviously can't count everyone, there could easily be around 200 people in here. They weren't kidding when they said it was mandatory. What could be so important to require these daily meetings?

"Let's sit down," I repeat.

Dominic keeps walking down the aisle until he finds a gap on a bench wide enough for the two of us to sit. The bench, though it has a maroon velvet seat cushion on it, is far from comfortable and it eerily reminds me of the community center where they purposefully made the chairs uncomfortable so we would stay awake during the territory meetings.

Now that we're seated, there are fewer eyes on us, though those seated nearby still glance at us with respectful courtesy. In the row ahead, sits Jerry, his familiar bald head bowed as if he's in deep thought.

"What do we do now?" I ask.

Looking around the large, old room as if he's seeking the answer, Dominic merely shrugs. Our upbringing in Potentia did not prepare us for this.

We eye the room nervously.

Finally, Silas—in what looks like an oversized black robe, but nicer—comes out to the stage and stands directly in front of the statue of the hanging man.

Everyone stills and the quiet conversations that were taking place cease instantly. Our Territory Leader demanded the same amount of respect when he would get our attention.

"Blessings be upon everyone in the room today. God has given us yet another beautiful morning to worship Him. Let us bow our heads in prayer," he says, and everyone follows his command.

We're about a second later than everyone else in complying. In this delay, I'm able to spot Jess and Allison around five rows ahead of us off in the corner. That was smart of them. We shouldn't have sat in the middle.

"Lord, we want to thank You for bringing us together this morning so we can honor You. Thank You for providing the food so we may nourish our bodies and have the strength to serve You. We ask that You continue to protect our people from harm and lead us into Your grace. In Your name we pray. Amen."

"Amen," the entire room echoes and I startle in surprise.

"Our Father..." he begins, and the rest of the people in the room join in with him in a monotone, unified voice. "Which art in heaven, Hallowed be thy Name..."

The prayer continues, but my attention drifts away from the words and instead focuses on the attitude of everyone in the room. They all utter the words together and seem to come through as one mind. They don't seem like 200 different people, but rather, the prayer comes from one voice. They all belong.

The chanting ends with another cohesive "Amen."

He gestures, raising his hands up, and the people all stand at the same time. Once again, Dominic and I are slightly delayed in following suit.

Silas looks around the room, seemingly making eye contact with everyone, though that's impossible with the sheer number of people in the room. Accustomed to his routine, everyone—even the children—remains quiet as he makes his pass through the room. I stare straight ahead, not blinking, waiting to see if he's going make eye contact with me.

Before he can, without a cue that neither Dominic nor I pick up on, everyone sits back down and looks up expectantly toward Silas, waiting for him to speak.

I've never seen anyone exhibit so much control over a group of people. Not even Dominic has been able to accomplish this. My brother shifts in his seat and drums his fingers on his thigh—a motion that, at least to me, gives away his unease.

"As many of you may know by now, we have been blessed with five new members to our compound. As they've come from the godless territories that have been subjected to the genetic manipulation, He has spared them from this disgusting marring of nature. God is good."

"God is good," the crowd says in unison.

From beside me, Dominic sits up straighter. Besides that slight movement, he stays perfectly still. It would be interesting to have seen Silas give this speech out in the territories. He would be eaten alive.

Literally.

I accidentally let out a bark of laughter, garnering even more attention. Dominic elbows me in the ribs, and I quickly adopt a more somber expression.

"While we shall not blame them for their upbringing, we must all pray for them to spot the errors of their ways and join us in the light. As we welcome them into our church, we must guide them away from their sinning ways. With His help, all things are possible. God is good."

From my sinning ways? Back in Potentia, the only girl I could get to talk to me was my mother.

"God is good," Silas's people repeat back to him in perfect harmony.

Everyone is paying such close attention. They seem to genuinely believe all of this. How low do they think our group is?

Laughing suddenly feels like the last thing I want to do. We're going to have to be careful.

Silas gestures to a person behind a large organ with golden pipes spread up through the wall. It's impressive architecture.

An unfamiliar melody rings out, and in that nerve-racking, single-minded organism that is this group, the singing starts.

"Praise to the Lord, the Almighty, the king of creation. Oh my soul, praise Him, for He is thy health and salvation…"

The song continues for a few verses. The lady next to me is singing loudly, as is everyone else, but she's off pitch. I bite back my laughter. She doesn't seem to realize how ridiculous she sounds. Instead, she's putting all of her energy into joining the crowd.

I'm unable to maintain focus on the words that they're saying. The atmosphere in the room is stifling with everyone blindly following along. Dominic's fingers continue to drum, though they're out of rhythm with the song. His eyes scan the crowd rapidly.

The song ends and immediately transitions to a more upbeat tune. The crowd sings out, the man's baritone next to me ringing through the halls. I look around in nervous wonder at the single body religion has created. If they're all on the same page here, how could there ever be any disagreement in any other avenue of life? Everyone is so in sync with one another.

The organ stops playing and everyone stands together. Dominic and I follow their lead, though Dominic takes longer than I do to get back on his feet.

"For today's sermon, I want to discuss the imminent destruction of the human's time here. Just as God has granted us our life, He can take it away. He has given us time and time again to honor Him justly, yet there are people who smother themselves in sin and succumb to the darkness."

The lady next to me nods. Everyone in this room is agreeing with Silas. I've never felt so out of place in my entire life. Even as an Unplanned in Potentia, it wasn't as odd as this. At least here, no one is pointing out how much I don't belong.

"Even if it may seem like sinners can escape God's wrath from time to time, He is indeed patient. The new members from the territories have brought with them joyous news. God has finally punished the sinners of the territories for their genetic manipulation and casting Him aside. The genetically mutated, or Planned as they call themselves, are all carriers of an illness that has broken out and sent them to eternal damnation. God is good."

"God is good," everyone repeats back to him with more enthusiasm than last time.

How is God good? Thousands of people have died. My friends and family have died. I don't understand.

"As you all know, there have been some creatures of sin that we suspected all along were coming from the ungodly territories, that have made their way to Veritas and took seven of our members' lives. They are a direct result of the genetically mutated experiments. We must stay strong and not let the agents of Satan take us from His path for us."

Dominic and I exchange a look and he raises one brow. I'm not sure who Satan is, but I doubt he had anything to do with the infection. Yes, it was a result of the genetic planning. However, the genetic engineers did that, not this Satan they speak of in such a hostile tone.

Silas wipes his brow of sweat. Leading a group of people this large must be hard work. "To warn us against the creatures of sin, God has sent us five unlikely people, who are all fortunate to be untainted by the genetic mutations. And as we must help save their souls, we must understand that He sent them as a tool to ensure we don't stray from our path of light and become tempted into the darkness. They understand how to destroy these demons to prevent them from spreading their disgusting infection."

"Now, let us pray," Silas says as everyone kneels and bows their heads.

"Lord, thank You for giving us another opportunity to honor and serve You. Please continue to provide us the strength to resist the evil temptations and sin that fight to get through the doors every day. In Your name we pray. Amen."

"Amen," the room echoes back to him.

Silas does his eye contact motion again and everyone remains still, waiting for him to finish his ritual. Once he finishes scanning the room, he gives one final nod and walks across the stage to an exit.

The trance is broken and the small chatter from earlier returns. That mindless energy doesn't entirely dissipate but buries into the surface, waiting to come back out at the next meeting.

The ball of tension in my stomach won't disappear. I'm not sure why their worship worries me so much. Maybe it's because Silas has exposed himself for having all the power that he does. Not only is he the political head of the compound, he's their religious leader as well.

While the territories didn't openly engage in any religious practices, a separation still existed throughout the political sphere, and it acted as a check to ensure one group didn't get too powerful. All the Territory Leaders were voted into office and reported to the President. Even her hands were tied if the Territory Leaders disagreed with her.

At Veritas, there doesn't seem to be any sort of separation. All of the power rests in the hands of one man: Silas. Whatever power anyone else has is smoke and mirrors. Even Jonah's authority is allowed by Silas. From the control he had over the group here during his prayers and hymns, I can't imagine anyone being able to question his authority.

"What did we get ourselves into?" Dominic asks himself quietly enough that even though I'm inches away from him, I almost can't hear him.

CHAPTER TWELVE

I double-check the number on the paper with the plate next to the door. Yes, it's supposed to be here. It's very secluded. I look around nervously, expecting someone to be playing a joke on me.

I'm either in the right place or I'm not. Standing here staring at the door isn't going to help anything.

I lightly knock on the door and wait. There's no response. I knock again harder—still nothing.

I let out a deep breath and open it. In the corner, a small figure is hunched over a box and wears the same blue pants that everyone wears with one of the obnoxiously bright yellow shirts I bypassed this morning. Without the door blocking it, I can hear the humming of an unfamiliar tune.

"Hello?" I call out.

The figure doesn't react and continues humming.

Jess used to hum whenever she was happy and content…whenever we were together. I can't remember the last time she hummed to herself. The knife that's been in my chest since Potentia twists again.

Maybe this person can't hear well. "Hello," I call out again, this time louder.

The figure jumps up and knocks her head on the shelf she was leaning under.

"Dammit," she cries out, holding her head in the spot she hit. With her other hand, she yanks out some cords from her ears and turns to face me.

Her hazel eyes narrow at me in accusation before a giant smile, revealing slightly crooked teeth, breaks out, making her look much more approachable.

"Are you the new person?" she asks, continuing to rub her head.

"Yes. I'm Elliot." I remain standing by the door, my arms awkwardly at my sides.

She pushes her dark hair behind her ears and steps closer.

"Nice to meet you, Eli. I'm Leah."

She smiles and holds out her hand, and I accept her nickname for me. Returning her handshake, I find it's surprisingly firm. She can't be more than an inch or two taller than Allison and is thin—smaller than even Allison.

"Isaac told me right before worship this morning that you'd be coming along. I totally forgot about it. If I remembered, I wouldn't have had my headphones in." She gestures toward the wires that are in her left hand.

"What are those? Were you calling someone?" I ask.

She raises one of her thin eyebrows in confusion. "What? Was I calling someone?" she repeats back to herself. Without warning, she starts laughing.

"Because they're called 'headphones,' right? That's why you asked that?"

Sheepishly, I nod. Her laughter continues to bounce across the room.

"No, I wasn't calling anyone. I was listening to music."

I keep looking at her without comprehension.

"Do you not have these back at the territories?"

I shake my head. Her eyes light up with excitement.

"I thought you were supposed to have all sorts of amazing technology. Here, listen to this," she says.

Leah holds the wires out to me. I lean my head down and she places them across my head.

Through it, a heavy melody plays with an electric beat. I smile at the sound even though I've never heard this song before.

"We have these back in the territories. They're wireless and we call them ear speakers," I say and lean away from the music.

"Ear speakers?" she asks and laughs again. "That sounds ridiculous."

I laugh with her. "It makes more sense than calling them headphones."

"We'll have to agree to disagree on that one." Leah sits down on one of the boxes and crosses her ankles.

I gesture toward the entire room. It's filled with boxes of various sizes with tall shelving hiding how big the room is.

I clasp my hands together. "Should we get started? What am I supposed to be doing?"

She shakes her head. "It's straightforward. We sort through the boxes that they bring to us and put them in the right places. It's super simple." She rolls her eyes.

"Where do they all come from?"

Leah shrugs. "They do food processing in another department."

I look around the room in wonder. For only 200 people, it's quite the operation to get everyone fed. The boxes seem limitless.

"Now, let's talk for a bit," she continues. "They won't send anyone to check on us since we're so far out."

"But shouldn't we get the work done?"

Another wide grin covers her face. "There's always going to be more work that needs to be done. It's never ending. That's not what life is about."

I sit down on the box across from her. It buckles in slightly but remains standing. "What's it for then?"

Leah's left eyebrow briefly flicks upward. "Living." She looks around the windowless room with all the shelves and boxes piled up everywhere. "Which we can't do in here."

It does seem gloomy in here. The artificial light is no real substitute for the light that used to pour into my grandparents' kitchen in the cabin. Nothing can beat that.

I frown. My family is buried at that cabin. I'm not sure if I'll ever make it back there. Everything at Veritas is so unfamiliar and foreign. Despite the uncertainty of life there, I miss it.

Misinterpreting my expression, she brings me back to the present with her chipper voice. "It's not that bad. I mean, we're pretty isolated out here, so like I said, no one checks up on us most of the time and we're able to do whatever we want."

"They won't figure out if we're not productive and working hard?"

She chuckles again. "Eli, I don't think anyone in this assignment has ever worked hard. They've nothing to compare us to. Trust me."

Her glint of rebellion is refreshing after this morning's religious exposure. Does everyone put on an act during those meetings or is she an outlier? Maybe I shouldn't have been as worried after the worship if everyone doesn't believe as Silas does.

"Uhhh, can I help you there, buddy?" she asks, drawing attention to the fact that I was staring at her.

I cough and break eye contact. "Sorry, I was thinking about something else."

"Now I know that you're absentminded and spacey. Great. They always send the best people out here." She winks to let me know she's joking. "Why did you request this assignment by the way?"

I'm surprised when I tell her the truth. "My mother worked in food distribution back in Potentia. I always hoped that one day I'd be able to join her."

"So you're a mamma's boy then. Where is she?"

I hesitate. Should I tell her she's under a mound of dirt with my grandparents who killed her? That might be a bit much.

"She's dead," I whisper back instead. It's still painful to say out loud.

Leah's smile instantly disappears, making her look like she did when I first walked in. "I'm so sorry. Sometimes I speak without thinking it through. I have a terrible filter. I should've guessed that from Silas's sermon this morning."

I'm not sure why I keep talking. Maybe it's to have someone listen. "My grandmother was infected and killed my mother right in front of me." My voice lowers even more. "We made eye contact as she died."

I drop my head and stare at my hands in my lap. When she died, Jess was there with me. Even though we had just met, she still managed to be the strength I needed to go forward.

Through all of the loss, Jess was always there. We gave each other support. It may have started with her giving me the strength, but our relationship eventually evolved so we could support one another. We were a team.

Leah tentatively moves toward me and squeezes my shoulder. I look up at her, wishing she were someone else, to find her looking down at me with an expression full of pity.

I shake my head to get rid of the emotion. I don't want her to feel like I need her to comfort me right now. I don't need her sympathy.

"Anyway, that's that," I say, no longer wanting to open up. Instead I stand up from the box and look around for inspiration on how to change the subject.

Luckily, she accepts my transition. She angles her head up as she scans my body.

"How tall are you, Eli?"

"Around five foot ten," I say. "Why?"

"You look tall standing right there."

She's awfully close to me. I take a step back and my foot hits a box. She eyes the motion and takes a step back herself to put some distance between us.

"I don't think anyone has ever told me I looked tall before. It must be because you're so short. What are you, five one?"

She straightens her shoulders and stands taller. "I'm actually five foot two, thank you."

I raise my eyebrow.

"Okay, with shoes on. Which I'm wearing right now so technically I'm not lying," she says again, her mischievous smirk back.

I bark a quick laugh. "You asked me why I wanted to work back here, but you didn't tell me yourself. Why are you here if you think it's gloomy?"

She bites her lips and sticks her face out like she's trying to get away with something.

"I have a big mouth sometimes and it gets me in trouble. I figured being isolated would be better for me." She sticks her tongue out. "Plus, one of my friends used to work down here and he said that you could get away with eating some extra food before it's logged to go to the Mess Hall. Speaking of which…"

Leah runs back to the original box she was looking through when I walked into the room and digs back through it.

"Aha!" she exclaims as she comes back out holding two wrappers. "I thought that's what I saw."

She sits back down and tosses me something. I catch it automatically and eye it curiously. I've never seen packaging like this before. We wouldn't use plastic to cover our food. Everything was always delivered in reusable metal meal packets.

She tears her pack and takes a big bite. "Go ahead and eat it. No one will notice they're missing two bars of chocolate." Her teeth are temporarily stained dark from her bite.

My eyes widen in excitement as I open mine. We would only get candy on special occasions. It wasn't deemed a nutritional part of a diet.

I moan when I take a bite of chocolate. It's delicious. No wonder some of the people here are a bit...fuller than those at the territories.

"This is amazing." I sit back down on one of the boxes opposite her.

"Like I said, there are some benefits to working here," she says and laughs at my expression. "You know, I've never spoken with anyone from the territories before..."

I chuckle at the enthusiasm in her tone. "What do you want to know?"

"How are things going so far? It's quite an adjustment, right?"

"That's putting it lightly," I admit.

"How old are you, Eli?"

"I'll be twenty-three in a couple of weeks."

"Oh, I have an older man with me then." She rubs her hands together as if she's planning something. "I'm nineteen," she tells me even though I don't ask.

"Cool." I'm not sure what else to say.

"The two women you came here with—there's the one with the baby and the tall, curly-haired one—are you with either of them?"

Even though I wish I could say something else, I reply honestly. "No."

I take another bite of my chocolate. It doesn't taste as good as it did on my last bite.

"Oh..." she trails off and takes another bite. "Is it true about the creatures of sin, as Silas said earlier?"

Reluctantly, I concede. "In a way. Something went wrong in the genetic engineering, and it created an infection that turned people into mindless creatures. We've been calling them the Letum."

Her eyes widen, though I can't tell if it's because of fear or excitement. "What are they like?"

I let out a breath of air. It feels like bad luck to talk about them here. "Like I said, they're mindless. They aren't people anymore."

"I assumed Silas was exaggerating again..." she tapers off.

"They're extremely dangerous. They've killed almost everyone from the territories."

She looks past me, deep in thought. I take another bite of my chocolate, trying to ignore the image of my grandmother ripping into my mother's throat, spraying her blood across the walls as she died.

"Honestly, I figured it was another one of his embellishments to scare us into following his lead."

My chewing stills as I carefully ask, "What do you mean?"

Leah shrugs again and keeps staring off into the distance. "His sermon was even gloomier than normal." She takes another bite of her chocolate. "He does that whenever there's some change throughout the compound." She gasps. "I'm so sorry. I shouldn't have said that. Please don't repeat it."

Already understanding what she means about lacking a filter, I say, "Don't worry. I won't say anything."

This suggests that he's using religion as a tool for power instead of truly believing in it, like he said. Leah's so young and full of rebellious spirit. Is she misinterpreting this?

Her voice brings me back to the present. "Well, do you like it here so far?"

I smirk at her change of topic. "It's nice to be somewhere safe, but things are different here from what I'm used to."

"Like what?"

She looks away in what seems like an attempt to appear less interested, though it's not working. Her curiosity about the territories is similar to how Carly idolized us.

You always want what you don't have.

"For one thing, Potentia—the territory where I'm from—doesn't have a foundation in any religion. This morning's church service was the first one I've ever been to."

I gauge her reaction to my words. I don't want to say too much and get myself in trouble. Luckily, she seems safe enough and gapes at my response.

"That's what they told us. Honestly, I thought that was a rumor they started to demonize you. Wow. I can't believe you've never been to church before in your life."

She looks at me with a new appreciation, then laughs loudly. Even though she's laughing at me, it doesn't appear to be mean-spirited, so I don't take offense.

"What's so funny?" I ask with a tentative smile of my own.

"You didn't even burst into flames when you walked through the church's doors. Man, what a disappointment!"

My mouth opens in shock. "Was that supposed to happen?"

She shrugs and wipes her tears with her left hand. "It's something they always said: if a nonbeliever tried to walk through His sanctuary, they would burst into flame once they passed through the doors. You don't believe in God though, do you?"

I shrug. "I've never put much thought into it. I was raised differently."

"Hmmm...don't let anyone else hear you say that," she says as she stares me down. "You don't look any different or like someone they warned us against—one of Satan's agents sent here to seduce me into sin."

She playfully nudges my side, smirking up at me.

"Can I ask you something, Leah?"

She smiles even wider. "Of course. What's up?"

"Who's Satan?"

PART THREE

CHAPTER THIRTEEN

The routine of Acroisia—or, rather, Veritas as they call themselves—is surprisingly easy to fall into. Every morning begins the same: a quick shower before heading to breakfast. From there, the daily worship takes place. I've learned how to...not exactly fit in during those meetings, but at least not stick out anymore. Dominic sits by me every meal and during worship, but besides that, I hardly ever see him. He doesn't ask me about anything going on in my life, and I don't care to ask him about his.

My birthday came and went without any major fuss. It's not right to celebrate when so many I've cared about aren't here with me.

Everyone here has accepted us, displaying a compassion and charitable nature that was not present in the territories. With so many names, it's been a challenge to keep up with everyone in their bright colors and refreshingly diverse faces.

Outside of the brief times I see Jess when I stop by every day to watch Josie, I only ever catch sight of her in passing. Allison, while she's always happy to see me, is a subdued version of her old self, always busy juggling her new work schedule and being a single parent.

While I was so dependent on them before we got here, we all drift apart, as anyone would when introduced into a much larger body of people. It's sad whenever I stop and think about it, but I've been busy myself with work—though it doesn't require much skill—and trying to make new friends and build a life here.

About a month following our arrival, I knock on the door to Allison and Jess's suite to trade off Josie-watching duty after work. It immediately opens.

Jess is wearing a navy, shapeless shirt with matching pants. It looks oddly similar to what our outfits were like in the territories though not as sturdy. She's wearing dark scrubs, as Leah called them when I asked. None of us have felt comfortable wearing any of the bright, vivid colors.

"Sorry I'm late. I was—" I hesitate as I don't know what to tell her. I can't admit that I lost track of time because I was with Leah. She'd get the wrong idea if I did.

Josie, lying on a blanket on the floor, cries out and lets me avoid giving an excuse. Jess instinctively turns, but Josie calms herself down without needing help and starts cooing into the air.

Callie, for once in the room during the day and not outside wandering the surrounding forest, pops her head up to observe the disturbance.

"Don't worry about it," Jess says. "Allison should be back soon."

She leaves the room in a hurry without saying anything else.

If she didn't have anywhere to go, she probably would have come up with some excuse to leave. Despite all we've been through, she still can't stand my company. She blames me for what someone else did. But I guess in a way, it was my fault.

Josie moans again, so I pick her up and she quiets down. She's probably one of the most spoiled babies. Allison, who has been fiercely protective of her, hardly lets her out of her arms. When she does, it's typically only with Jess or me. She still won't let her go to daycare, which is all right by me. I enjoy my afternoons with her.

Josie relaxes in my arms and closes her eyes. Carefully, I sit down on the couch. Callie, with a small moan, walks over to lie companionably next to me on the floor. With Josie peacefully sleeping on my chest, I lay my head back. After a few moments of us not moving, the motion sensor lights turn off and put the room in comfortable darkness.

The lights come back on again and I startle awake, trying to remember where I am. Josie protests at my movement, and Allison calls out, "Everything okay?"

Careful not to disturb her even more with my movements, I sit up and rub my face with my free hand.

"We were taking a nap," I call back as I adjust to the light.

Allison walks over, wearing the blue jeans, as Leah told me they were called, and a plain black T-shirt. She looks tired.

Callie jumps up with excitement and licks her hand in greeting.

"How was your day?" I ask as I hand Josie to her outstretched arms.

She smiles down at her daughter and sits on the cushioned chair in the corner of the room. "It was pretty hectic. Kids are exhausting."

I chuckle. Kids on the public transportation or at the territory meetings were always obnoxious.

"I bet," I say.

Allison's shoulders are slumped, making her appear even smaller than usual. She has dark circles around her eyes.

"How are you, Allison?"

She yawns. "I'm fine—just tired."

I don't want to play around with what I'm asking, so I bring up the topic I want to talk about.

"I miss Matt," I say. "When I'm here watching Josie, I feel guilty that I'm able to spend time with her when he's not."

Allison drops her attention to their daughter. "It still doesn't feel fair."

"No, it doesn't," I say and hold off, waiting to see if she's going to open up.

"Sometimes, I forget that he's dead—never for long—but enough where the darkness lifts and everything's possible again," she says at last. "Then I remember and crash back down."

She continues to stare down at Josie, her eyes darting around her small face. "It helps when Josie is with me because I can look down at her and see him. She's proof that what we had was real and existed. The life we had together is so far gone from what it's like now. The problems I thought we had back then were meaningless."

"So much has changed," I say, pausing again.

"I'm Unplanned. As such, I grew up constantly discriminated against and told I couldn't do the things I wanted or love who I loved..." She wipes an escaped tear from her cheek. "But whenever I was with Matt, it didn't matter. He made everything okay. We were together. We hadn't figured out what we were going to do about my pregnancy with his parents' high-levels at Robur, but it would have worked itself out. He could always calm me down and make sure I wasn't taking anything too seriously." She tries to smile at the memory, but her face falls again. "Now he's gone and has left me in a whole new world."

"Did it make it better or worse that Dominic brought him back for such a short amount of time?"

"Elliot," she starts and pauses to collect her thoughts. "No matter what else Dominic has done, I'll forever be indebted to him for letting Matt meet his daughter. And for…" She takes a deep breath. This time, she allows the tears to fall down her delicate features. "I got to say goodbye." Her voice breaks.

I stare down at my hands to avoid eye contact. I only knew Matt for a couple of months, but it felt like it had been so much longer than that. I risked everything to bring him back, and we're still struggling with the consequences of that action, but Allison is right. We got to say goodbye.

"It's not fair that it happened to him," I say to repeat her earlier statement. "He was such a kind person."

"Matt should be here for this," she says and sniffs, her face already getting red and blotchy. "He would have been such a great father."

"He absolutely would have."

"That's the only thing keeping me going these days. Matt would be so mad at me if I gave up. I have to be strong for Josie. I'll have to get through it somehow."

"I wish there was more I could do to help," I say.

She brings the baby closer to her chest. Josie moans at the movement.

"Talking about it is almost a relief. Besides Jess and your brother, no one else knows exactly what happened. Sometimes, I want to talk about Matt to make it seem like he was here and I'm not going crazy with the memories we shared together."

I look into Allison's eyes again. Her face is painted with grief, and she lets out another deep breath and stands up straighter.

"I don't know what I would do without having you all here…if I were truly alone. Jess and I have been able to lean on each other. Thank goodness we're sharing this suite together, so she's forced to interact with me." Allison wipes her tears away and attempts to laugh. It comes out as a choked noise and she immediately cuts it off.

It hangs in the air, along with what she gave away about Jess. She's still struggling.

"How's she doing?"

"Jess is better," she says.

It wouldn't take much for Allison to say she was doing better. I think back to Jess, naked and vulnerable in the shower, the cold water trailing down on her broken body.

Better doesn't mean she's doing well.

"Do you think…" I start and stop as I struggle to complete my thought in a way that doesn't sound pathetic. When I can't come up with a good way to express it, I bluntly ask, "Do you think we'll ever get back together?"

Allison coos at Josie to quiet her fresh cries. Over the noise, she says, "I don't know, Elliot." She transfers Josie to her other arm to calm her down. "She still needs more time to heal and remember who she is."

I shake my head and clench my jaw. "I'm not the one who hurt her. Why is she punishing me for something I didn't do?" I spit it out, shocking even myself at this sudden anger.

Allison mutters, "Elliot…"

I throw my hands in the air and continue. "She shouldn't be treating me like this. I thought I meant more to her."

"This isn't about you," she states.

I close my mouth at her expression. She looks so disappointed. I drop my head in shame, thankful Jess wasn't here to witness my outburst.

"I know, I'm sorry."

Allison shifts Josie as she cries out again.

Speaking quietly with the irrational belief that if I say it too loud, it may become true, I whisper, "Should I have any hope?"

Her eyes break away before returning to my face. "She's going to have to eventually find a way to let you back in."

"Are you only telling me that to make me feel better?" I ask.

Allison opens her mouth to respond, but Josie's cry cuts her off.

"Thanks for watching her. I don't mean to be rude, but she's probably hungry now." She stares at me meaningfully.

"Right." I stand up, disappointed that she didn't answer. "I'll see you down at dinner?"

"I'll meet you there in about an hour or so. Does that work?"

"Sounds good," I say and leave their suite.

My unanswered question lingers in the air.

CHAPTER FOURTEEN

I let out a sigh of relief as I drop the heavy box of canned fruit on the shelf. When Leah packed it, she must not have been thinking about how heavy it would make it for me. Or, she didn't care. Probably the latter.

"Next time you do these, please remember I don't have superhuman strength. I can only lift so much," I call out to Leah, who is singing to herself as she packs another box.

She pauses her song. "Did you manage to get it done?"

"Well, yeah."

"Then what's the problem?" she asks through light laughter. "Sure, being mutated comes with the risk of turning into a monster, but what's that compared to a little extra strength at a time like this?"

She's lighthearted about it now, but what if she found out about Dominic…and maybe Jess?

"Funny, Leah," I say, trying to keep my tone light. "You know none of us were actually genetically engineered. So take it easy on how heavy you make the boxes."

She rolls her eyes, though her face is still lit up in amusement. "Don't be so serious all the time, Eli. I'm making a joke."

It's hard to be mad at her for anything. She's too playful to ever take seriously.

"One of these days, I'm going to drop something on my foot and you're going to feel badly about it," I say.

She looks up from her box and bites her lip in an attempt to hide her smile. "Eli, if you ever drop one of those boxes on your foot, I'm pretty sure you're going to be the one who feels bad."

I shake my head, fighting back my amusement. "You know what I'm trying to say."

"I'll tell you what. I'll put one less can in the next one. Sound good?" she asks as she continues to place the cans inside her next box.

"It's a start." I walk over to grab another box to place on the shelf.

"I aim to please," she says.

"Umph," I mutter as I pick up the box. "This is even heavier than the last one."

Leah looks at her watch. "Oh, look at the time. Our shift is over. Looks like that's the next person's problem."

She stands up, her box only partially packed, and stretches her arms.

The clock on the wall says we still have over an hour before our shift is up. "Not so fast."

Leah throws her hands up in the air. "Oh come on, Eli. Don't be lame. No one will know." She sticks her lips out in an exaggerated pout.

I can't help but laugh. "At least help me move this box back to where it's supposed to be. It will only take a minute."

She lets out a dramatic sigh as she walks over and picks up the other side of the box. "You're such a martyr. It's disgusting."

She's too much to handle sometimes—in the best way possible.

"What can I say? I aim to please." I repeat her earlier phrase, and she rewards me with another burst of laughter.

When we get the box to its rightful place, I stretch back from the long day of moving everything around while she sat and packed up for me.

"I'll see you tomorrow then," I say.

She waves as she brushes her hair out of her face. I turn and walk out of the room, looking forward to resting before dinner. Hopefully Josie will be tired and willing to nap with me while we wait for Allison to get back.

"Hey, wait up," Leah calls out as I'm about to turn down the hallway.

I lean against the wall. "Yes?"

"What are you doing for the rest of the afternoon?" she asks.

I thought she already knew this. "I'm going to watch Josie for Allison, so Jess can get to work."

She rolls her eyes and closes the door behind her to lock up. "I mean after that, silly." She catches up, and the two of us walk together down the hall.

"Oh." I shrug. I usually don't do anything after that but go back to my room and wait for dinner. "I don't have anything planned."

Her wide grin highlights her one dimple. "Perfect. A group of us are going to play football. You should join us."

"Play what?" I ask.

Her laughter bounces off the walls of the narrow hallway. "It's a sport. It's a lot of fun, and it'll be a good chance for you to meet some people."

I guess it would be nice to make some friends who don't remind me of all the terrible things that have happened.

"How do you play?"

"There are two teams, and you're either trying to score or trying to keep the other team from scoring. You basically throw this oval ball back and forth and try to get in the end zone to score."

I tilt my head. "You throw it?"

"Mmmhmm."

"Then why is it called football?"

She bites her lip to hold back another snicker. "I guess it doesn't make much sense. It's another one of those names that we've always used but never thought much about it. Did you not play any sports in the territories?"

Not wanting to admit that I had been taken out of my physical education classes because it was deemed no longer important for my future, I dip around the question.

"We didn't spend much time doing activities only for fun. Everything had to serve a purpose," I say.

"That's boring. How did you last so long there before you left?"

I rub my forehead. Now that I've seen life outside of Potentia, there are so many things that sound bizarre that I accepted without question. In the territories, I had no control over how my life would be. It was predestined from the moment my mom decided to have an Unplanned child—without letting my father know.

I smile at the thought of my mother. She had a bit of a rebellious nature in her as well. I wish I would have recognized that in her sooner. What would she think about how much everything has changed?

"Eli?" she asks. "Anyone home?"

I blink a couple of times and reestablish eye contact with Leah, reminding me of her earlier question.

"I didn't know anything different," I say. "That's how things were."

"The territories sound horrible. I would have left way sooner," she states.

She's so naïve about how things are. She's spent her whole life sheltered, and most of her views stem from her upbringing.

Then again, so was I.

Looking at the rebellious glint, she's not entirely a product of Veritas. There's something else there.

We pass the Mess Hall to the left of the hallway. Pots and pans are clanging against each other as the kitchen staff prepares for tonight's meal.

"So will you come play with us? I promise you'll have fun," Leah says. "We'll be in the field to the west of the compound until it gets too dark."

"How do you get past the walls?"

She shrugs. "Joseph is working security and he doesn't care as long as we come in before it gets dark." She smiles again. "What do you think? You in?"

"Sure," I say. She immediately lights up with excitement. "I'll be out there as soon as Allison gets back."

"Perfect." She skips ahead through the hallway. "I'm going to go change. Make sure to dress properly."

"How does one dress for football?" I ask, but the only response is her laughter as she runs ahead.

As she passes the corner, she almost runs into Jerry. He glares at her as she passes and mutters to himself. When he spots me, his expression softens as he waves.

I bite back my own laughter at his response. Even though she's lived here her entire life, it doesn't seem like Leah has ever understood how to fit in. Or, maybe she has, yet she chooses to stand out.

Knowing the hallways now, it's not as confusing as the first day Isaac showed us to our rooms. I easily navigate the various turns as I focus on the game of football that I agreed to play. It appears simple enough, but I'm sure I'll have problems with it. Throughout every sport or physical activity back in Potentia, I always lagged behind.

When I knock on the door, there's no answer. Right before I'm about to knock again, Jess opens the door, looking confused and still in her casual clothes.

"You're here early," she says.

I glance at the clock in the corner of the room. Even with the conversation with Leah, I'm still almost an hour earlier than I normally am.

"I can come back if you want," I say, staying in the hallway.

"Don't be silly." She opens the door wider. "Josie is sleeping in her crib in their room right now. If we're quiet, she may sleep all the way through your watch. Lucky her, I wish I could nap."

I go inside and sit on the couch. "I could use a little bit of rest myself. It was a long day at work."

A smile—the one that I've missed so much—plays at her lips as she glances meaningfully at the clock while she remains standing. "Was it?"

I rub my face, feeling my newly grown beard, and laugh lightly. "Fair enough."

We make eye contact. She furrows her brown eyes in concentration. With the lighting in the room, her freckles stand out across her nose. I want to walk up to her, take her in my arms, kiss her, and reclaim her as a part of me.

Her eyebrows flicker upward. She turns away and says, "I'm going to finish getting ready."

"Sure," I mutter and stare at my hands. What did she see in my expression? Am I that much of an open book that she can tell everything I'm thinking?

I can't apologize for wanting to be with her. I can't turn that part of me off no matter how much she wants me to.

Her door reopens and she walks out, wearing light green scrubs. They're ill-fitting and hide her figure.

"Since you're here early, I'm going to head down and see if they need me."

"Okay. I'll see you tomorrow," I say, trying to ignore that I drove her away—yet again.

She leaves the room without saying anything else. We've probably only seen each other about an hour total in this last month. I still want us to be together again. I doubt any amount of time will ever change that.

Relationships are supposed to be two people, working together to make it work. Shouldn't I get a say in whether we should be together or not? My voice in the matter was snuffed out the moment I took her to my brother and let him abuse her. After what I did, maybe I don't deserve her.

I rub my forehead, trying to get rid of the headache that's threatening. I lean back against the couch and fall into an uneasy slumber until Allison returns.

"Are you ever not sleeping?" she asks. It seems like she finds me napping this way almost every day unless Josie is being fussy.

I rub my eyes to fully wake up. "I needed to conserve my energy for this evening."

"What are you going to do?" Allison asks.

"Leah invited me to go play some game called football with her group of friends. I'm meeting them out on the west field."

"You've been talking about Leah a lot," Allison says as she carefully watches my expression.

I try to keep it neutral. "We're friends. You'd like her. She's short like you."

"Oh?" She smirks as she goes into her room to check on Josie, who is somehow still sleeping. "She sounds lovely then."

"You can come out, too—if you'd like. You could bring Josie out and watch us play," I say. I feel guilty for leaving her though there is no reason why I should.

She shakes her free hand in the air. "No, you go have fun, Elliot. It's been a long day, and I would prefer to relax."

"Okay. Next time, then?" I ask as I walk toward the door.

"Maybe. Be careful, Elliot," she says as I leave the room.

While it is nice to have the safety of four walls, I miss the feeling of the sun beating down and the fresh air. I'm excited to get outside and out of the compound—even if it's only for a couple of hours.

CHAPTER FIFTEEN

Wearing what I hope is appropriate for a sport I've never heard of before, I walk out to the west field in a plain white T-shirt, loose shorts, and some athletic shoes. There are definitely some odd things about Veritas, and it's been an adjustment so far compared to life in the territories, but their clothing options are a lot comfier and more casual. People here aren't automatically labeled for what they do based on what outfit they're wearing. It's nice.

The sun is still high in the sky, though it's beginning to set. I blink as I adjust to the light.

I hadn't realized how much I'd missed being outside.

Several figures are running down the field, the sun making it hard to distinguish any specific characteristics. I wish I had been able to convince Allison to come down with me. It's awkward trying to join a group when I only know one person. Do they even know I'm coming?

The figures break free from the invisible line they were all standing by and run toward the north where there are cones laid out in the distance. A tall figure throws the ball, creating a shadow in the sky, and it falls into the arms of a smaller figure about five yards ahead of him.

The figure takes two steps before someone else comes and places two hands on her. Without anything else, the play stops.

"That's a first down," a deep voice I don't recognize declares.

They all move closer to where the person with the ball stopped and look to the sideline where another cone is marking some spot.

"Barely," Leah's familiar voice says begrudgingly.

"Hi everyone," I say. They turn their attention my way.

"Eli's here!" Leah calls out.

I wave and hope I don't look as awkward as I feel.

She laughs. "Stop standing there and looking so weird. Come join us."

Guess not. Count on Leah to call me out like that.

The taller man who threw the ball earlier eyes my size appraisingly. "Leah said you were tall, but she's so short that didn't mean much coming from her," he says as he rubs his stubble.

Everyone, including Leah, bursts out laughing as she playfully punches him in the arm. I smile along. Everyone is here to have a good time. There doesn't seem to be any underlying motive.

"I'm Thomas, by the way." He sticks his hand out.

"Elliot," I say as I shake his hand, recognizing him as someone who helped direct me through the maze of hallways during my first week here.

Thomas brushes his dark, shaggy hair out his face. "We're down one person so we'll take you on our team. We could use the help."

"I'm not sure how much help I'll be," I say. "I've never played football before."

The person standing next to Thomas, pipes in. "Can you run?"

I shift my attention to him and back to Thomas. They must be related, though he's a couple of inches shorter and a few years younger. They both have the same piercing green eyes.

"If I have to," I admit, thinking of the time Jess and I were sprinting from the large group of the Letum before Matt and Allison rescued us.

Leah bites back her laughter. "He'll be fine," she says. "He's being modest. You know, trying to trick the other team into thinking he's not a threat."

The other team, who all are—refreshingly—very diverse, eye me in judgment as if they're trying to guess how fast I'll be. Even though I've been judged on my physical shape my entire life and I'm used to it, it's always been on the negative side. Out here, away from all the strict genetic planning, the quick judgment is favorable. It's strange.

"Eli, you must be wondering who the hell everyone is," Leah says. "Let's get the introductions out of the way so we can play."

The younger version of Thomas—who can't be more than sixteen or seventeen—sticks his hand out for me to shake. "I'm Jordan," he says.

The shortest male there, only beating Leah by a couple of inches says, "Zach."

"Peter," the figure closest to me says, his eyes open and kind.

To his other side, a balding, squirrely looking man introduces himself. "I'm Simon."

"On the other team, you have Nathan, Clement, Isaac, Abby, and Mary," Leah says quickly as she gestures impatiently toward each person.

"Nice to meet you all," I say, already forgetting almost everyone's names. Isaac smiles his familiar, good-natured grin.

Thomas claps his hands together. "Let's get started."

Both sides get together in loose huddles. Leah gestures me over, so I squeeze in with her group.

"Okay, let's take back control of the game," Thomas says, clearly the leader of the team. "Now that we have Elliot here, we can play man-to-man instead of zone. Let's play a tight defense."

Everyone murmurs in agreement.

"What do you want me to do?" I ask.

"Don't let Isaac catch the ball," Thomas instructs.

"Right." I roll my shoulders back in anticipation. This is going to be fun.

"One more thing, Elliot," Thomas says. "You can't touch him unless he has the ball. Otherwise, it's interference."

"He's ready," Leah says. "Stop micromanaging our team."

Thomas raises his eyebrows but bites back his response.

We spread out across the field. I line up with Isaac on the other side. I'm not sure what to expect, but everyone is having fun.

"Hike," a man from the other team calls out—either Nathan or Clement—and sets the play in motion.

Isaac kicks forward and sprints down the field. Because I wasn't expecting his quick takeoff, he gets a head start on me.

I turn my body and run after him. Leah sprints next to me, chasing after one of the other girls.

Isaac got past me initially, but I'm faster and quickly close the gap between us. His eyes dart up and follow the motion of something. I turn my head in time to see the football flying in the air toward us. With the height advantage I have over Isaac, I throw my hands up and bat the ball down.

It spikes against the ground. From next to me, Isaac cusses. My eyebrows shoot up at the language in this religious society.

"Good D," Jordan says.

I'm not sure what he means, but his enthusiasm suggests he's complimenting me. "Thanks," I say.

Leah catches up and pats my back. "Nicely done!"

"What's a D?" I whisper to Leah.

She shakes her head in suppressed laughter. "Sometimes, I forget that you're not from here—then you ask something like that and make it so obvious. He was complimenting your defense by not allowing Isaac to catch the ball."

"Oh," I say and return Jordan's carefree grin. "What now?"

"Now we do it again," Leah says and runs back to the original starting point.

"Man, I thought I had you for a second," Isaac says as we jog back together. "You're pretty quick. Leah was right about that."

He pats my back and runs toward his team's huddle.

Still smiling, I rejoin the rest of my team.

"Same thing?" Jordan asks his older brother.

"Worked last time. Good job, Elliot," Thomas says as he tilts his head in my direction.

"Beginner's luck," I say. "I have no idea what I'm doing."

Peter says, "Natural athleticism and hand-eye coordination will take you a long way."

I open my mouth to argue with him and close it. Huh.

"Let's get them again," Thomas says and claps his hands together.

I take the same spot on the line. When they hike the ball, I'm ready. I don't let Isaac get his jump start and keep him covered. This time when they throw the ball, it's aimed at the girl Leah is guarding.

Because this play is on the other side of the field, Isaac stops moving to watch. The two of us stare at the ball as it falls short of its target. Leah somehow manages to duck under and catch it.

Isaac cusses again, though he laughs instantly. "Looking at her, you don't expect it, but she always manages to make plays like that."

"She's something else," I admit as she jumps up and cheers. Thomas runs and picks her up in celebration.

"She is," Isaac agrees. His tone is more serious, causing me to shift my attention back to him. "We're all protective of her. We don't want her getting hurt."

My eyebrows rise at the implication of his statement. "You don't have to worry about me," I say as I redirect my attention to her.

"You sure about that?" Isaac asks.

Before I can respond, he runs back to his team and joins them in their huddle.

I've never considered myself athletic or fit. Quite the opposite in fact, but I now realize that it's all relative. Playing football with everyone from Veritas, my athleticism stands out. Next to Dominic or someone else Planned, I'm completely inferior physically.

That must be because while I'm Unplanned, both of my parents were Planned—and their parents before them—so the genetics were in my favor. At least I was Unplanned in the generation that created the Letum.

❦

We huddle as we choose our next play almost an hour later, all five of us breathing heavily in the close circle. The light is fading. We're in a hurry to get as much play in as we can. I can't get rid of my grin; it's nice fitting into a group. And running for something other than my life is a nice change of pace, too.

"If I throw it out to you on the right side, do you think you'll be able to run past them?" Thomas asks me as he wipes the sweat away.

I pop my head out from our huddle and eye the distance. We're probably about fifty yards away from the end zone. They've been playing man-to-man and so far, I've been able to outrun Isaac.

"Of course he can," Leah pipes in for me, her voice, filled with excitement. "Have you been watching him out there? He's killing it."

I smile at her confidence. "I got it," I say.

Thomas claps his hands. "Okay, Zach, I'll fake it to you on the left side and then throw it over to Elliot."

"I'll be with Eli to block for him if I need to," Leah adds.

Thomas and I both eye her small height and laugh.

"You're going to block for me?" I ask.

With a giant grin, Leah shrugs and nudges me in the side. "Anything's possible, right?"

I look around at the group of people—though I guess I could call them my friends now—who have accepted me. Meanwhile, my mother and grandparents are buried in the dirt thousands of miles away.

Anything is possible.

"Let's do this," Isaac calls out from the other team, snapping my attention back to the game. I want to win. Even his typical easygoing nature has been overshadowed by his competitive edge.

I run off the right side and stand at the line of scrimmage. Leah follows and stands about five feet to my left.

Thomas snaps the ball as I dig into the ground to get a good jump start.

After three long strides, Thomas executes our plan and gestures like he's going to throw to Zach. When Isaac takes the bait and reacts, Thomas jerks his body toward me and throws the ball.

The ball wobbles slightly in the air, making it harder to catch, but I still clutch it in my arms. I take off toward the end zone.

Even though there's no defensive player around who can catch me, Leah runs with me all the way as we break away and score. I get to the end zone about ten yards before Leah reaches me.

Even from this far away, Thomas's cheers of celebration are easily heard and echo louder than the groans coming from the other team.

We cross the cones and hunch over as I try and catch my breath. Right next to me, Leah is doing the same thing. Even though I'm apparently in pretty decent shape, sprinting fifty yards is still a lot of work, especially after spending so much time indoors recently.

"Good job, Eli," Leah says through shallow breaths.

I hand her the football. "You didn't have to run all the way with me."

She raises her eyebrows and tilts her head. "I take my job seriously. I promised I would block for you, didn't I?"

I gesture around to point out the lack of opponents next to us. "I'm not sure how I would have made it here without you."

"That's all I'm saying."

Leah tosses the football back to me and starts to walk back toward the rest of the players. Once we broke away, everyone on the other team gave up and—smartly—saved their breath and energy for the next play.

"Are you having fun?" she asks as we walk back.

I play with the football in my hands. "I am."

She leans in and hits me playfully with her shoulder. "Why do you seem so surprised? That's insulting. I told you that you would like everyone."

I shrug and don't respond. How do I tell her that this is everything I've wanted and feared? I've waited my whole life to be accepted into the community but worried what it might cost me. Their morals and sense of righteousness may not be the same of those back in the territories, but they can still be extreme.

"Hurry and bring the ball back. It's going to get dark soon," Zach calls out, causing us to lengthen our strides.

The sun is slowly going down, ready to rest before another hard day of work tomorrow. We probably only have another ten minutes or so before it gets too dark to play.

We're about twenty yards away, the whole group watching us jog back, when a figure walks up behind them.

It must be someone else wanting to join our game, though I don't recognize who it is. The teams are even right now so we will need to sit someone out.

The figure stumbles on something. My stomach churns at the sight of its awkward movements. It's one of the Letum. Over time, it's made the long journey, probably searching for some form of sustenance other than its own body, all the way up to this compound.

I drop the ball and sprint forward—even faster than when I was running to the end zone—and call out, "It's one of the Letum!"

Leah, even though she doesn't understand what's happening, tries her best to keep up. My legs are much longer than hers and I leave her behind.

The Letum gets closer to the group as they all stare back at me in confusion—not understanding that their lives are in danger. From a distance, they can't make out what I'm saying and instead only hear the desperate tone. I'm trying to warn them...and I'm only a distraction that's keeping their attention focused in the wrong direction.

"Behind you!" I call out again as I dig my feet into the ground in an attempt to close the gap between the Letum and me as soon as possible.

Jordan turns his head just as the Letum grabs his arm. He screams while the rest of the group shrinks away. The Letum dips his head down toward Jordan, who tries to pull away.

It's like I'm in one of the nightmares where no matter how hard I try to run, I can't move fast enough, like a month ago with Josie. While it can't have been more than a few seconds since I spotted the Letum, it feels like it has been much longer. I wish I could teleport these last ten yards so I could stop the infected creature's desperate attempt at Jordan's flesh.

Thomas is the first to react and jumps forward to tackle the Letum from the side. The two of them fall to the ground with Thomas pinning its head forward in the dirt—the only thing fortunate about this situation.

I finally reach the rest of the group. Through the confusion, everyone is still backing away in terror from the Letum, while Thomas keeps its head in the ground. It's wearing the white leisure outfit of the territories, though it has long since torn and is smeared with blood and mud.

"Move your hand, Thomas," I say.

"What? No," he says. "I'm keeping him down until we get someone to take him to the cells to answer for this attack." He crinkles his nose. "God, he smells horrible. What's that? He smells like a dead animal."

"Move your hand, Thomas," I repeat.

This isn't a conversation we're going to have. This is something that needs to be done.

He opens his mouth to respond but closes it again once we make eye contact. Carefully, he moves his hand off of its head.

It lifts up and moans disgustingly. Like so many of the other Letum, its lower lip is torn away. Its broken, rotting teeth have dirt and grass smeared into them now, along with fresh blood. It looks up at me with an empty, yellowed glance that shows no recognition of anything. The man it used to be is long gone.

I slam my boot down on the Letum's decomposing skull, causing its head to explode. Chunks of its scalp, with hair and parts of its brain attached, fly through the air, landing on Thomas and me.

Leah screams.

Jordan's voice trembles as he asks, "What the hell is going on?"

Now that the threat is removed, I break my attention away from the Letum and Zach's horrified expression.

Jordan's hand clutches his left forearm with blood seeping through his fingers. Everyone is staring from him to the mutilated body of the Letum, eyes all bulging in a similar state of shock.

I drop my head. I wasn't quick enough.

Everyone is looking at me for an explanation. They're looking at me the way people used to at Dominic. I blink back my surprise.

I don't have any answers for them that are going to be satisfactory. Instead, I tell the horrible truth.

"That thing, the one I called the Letum, is one of the infected creatures from the territories. The virus that caused him to turn took away all of its humanity and it is no longer human." I take my shirt off and hand it to Jordan. "Put this over your arm and apply pressure."

Trembling, Jordan asks, "Why did he bite me?"

"The Letum need human flesh to survive. When they can't find any, they consume their own, which is why they smell so terrible. They're decomposing with every passing moment."

When Dominic originally shared that information with Jess and me, our expressions of disgust were likely similar to everyone's here.

Thomas has finally gotten back to his feet and wipes his face on the sleeve of his shirt. His eyes are wide in panic. "How is the infection spread, Elliot?"

"It's not spread in any way that you were exposed," I say, not wanting to fully answer and seal Jordan's fate.

"What about me?" Jordan asks.

If I tell him now, he's going to freak out and that will spread faster than any infection. He should go to an environment where he can be controlled. I need to take him to Dominic.

"Let's go inside to the infirmary. We'll get you some help there, and I'll go find my brother. He understands this infection a lot more than I do," I say.

Jordan's panic bubbles to the surface. He swallows his fear and nods.

I make sure I'm the last one in the group as we walk our funeral march back inside. Luckily—if I could call anything about this incident lucky—the Letum traveled alone and no other creatures stalk us through the rapidly diminishing light.

Even Leah is subdued and doesn't say anything as we walk back into the compound.

The football remains behind on the field—forgotten.

CHAPTER SIXTEEN

Jess's eyes widen when she sees me. The scar on my chest shines brightly, a stark contrast to the blood and gore on my arms and face.

"Elliot, what happ—" she starts.

Thomas walks through the door with his arm around his younger brother, who is getting paler—probably from the combined blood loss and shock.

"He was bitten," I say.

Her eyes dart to my bloody shirt on Jordan's arm. The understanding filters through her face, causing it to go neutral.

An older woman peeks around the corner. "Do you need any help? Should I send for—"

Jess cuts her off. "No, that isn't necessary. Tend to your patients. I'll handle this one."

"I don't think it's serious," Jordan says, the panic rising in his voice. "It isn't too bad."

"Come sit down," Jess says as she gestures toward a patient table.

"He's going to be okay, right?" Thomas asks, gathering her attention.

Jess stares at the gore on his person before looking at me. "Elliot, go get Dominic," she says.

I don't wait on her to say anything else and push back through the door. Everyone from the football field is waiting outside. While their faces are all so diverse, they all have similar furrowed expressions.

"What'd they say?" Zach asks.

I don't answer and push past them.

"Where are you going?" Leah calls out.

I ignore the question and continue on. Once I am through, I start jogging down the hallway. My brother is probably at the gym right now. He likes to do that in the evenings. If not, he'll be in his room.

Footsteps are following me, a lighter echo than my own, keeping pace with my jogging.

"Eli, stop," Leah says.

The terror in her voice causes me to stop and wait for her to catch up.

"Where are you going?"

Keeping my back to her, I say, "I need to find my brother and bring him to Jordan."

"Why?"

There's nothing I can say to reassure her now. Anything I could say would be a lie. I take a step forward, but Leah's touch on my bare back stops me again.

"Talk to me," she begs. "What's going on?"

The desperation in her tone reminds me of my attempts to get Jess to let me in, though not as extreme. Knowing the information I'm about to share is only going to make it worse, I turn around.

Leah takes in my expression, closes her eyes, and lowers her head. When she reopens them, she whispers, "Why are you looking like he is about to die?"

"Leah, when someone is bitten, they turn into one of those creatures. Jordan is infected now."

"He's a kid," she says. "He's only sixteen."

I shake my head, wanting to rewind and stop these fifteen minutes from ever happening. Why were we so naïve to think we would be safe from the Letum here?

"It doesn't matter," I say.

Leah runs her hands through her dark hair in thought. "Why are you getting your brother? Do you think he can help?"

While he may have been able to make a difference if we were in Potentia, he doesn't have what he would need here. When he turned Matt back, he used all of the cancerous cells he brought with him.

I want to give in to her hope, but I can't pretend it's there. "He can't save Jordan. I'm getting him because he understands it better than any of us. He…" I catch myself right before I admit he was a genetic engineer and keep up the façade of our lie. "He overheard genetic engineers discussing the virus. He needs to be there."

She narrows her eyes and looks like she's about to question me further. Before she can, I turn and head back down the hallway in a run. This time, she doesn't stop me.

I ignore all the questioning looks as I run through the compound in a desperate search for my brother.

I push through the gym doors and scan the room. Some of the other men who work security are here. I recognize the oldest, though we've never spoken. Dominic has pointed him out to me before as someone working with him. They laugh at my entrance but stop once they see my expression and the blood covering my arms and face.

"Dominic?" I ask, slightly out of breath.

The man closest to me gestures toward the back corner where my brother is lifting weights. "He's over there."

I rush toward him, and he looks away from his weights to study my appearance. "Who?" he asks.

"A sixteen-year-old," I say.

Dominic keeps staring at my chest—at the scar he put there when we were younger.

"Where?"

"We were in the field on the west side of the compound," I reply and cross my arms over my chest, blocking his view and bringing his attention back to my face.

"How many were there?" he asks.

"Only one," I say.

He stands up and wipes the sweat off his face with a small towel. "How long ago did this happen?"

I take a deep breath and try to get all the information he's going to want in one answer. "It happened about ten minutes ago. He was bitten in the arm before I could take care of the Letum. He's with Jess in the infirmary. She asked me to come get you."

His eyebrows flicker upward. "Lead the way, little brother."

We leave the other men staring stupidly at us.

While I may have been quick compared to everyone else I was playing football with earlier, Dominic has no problem keeping up with my hurried pace. With him on my heels, I push myself to run even faster, almost knocking an old man down when I pass the last corner. His frustrated yells weakly follow me but not for long.

Leah is waiting with the rest of the football group right outside the doors. Most of their eyes widen at the sight of us. While I have lean muscle, it's nothing compared to the physical aspect of Dominic in his workout tank top. If they thought I was tall and athletic earlier, they're probably rethinking that assessment.

They break away and let us enter without any questions, which surprises me. They must be itching for information right now. Their faces indicate Leah must have told them Jordan's fate.

"I am Dominic, Elliot's brother," he says to introduce himself.

Thomas returns his attention to his brother, who is now violently throwing up in a bucket and hasn't noticed our entrance yet.

"Step outside while I examine your brother," Dominic says.

"No, I should stay here," Thomas replies.

"This room is small and getting crowded. It will only take a moment."

Thomas looks at me.

"It won't take long. Go outside with the others. I'll come get you when we're done," I say.

Though he looks like he doesn't want to listen, he leaves the room with one last peek over his shoulder.

Dominic continues to stare at me. "How long have you known him?"

"Just met. Why?"

Dominic frowns. "He was looking at you to lead him."

I shrug, not wanting to think too much on the change in dynamic. It's a lot of responsibility to take on, and I'm obviously not doing a good job at it—look where we are.

"Come on," I say, and we walk back to Jordan.

Jordan has regained some control and now leans back. Jess, holding a needle in her hand, swoops in and gives him some medication through the IV she's placed in his arm.

"What are you giving him?" Dominic asks.

Jess tenses at his question, but when she answers, her voice is calm enough. "Some anti-nausea mediation."

His eyes flicker on her briefly before focusing his attention on Jordan. He walks closer to him and examines the bite mark on his arm.

"Something's wrong, isn't it?" Jordan asks, his lower lip trembling as he tries to fight through his fear, though he's doing a poor job of it.

Dominic nods. "If I had some medicine and technology from the territories, I would be able to give you more time. However, I do not have what I need with me here. There is nothing that I can do to fight off your infection. Do you understand?"

Jordan's hands shake. "What's going to happen to me?"

"Do you remember the creature that bit you?" Dominic asks. His voice is surprisingly patient.

"Yes."

"After you die, you will turn into one of those creatures," Dominic says.

Jordan looks between all three of us with a desperate hope that one of us will say something else. He gasps and Jess steadies the bucket for him to throw up again. The sound of his dry heaving fills the room. Unable to watch, I turn my head and try to escape—at least mentally—from the situation.

However, the noises he's making are too similar to when Matt was sick and turning that fateful night. It's all too easy to imagine I'm back in that cramped bathroom with Matt, oblivious to what's about to happen.

Jordan lets out a long sigh. From the corner of my eye, I see Jess move his bucket back to the floor. I return my attention to the doomed teenager.

"How long?" he asks, voice hoarse from the straining.

Dominic stares down at him, his mask hiding all of his thoughts. "You are turning now. I do not anticipate you making it through the night."

Jordan looks up at the ceiling as he struggles with his emotions. Still not making eye contact with any of us, he whispers, "There's so much more I was planning on doing." He turns his gaze to me. "You have to tell my brother and bring him back in with me. I don't want to be alone."

I place my hand on his shoulder and squeeze. "Of course. I'll be right back," I say.

Looking so young and afraid, he stares back at the ceiling. Dominic takes a seat next to him and waits.

"I'll go with you," Jess mutters as she follows me out of the room.

We open the door to find Thomas sitting on the floor with his head in his hands. At our entrance, he jerks to his feet. His attention is focused on the closed door behind us.

Jess says, "You should get your parents."

"They died when we were little," he mutters, still looking past Jess's shoulder toward his brother.

"Any other family here?"

Still distracted, he responds, "It's the two of us. Why are you asking?"

"Thomas…" I start and place my hand on his shoulder.

Thomas jerks at my touch. He shakes his head in disbelief. "No… No…No…"

"I'm so sorry," Jess says.

"No, you're wrong. Stop looking and acting like he's going to die. Some crazy person bit him in the arm. That's all."

"That's how the infection spreads. What attacked him wasn't a person anymore. If we don't do anything, that's what's going to happen to your brother," Jess says.

Thomas's panicked eyes dart between the two of us. "What do we have to do?"

"He's dying," I tell him. "When he does, he's going to turn into one of the Letum. We can't let that happen."

He chokes back his emotion while his voice cracks. "He isn't dying. We were playing football and having fun. There has to be something we can do."

"There's nothing we can do," I say, although there might be something if we had access to all of the medicine and technology in Potentia. It would be a temporary fix, but it would at least buy them more time.

"Can't we clean it?" Thomas asks.

"The infection has already spread," Jess says.

"Then cut off his arm. Stop the infection," Thomas says in absolute desperation, his voice rising.

"That won't work," Jess says and places her hand on his forearm. "You need to go spend what time you have left with your brother and say goodbye."

He shakes his head. "I'm supposed to protect him. This isn't happening. This is a nightmare."

"This is what life is," Jess says.

Thomas clenches his jaw and shakes his head again.

"Go be with him while you can," I say.

Though it's clear he doesn't agree with our assessment—at least not yet—he walks past us and into the small patient room.

The door automatically shuts behind him. Jess leans against the wall and brushes some escaped hair back behind her ear.

"The noises he was making…" I let the thought float in the air.

She rubs her forehead and sits down. "I know. I'm glad Allison isn't here."

I sit opposite her, both of our legs spread in front of us, our feet almost touching.

Every time I think we   are   past   Matt's   death   and   safe, something like this happens. As horrible as it sounds, even though it's terrible that Jordan was bitten, I only met him today. It's not like him dying should be anywhere as painful as losing my mother, Chris and Andrew, or even Carly. Yet, Jordan is still a person. Do I not care as much anymore?

I let out a deep breath at that musing. This isn't something I want to start affecting me less.

"Will it ever end?" I ask.

The two of us look at each other. Her brown eyes are so beautiful, despite the pain in them. More than anything, I want to sit next to her and pull her into my arms. I want to give her support and take hers.

She drops her eyes again. "I hope so."

We sit in silence, neither of us feeling the need to say anything, probably because there isn't anything to say. All of our hopes for the future won't change the reality of today. No matter how far we get from the infection the genetic engineers forced upon us, we can't truly escape it.

The door opens, snapping my attention to an alarmed Jonah. He spots us on the ground and straightens his shoulders.

"Silas has requested that the two of you and your brother come see him immediately," he says.

I let out a sigh and stand. Of course he's going to want an explanation about what happened. He's going to have to answer for it.

"Jess should stay with Jordan. It wouldn't be a good idea if we left him alone," I say.

"I am to escort all three of you," he says and walks through us to get to Dominic.

Jess shrugs. "Jordan won't be turning for another few hours. Let's not waste our time arguing with him. The sooner we share our story, the sooner we'll be back here to monitor the situation."

Dominic must have reached the same conclusion because he joins us, looking annoyed, and exits the infirmary. Jess and I follow him out while Jonah takes the rear, making sure we don't stray from our path.

Dominic keeps a quick pace, to the point where I'm almost jogging to keep up, and bursts into Silas's office without knocking.

Sitting behind his grand desk, Silas blinks at our abrupt entrance and says, "Thank you, Jonah. Please leave us."

Jonah's face falls, but, as always, he follows his orders.

"How did it get here?" Silas asks without preamble once the door closes behind him, taking away what limited light the hallway provided.

Even though there is a the window behind Silas, nothing comes through it as darkness has fallen. The small lamp on the corner of the desk is the only source of light. It casts half of Silas's face in shadows, giving him a dangerous edge.

"It must have walked here from one of the territories," Dominic responds as he sits down in one of the chairs opposite Silas's desk.

I gesture toward the other chair for Jess and she sits down, with me between the two of them.

"But it was alone?"

"Yes," I start and have to clear my throat. "There will be more."

He shakes his head and rubs his forehead. "I thought we would be spared from the devil's agents. Jordan must've sinned."

Jess jerks her head up. "He's sixteen," she says in disbelief, her voice raised. Even Dominic looks surprised.

Silas continues as if he didn't hear her. "I must push the message of God even harder tomorrow morning. I'm not getting through to everyone."

"We need to start a watch and teach everyone how to protect themselves," I say. "Otherwise, there are going to be more attacks and deaths."

Jess nods while Silas shakes his head. "I must pray on this issue. God will lead the way."

"We cannot rely on prayer to eliminate this problem," Dominic says.

"You have come from the territories where everyone has completely disregarded religion, so I'll try my best to ignore your comment. Soon enough, boy, you will learn that through God, everything is possible." Silas's voice is even, but there's a sharpness to it.

Dominic's fingers tap on his thigh. "I've been listening to your sermons and I understand where you're coming from."

"Then why are you questioning me?" Silas asks as he stares at Dominic, not blinking.

I tilt my head slightly at his words. Dominic isn't questioning him; he's doubting his God. Can he not tell the difference?

"Prayer alone will not protect you from the Letum, but I can. Let me get a group together to train to ensure no one else gets hurt. God sent us here for a reason. That's what you believe, isn't it?"

Silas rubs his chin, where his stubble from the long day is starting to show. "Are you playing me now, boy, or do you believe that?"

"Does it matter as long as it is what you believe?"

Silas's eyes flicker toward the Bible on his bookshelf in the corner of his bare room. He stares at it in deep thought.

None of us make a noise. The only sound in the room is the light ticking from the grandfather clock in the other corner. Its noise becomes louder with each passing second. Dominic's fingers continue to tap against his thigh.

Silas lets out a deep breath and finally breaks the pause. "I don't want a watch all day. It will cause panic throughout the population. I will, however, permit your group to conduct a daily walk around the compound to watch for any of the sinful creatures."

"That isn't enough," Jess says. "It won't catch them all."

"I agree," I say. "This isn't going to cast a wide enough net. We also need to start training members of your compound on how to adequately protect themselves."

Silas raises his hand to silence us. "This is what we'll start with. If there proves to be a greater need, we can revisit this conversation. This will be my compromise."

"Very well," Dominic concedes. "Anything else?"

Silas shakes his head and motions for us to leave. "That's all."

The three of us walk out of his office. Once the door closes behind us, I let out a deep breath and feel some of the tension leave.

Jess says, "I need to check back in with the infirmary. I'll stay with Jordan through the end and make sure he's taken care of."

"Do you want me to wait with you?" I ask, hopeful she will accept my offer.

Instead, Jess shakes her head. "There's no need for two of us to have to witness this. I'll handle everything. Can you let Allison know that I may stay late at work today?"

"Of course," I say. "If you change your mind, let me know and I'll come join you."

Jess quickens her pace to move ahead of us. As I watch her walk away, I can't help but feel a twinge of disappointment. When we were sitting across from each other earlier, it almost felt like an echo of our connection was starting to come back, brought from our shared pain of the past.

Jess turns the corner, leaving my field of vision.

"We will start tomorrow during their church service," Dominic says, breaking my line of thought. "If I ever have to go to another one of those, it will be too soon."

While I agree with him, it doesn't seem like a good idea to miss the religious service. "Won't that isolate us from them?"

Dominic shrugs. "We already are."

I'm finally starting to fit in somewhere. I'm not sure if I want to work against that so soon after making friends. Well, after I let the Letum get to Jordan, I guess I'm not sure where I stand.

"I don't know..."

Dominic stops walking and scoffs. "Oh, wake up. These people are idiots. Their concept of sin is the most ridiculous thing I have ever heard of." His fingers twitch. "It completely discounts the bigger picture. They say if you do one small thing, you're damned? That's it?"

"One small thing..." I repeat. "You mean like killing someone?"

His eyes darken. "If killing someone leads to saving more lives, then it was for the greater good. Their God should show some appreciation toward me, not send me to whatever hell they blab on and on about."

Dominic breathes heavily out of his nose, eyes narrowed.

I take another step forward and turn my head away from him. I'm not going to get him to change his mind. What's the point in trying? I've heard his justifications before.

"Even if you believe that," I respond, "you still think this is a good idea?"

Despite not directly looking at him, I can sense his steely gaze piercing me. "You have seen how everyone acts during the services, right? I would be surprised if anyone notices if we are not there. They are all too focused on Silas and his messages of their hateful, vengeful God."

"Won't it bother Silas if we don't go? Surely he'll notice," I say, thinking of his focus on his Bible when we were in his office.

"Silas knows we do not believe, and he is not doing anything. He firmly trusts that God sent us here for a reason and is trying to figure out exactly why that is. He is not concerned with saving us—as he always claims—he wants to make sure he stays in power."

PART FOUR

CHAPTER SEVENTEEN

A week later, I yawn as I sort through a box full of fresh fruit. Dominic and I have been getting up even earlier than usual to make sure we have enough time for our morning walks around the compound. After the first day of not finding any of the Letum, we've been alternating mornings—partly because we're both confident we can handle anything individually—and also as a result of my disdain for his company.

Like every check before, this morning yielded nothing.

While I'm glad no more of the Letum have reached us, it's going to take a lot more exposure to the Letum for Silas to finally acknowledge how much of a threat they are to us. The more I think about it, the more it's like he appeased us with his so-called compromise. He didn't give anything up, only our own time.

Footsteps echo down the hall toward our room as we sort through the most recent boxes of food.

Leah pauses. "Who could that be?"

I frown. The next shift isn't supposed to be here yet. "Maybe the next group is getting here early?"

Even as I say it, I know it's not right. There's only one set of footsteps coming down the hall.

The footsteps get louder and louder until a figure steps through the hallway. It's Jonah. Leah tilts her head as her eyes meet mine. What's he doing down here?

"Excellent," he starts. "I was hoping to find you here, Elliot."

Not sure how else to respond, I say, "This is where I'm supposed to be during my assigned working hours."

Behind me, Leah snickers. Jonah glances her way, and she quickly gets herself back under control.

"We haven't had a lot of opportunities to speak, so I wanted to make sure you were comfortable. Do you have any questions or any concerns I can address at this point—especially considering recent events?"

"Um..."

He laughs good-naturedly at my response, but the laughter doesn't quite reach his eyes. They're still empty and stern.

He continues his speech. "As Silas mentioned when you first got accepted into the compound, our culture is the most important aspect of who we are. It's what makes this such a great place to live."

"It appears to be working for you," I respond evenly.

There's still something wrong about his smile.

"Now, the growth that we've had since the Civil War between the godforsaken territories that you grew up in has been the easy part, by far. What we're most proud of is our people and the impact we're able to have. I'm glad you're going to be able to join that to be a productive member of our family."

Even though everything he's saying is the right thing, something is off.

He studies me, calculatingly. If he's going to look at me like that, then I'm going to try to better gauge who he is as well. Two can play this game.

"I guess I do have one question for you, if you don't mind." I say.

"What would you like to know?"

"You're acting a little on edge. What's going on?" I ask, curious how he's going to respond.

He flashes that same insincere smile and takes a seat on one of the full boxes by the door.

Speaking with his hands, he begins his tangent. "It's no big deal or anything to worry about. We're as stable and secure as ever, I assure you. Some other people around here are overstepping their responsibilities. They're trying to push their power and take control of areas in which they've no right. Simply put, they're walking around like they own the place. They're getting such big heads. Don't they know who I am? Don't they know I sit next to Silas every day? I can tell him any story I want to."

He pauses and collects his breath. "But, I don't. Because even if they don't have my back, I'm going to support them. It all eventually comes back to you, don't you agree?"

Mind racing at all that he's said and the light it sheds on his character, I say, "Yes, I do agree."

"I hope this chat was helpful for you. I want you to know you can always come to me with anything that you need. I'm here to support you."

I don't trust a single word coming out of his mouth.

I purposefully refuse to make eye contact with Leah. Out of the corner of my eye, I can see her shaking with suppressed laughter that she quickly turns into a cough.

"Yes," I say. "I appreciate you speaking with me. It was enlightening."

Yet again, that smile of his flashes across his face as he stands up. "That made my day. If I can enlighten one person, that means my day was well spent."

Now, I'm biting my tongue as well. Is he so socially stunted that he doesn't understand how ironic this conversation is?

"I know how important it is to have a balance between work time and leisure. Why don't the two of you go to lunch and call it day? I'll join you in a bit. I want to browse around here first. I haven't been in this area of the compound in too long."

"Thanks, Jonah," I say in relief. I need to get out of this room before I start laughing openly.

Leah grabs my hand and pulls me toward the door to leave. "Yeah, thanks."

The door closes behind us and Leah's eyes are frantic as she tries to hold in her amusement.

"Wait until he can't hear us anymore," I warn, though I'm struggling to hold in my laughter.

Leah waits until we pass the corner before her laughter echoes throughout the space. "Can you believe he said that?" She snorts in amusement, her dark hair bouncing as she almost skips down the hall.

Although a big part of me is horrified that he said it, that doesn't stop me from laughing with her. "What was he thinking?" I ask as I walk down the hallway toward the Mess Hall with her.

"The best part is…" Another wave of hysterical laughter takes over her body. "The best part is…" she continues. "He was absolutely serious. He didn't say it as a joke. He truly holds himself in such high regard."

"How did he get in a position of power? I don't understand it." I shake my head in disbelief.

It doesn't matter what the foundations of society are like; shitty people always find a way to make it to the top.

Leah gasps and makes an exaggerated horrified expression. "Eli, how could you ask such a question?" Her mouth twitches. "Don't you know who he is?"

"Unfortunately, I think I do," I mutter as her laughter continues to ring out against the walls.

She wipes the tears from her face and companionably locks her arm with mine. Even though she probably wants more than I can give her, I don't pull away. It's nice not to feel alone.

The noise of the rest of the compound gets louder as we turn another corner.

"They all have such big heads. Don't they know who I am?" Leah repeats under her breath again as she chuckles in disbelief.

We walk into the Mess Hall, arm in arm, and Silas's calculating eyes watch us from the center of the room where he's conversing with a large group.

I look away from Silas's group of lackeys to see what meal they're serving today for lunch. Whatever it is, it smells better than normal. They've splurged and cooked up some type of meat.

The innocent sound of Josie's cry catches my attention. About two tables to the right, Jess is holding Josie in one arm and trying to eat with the other.

Her hair is up in a messy bun, though some of her dark curls are sticking out, uncooperatively. Her face is flushed as she peeks down at Josie. This is the healthiest she's looked since we left for Potentia. She's absolutely beautiful.

I instinctively unlock arms with Leah and turn to the right.

"Where are—?" Leah starts, but the noise of the loud, fake-sounding laughter from one of Silas's companions cuts her off.

As I approach Jess, her eyes dart up. She automatically tenses but relaxes once I sit down across the table from her.

"Where's Allison?" I ask as nonchalantly as I can.

She looks beyond my head toward the hallway and shrugs. "She said she would be right back, but that was twenty minutes ago."

Josie fusses as Jess tries to take a bite of food and moves too much for Josie's liking.

"Here, let me take her for a bit while you eat," I say and reach across the table.

Jess gently hands Josie off. Not wanting to sleep but perfectly content to stare openly at the world above her—she's started to track things with her eyes—she settles down.

"You're good with her, Elliot."

Jess stares intently at me, her forehead puckered. Her guard quickly shoots back up once our eyes meet and she takes another bite of her meal.

"I haven't forgotten my promise to Matt," I whisper.

What would Matt think of us being here? We're safe from the danger of the Letum, though I suspect the politics of the compound aren't going to stay contained forever.

"Eli, why did you run off so quickly?" Leah asks as she sits down next to me. She places a plate of food in front of me.

Jess's nose crinkles and she leans farther away. I shoot her a worried glance, but Leah keeps talking and grabs my attention.

"They let me take a plate for you, because, well, they know who I am."

I chuckle. "Jess, have you met Leah yet?

"No, she hasn't," Leah answers for her and puts her hand out for Jess to shake. "I'm Leah, by the way. Eli and I work together."

Jess watches Leah as she gets closer to playfully grab Josie's tiny feet.

"Jess."

Leah leans in close, her easy comfort with me obvious to anyone half paying attention—and Jess is doing much more than that. I can feel her eyes on every motion between us right now.

I cough nervously and shift to my right a bit, trying to put distance between Leah and me. Unfortunately, she's oblivious to my desire and rests her hand casually on my arm.

"Well, it was nice to meet you." Jess gestures toward Josie. "I can take her back now, Elliot. I should probably try to find Allison. Since it's one of her off days and I don't need to watch Josie for her, I picked up an extra shift this afternoon."

"I don't mind waiting for Allison to come back. I have plenty of time," I say.

"Well, okay," Jess says as she takes her plate and starts to walk away.

"Wait, Jess," I call out, not sure what I'm going to say.

She freezes and turns back around to face me. Away from the stresses of captivity and being stuck in close proximity to Dominic, her face has filled out as she's put back on the weight she'd lost.

"Yes?"

"It was nice to see you." I try to find the right words to articulate what I want to say without making her uncomfortable. "You look good."

Her eyes dart toward Josie in my arms. "You do too, Elliot," she says so quietly, her voice almost doesn't carry over the noise of everyone else talking in the large room.

She tucks some of her escaping hair behind her ear, her guard fully up, and walks away from me.

"I hope I didn't interrupt anything," Leah says, bringing my attention back to our table.

I awkwardly grab a bite of the crushed beef and say, "Of course not." Although, I wish Jess and I could be alone again—even if it's surrounded by most of the compound eating lunch.

"She left pretty quickly after I sat down."

I don't think it was because Leah sat down. She always leaves whenever I get close. She's apparently doing just fine without me.

When I don't say anything, Leah continues. "The two of you obviously have a history—more than you've let on. Why haven't you spoken much about her before?" She plays with the food on her plate.

I shrug, not wanting to talk about it. Luckily, Allison spares me from having to answer.

"Elliot, have you seen Jess? She's watching Josie..." She trails off as she spots her daughter in my arms.

"Safe and sound," I announce, happy to have avoided Leah's question.

"Thanks for that," Allison reaches down and takes Josie. She smiles as she spots her friend down the table. "How's it going, Catherine?"

Sitting at the other end of the table, among a large group of middle-aged men, Catherine holds Jeremiah. "Hey, Allison. Still on for tonight?"

"I wouldn't miss it," Allison says. "Josie and I will be over after dinner."

Catherine puts Jeremiah's hand up as if he's waving. "We'll see you then."

Allison returns her attention to us, still smiling. "And how are you doing, Leah? Keeping an eye on Elliot for me, I hope?"

Leah laughs good-naturedly. "Of course! Though I think he's watching out for me too. At least, I like to believe that." She playfully pokes my side.

Allison raises an eyebrow. "We need to get together one night—the two of us. It'll be nice to get to know you better. We haven't had that chance yet."

"That sounds lovely." Leah beams.

I'm glad Allison is reaching out, regardless of her motives. It would be good for her to make more friends, especially with someone as great as Leah.

"What took you so long?" I ask.

Allison sits down where Jess was. "I ran into Dominic."

This time, I'm the one raising my eyebrows. I didn't know the two of them were in contact. "What does he want?"

"He was checking in on how everything was going...with everyone." She eyes me nervously, gauging how I'm going to react.

Why would she entertain anything he has to say? That's the benefit of staying in a large compound; it's a lot easier to put some space between each of us.

"If he wants to know anything about my life, he can ask me himself," I say.

Allison glances at Leah's confused expression before returning her attention toward me. "He wasn't asking about you, Elliot," she whispers.

He certainly doesn't deserve to know anything about Jess's life either. I want to say as much, but Leah doesn't need to get involved in any of this drama.

"So..." Leah begins, trying to break the tension. "Josie's such a perfect blessing. She's precious."

Allison offers her a tight smile at her compliment.

Leah looks up at Allison, unfiltered excitement in her expression. "Can I hold her?"

Allison's eyes widen and she bites her lips. She takes a deep breath and nods. She walks back around the table to set her in Leah's arms.

"Make sure to support her neck," I say. Leah's motions aren't as confident as I would have liked for her to be holding Josie. To be fair, she hasn't had the practice that the three of us had.

"Don't worry, I have her," Leah says and she smiles down. "She looks a lot like you, Allison."

Allison chuckles as she sits back down. "You think so? I think she looks more like her father."

I stare down at Leah's arms. Josie's still a balance between them. She has the same small nose as Allison and Matt's wide mouth. It's an interesting combination.

"The two of you have the same chin." Leah smiles warmly at Allison. "If you don't mind me asking, what happened to her father?"

Allison lets out a deep breath. "He got infected and turned."

Leah's shoulders slump. "I'm so sorry. I can't imagine how hard that must've been for you when he was bitten."

I instantly tense up at the change in conversation. Before I can stop her, Allison, out of habit, responds, "He wasn't bitten."

Leah holds Josie farther out from her body.

"What are you saying?" Leah asks, looking at Josie in horror.

Allison tries to backtrack. "No, I'm sorry, I misspoke."

When she speaks again, Leah's voice is raised, carrying over the normal chatter of the group closest to us. "Was her father genetically mutated?"

The group of five men eating next to us, including Nathan and Adam who work in security with Dominic, fall silent. Leah continues to stare at Josie in horror.

I hold my hands out. "Leah, hand me Josie."

"No, of course not," Allison says, though the panic in her voice betrays her.

"Dear Lord," Leah exclaims. She holds Josie out as far from her body as possible.

"Please stop talking. Everyone is—" I start.

"Who was genetically mutated?" Nathan's stern voice rings out, making sure everyone in the room is aware of the situation.

Next to him, Adam shifts so his body is covering Catherine and their son.

The group nearest to us steps closer, preventing Allison from moving. She eyes the table separating her and her daughter with dread.

I repeat my request louder. "Leah, give me Josie."

Bordering on hysterical, Leah stares at me in horror.

"She said the baby's father was mutated!" Nathan replies.

"No, that's not what I said," Allison says.

"The baby could turn into one of the monsters," Catherine, forgetting her relationship with Allison, calls out, waking up Josie, who lets out a long, healthy wail.

Allison flinches in reaction to her daughter's cries, but there's nothing she can do. There's a physical barrier between the two of them.

"Leah, look at me," I say, urgently enough to finally get her attention through all the screams of protest spreading through the Mess Hall. She breaks her eyes away and stares at me, no reason in her expression. "Hand Josie to me."

"But—" she begins.

My heart races in my chest. The energy in the room is turning against us. I must get Josie into my arms now to protect her.

"Trust me. Hand her to me."

Josie is now fully utilizing all of her lung capabilities to let everyone know she's unhappy with the amount of noise.

Reluctantly, still holding Josie out as far from her body as possible, Leah gives her to me.

I breathe a sigh of relief even though this is only beginning.

With all the shouts of fear in the large room, I can only read Allison's lips as she mouths, "Leave."

Even though I promised to look after Allison, I take a step backward toward the exit of the room. Josie is in much more danger.

I turn around, taking one last glance at Allison, and take two steps before I spot Jonah blocking my exit. I exhale loudly.

We're trapped.

"She's a ticking time bomb!" Another hysterical person calls out.

I look around in desperation, hoping for some inspiration on how to diffuse this situation.

Leah's eyes shift between Josie and me, an even deeper fear etched on her face.

She was afraid when Allison slipped that Matt was Planned, but that was an unrealized fear. With this new terror, she can sense the vibe that's spreading through the room, more contagious than any infection.

Leah puts her hands out in front of her and mouths, "I'm so sorry," and backs up into the crowd.

"Everyone be quiet," Silas's voice echoes throughout the Mess Hall. He silences all the raw panic but doesn't take it away. It's still present in the body language of everyone here, in the way Nathan clenches his hand and stares murderously at Josie in my arms.

I instinctively take steps away from him to return to the table where we were innocently eating our lunch. Allison's fresh tears are spilling down her face. She's still trapped on her side of the table, unable to get to her daughter.

Silas's arms are crossed in disapproval. "Allison, did you lie when you entered our compound? Are you Planned?"

"No, I'm Unplanned—like you and everyone else here," she responds.

"Was your baby's father Planned?"

Allison opens her mouth to speak and closes it again. Her silence is answer enough.

"Jonah, seize the child."

"Out of my way," Jonah calls out as he pushes his way toward me.

I don't know what to do, but I know one thing: he's not getting this child from me willingly.

Sharing the same chain of thought, Allison takes advantage of the distraction and climbs over the table, knocking my food onto the floor.

"Let me hold my daughter," she whispers.

Happy to have both of my arms free for the inevitable physical confrontation that's about to ensue, I hand her off.

"Stay close," I whisper back.

"Stand down," Silas instructs. "The baby is a danger to all of us. We can't accept that risk."

Jonah has reached us and holds one arm out to take Josie, while the other rests on the holster for his gun. I shake my head. We're not giving her up.

"The baby is not a danger to anyone," another familiar voice rings out.

Dominic pushes his way past a startled Silas and steps in front of me, blocking Jonah from reaching Allison. While Dominic joining us is certainly helpful, we're still severely outnumbered. It doesn't matter how strong he is; even he can't fight everyone at the same time.

"It does not matter if a baby's parent is Planned as long as the other is Unplanned," he says loud enough to ensure everyone in the hall hears him. "And if you think I am going to let you take her, you are going to regret that decision quickly."

Dominic stands to his full height, all six foot four of him, and easily towers over Jonah, who is a small man—in more ways than one. Even though Jonah hasn't witnessed how dangerous Dominic can be—as I have—his eyes dart toward Silas.

"How c-can you be so positive?" Jonah asks, his tone overly sharp, though the stutter gives his nerves away.

I hold my breath in hesitation as to what he's about to say. He can't explain he was a genetic engineer or he'll doom himself. He can either admit who he is and hope they listen or walk away and protect himself.

He turns his head to make eye contact with Allison. Dominic lets out a deep breath and squares his shoulders again.

"Because I was a genetic engineer at Potentia and studied the infection extensively. That being said—"

Silas's emotionless voice cuts him off. "You lied to us. They would never have let an Unplanned work in their precious laboratory."

"Yes, I am Planned," Dominic admits.

The entire room explodes in shouts of protest. I can't make out a single word; it's deafening.

Silas speaks to Jonah. "Seize him. Go find the other one, too. Bring them all to my office and keep them under guard."

Eyeing his chances with the crowd or in a calmer environment, Dominic motions for Allison and me to follow Jonah. I walk out of the room first, with Allison and Josie behind me, Dominic bringing up the rear.

What did we get ourselves into?

CHAPTER EIGHTEEN

We file into Silas's dark office. The only light is coming from the tall window behind his desk. For someone claiming to have an open-door policy, we're only here when something goes wrong.

"I'm going to go find the other." Jonah pauses before leaving the room. "Joseph and two armed guards are at the door. If you try to exit the room, you will be shot without hesitation."

Jonah closes us in the room to await our fate.

"Shh...it's okay," Allison coos to Josie.

Her attempt to calm the crying baby sets me even more on edge. Doesn't she understand the danger we're in?

"What do we do?" I ask Dominic.

He scans the room, avoiding eye contact.

"I had to expose us all, or they were going to kill Josie. There was no other option," he mutters, running his hand through his light hair. His gaze shifts toward Allison.

That's more startling than anything else that has happened today so far. Why did Dominic sacrifice his own self-preservation? This doesn't add up.

"What do we do?" I repeat myself.

Josie finally settles down and lets herself be comforted.

Dominic glances one last time across the room. "We could break the window and try to get out before the guards outside the room hear us."

Though the window is high, we could use his desk chair to help us get through it. The desk could be moved to block the door. We may have enough time to escape. It might work, but where would we go? We'd have to figure that out, but that could happen later.

My body tenses in expectation of what we need to do. Then, I freeze, realizing the plan won't work.

"We can't leave Jess," I say.

"No, we can't," Allison says now that she's able to contribute to the conversation.

I open my mouth, prepared to argue against whatever greater-good rebuttal Dominic is going to claim.

Dominic looks away from Allison and agrees. "No, we can't."

I exhale the breath I was holding. I tilt my head as I examine his anxious expression. What is his game right now?

For the third time, I ask, "What do we do?"

Dominic turns to me in anger. "What do you want me to say? I'm not your savior. I'm not responsible for you. What do you want from me?"

My eyes widen at the sharp tone of his voice. "The only reason we're in here is because of you. So figure it out."

He opens his mouth, preparing to respond.

"Dominic," Allison's voice rings through the room, and its effect is instantaneous.

My brother takes a deep breath to steady himself. A forced calm resonates through his expression.

"I need to prove that we are more valuable to them alive than dead. That is our only chance. Let me do the talking," he says in no more than a whisper.

There's no other option. I have to trust Dominic to get us out of this mess—even if I don't understand his motive.

We enter a contrived silence as each of us calculates the odds of survival. While Allison and I should be safe, Josie and Dominic are in severe danger. Even though Jess has never explicitly stated whether she's Planned or not, she looks like she is and that could be cause enough. I never thought I would be thankful for my lesser physical attributes.

Dominic's strong jawline is clenched in anticipation. Maybe they'll get rid of him so I don't eventually have to. I shake my head to expel my thoughts about him. It's too complicated to get into right now.

The door squeaks open, and Jess's alarmed face stares into mine. Jonah and Silas follow closely behind her. Jess stands to the left of Allison, so Allison is between the two of us, with Dominic on my right.

"Should I come in?" the first guard asks.

Silas studies our body language. "If you hear any noise, come in immediately. I don't imagine we're going to have a problem. Are we, Dominic?"

Even though he only addressed Dominic, both of us shake our heads.

Confident in his motions, Silas turns on the light, causing all of us to blink as we adjust from our accustomed darkness, and takes a seat at his desk. Jonah stands close behind, his hand hovering around his gun holster. No matter how calm Silas seems, Jonah contrasts him and keeps me tense.

Silas studies each of us, his eyes finally resting on Dominic.

"Who all among your group is Planned?" Before Dominic can reply, Silas continues. "Don't lie to me. If you do, you will jeopardize everyone's life here."

"I am, sir, as is Jess."

"She may not be," I immediately interject. How could he throw her under like that when she's never confirmed or denied it?

"When everyone was at the genetic engineering building..." Dominic starts.

My jaw clenches. He's skating over the fact that he held us captive.

"I ran tests on everyone to learn as much about the virus as possible," Dominic continues. "When someone is genetically engineered, we alter an insignificant piece of their DNA. It is a way of marking them, if you will, to ensure that even if one moves territories, we can still keep track of who is Planned or not."

Jonah's fingers twitch above his gun.

"I ran this test on Jess and found the marking integrated within her DNA." Dominic pauses to look me in the eye, so I can see the truth in his words. "Jess and I are the only ones who are Planned."

Jess's eyes—still guarded—betray her dull acceptance. She thinks we're about to get killed. The worst part is there's almost a sense of relief coming from her.

I don't accept this fate. I subtly shift my body stance so I'm closer to her and Allison. Jonah narrows his eyes, but doesn't say anything.

As calm as ever, Silas says, "When my grandfather founded Veritas after years of searching for a new home, after your ancestors pushed science further and further until they eventually lost their humanity, the people put their trust in him to protect them and keep them safe. Though the Civil War was over, the danger was always lurking in the shadows. For how can anyone truly be safe when there is such savage genetic manipulation?"

I expect Dominic to respond, but he remains silent and lets Silas finish.

"Sadly, our fears were realized once the cruel, inhuman Planned created a weapon even more dangerous than the bombs they used to drop on us: they created the infection."

Still not breaking eye contact, Dominic flinches at the last statement. He may not have been part of the genetic engineers who isolated the gene that caused cancer and thus created the Letum, but his biggest pride and accomplishment was being a part of that team. How is he accepting all of these attacks?

"Though we've taken our losses, I've kept us safe and strong. While the territories destroyed themselves from within, we still stand." Silas's voice gets even lower. "So tell me, Dominic, why shouldn't I kill you? You're a risk to everything I've built here."

Dominic steadies his shaking hand and responds with surprising calm. "If you want to maintain the status quo, you should."

"What?" I breathe, unable to help myself. Out of all the things he could have said, that's the most shocking.

Jonah's fingers continue to drum against his holster. He's itching for the chance to get to use it—to feel that power.

"You do not strike me as the type of man who wants his legacy to be that he kept the status quo though, are you?" Dominic asks, starting to gain back his confidence.

Silas raises an eyebrow. "What are you trying to say?"

"If you want to truly be remembered for pushing Veritas ahead, you need me."

Jonah snorts. "You've got to be joking. Silas, let's finish this now. Don't listen to his madness."

Silas raises his hand to silence Jonah. He studies Dominic, somehow, even closer. The stillness in the room is uncomfortable. Every quick beat of my heart reminds me that there are some in the room whose heartbeats may be running out.

Finally, Silas speaks. "Why do I need you?"

"You need to visit the territories—specifically Potentia. I can help you bring some of that technology back here so you can advance your population."

"You mistake me, boy. As long as I live, there will be no genetic manipulation occurring in Veritas," Silas spits back.

Amazingly, Dominic smiles. "No, you mistake me. I am not offering to set the genetic engineers up here. You were right—we should have never allowed our society to mess with the will of God."

Jess jerks her head toward Dominic, eyebrows furrowed. I don't understand it either. Is this my brother speaking?

When Silas doesn't respond, Dominic continues. "What I can offer you is to help bring over the other areas of technology, from our renewable resources to even our weapons, so you can protect your people. Think how much you have learned from tearing our vehicle apart." He pauses to let his words sink in. "All of that technology is sitting, unused, waiting for someone to come take it. If you are not going to use it, someone else will. What happens when that person decides they want your compound? If they have the superior technology, how will you protect your people? It'll be like the Civil War all over again—and your people will, once more, be the losers."

Jonah looks toward Silas for instruction, his hand finally going away from his gun.

"I have been watching you, Silas, and the type of leader you are. It is so obvious you care about your people and have done the best you can for them," Dominic says. "You would not be sucked into the power and let the technology take over. You would know when to stop."

Silas rubs his chin. "The entire Mess Hall heard you admit that you're Planned. What do I say to them when they panic thinking you could turn at any time?"

Dominic takes a deep breath. "The likelihood of one of us turning is fairly low. It is the same odds as an Unplanned developing cancer."

Quietly, Silas whispers, "My mother died of cancer."

Changing tactics, Dominic says, "You tell them the warning signs of someone about to turn. It is pretty straightforward—basic stomach flu symptoms. If any of us starts to throw up or even have a fever, you know we are potentially turning. There is a warning before it occurs."

Silas leans back in his chair and studies each of us, eyes lingering on Josie sleeping in her mother's arms.

"Jonah?"

Jonah jerks his head toward Silas. "Yes?"

"You have one week to prepare for a trip to Potentia. You're to lead this trip," Silas instructs.

I exhale the breath I've been holding. Somehow, Dominic bought us time.

"No," Dominic says.

"No?" Silas asks.

"I will lead the trip."

What's his endgame? He's walking down a slippery slope and in doing so, putting all of our lives at stake.

"You're not in a place for negotiation, boy."

Dominic walks closer to Silas's desk and stares him down.

"If we're going to do this, we're going to do it my way. I'm the one who understands Potentia and where the technology is. I've also spent time in the territory after it was overrun. I know the safe places." He pauses and looks toward Jonah. "I need someone who I can trust to back me up. Elliot will come along and be my second in command."

He's never put much esteem in me, yet here is he, trying to put me in a position of power.

Jonah opens his mouth, but Silas shakes his head, cutting off any objection.

"I'll allow you ten total people, including yourselves. You may choose two, along with whoever else I decide will join you." With one last penetrating gaze, Silas concludes. "You may leave."

Allison, Jess, and I instantly turn to the door, anxious to get out of the room, but Dominic remains frozen.

"Yes, Dominic?" Silas asks.

"Allison, Jess, and the baby will remain here while we are on the mission. If I come back and even one hair is damaged on their heads, I will use that technology to blow this place to oblivion. It won't matter what your grandfather once founded—no one will even remember he existed."

Jonah slams his hand back down to his gun.

"To be clear, are you threatening me?" Silas's eerily calm voice rings through the room.

"Yes, sir, I believe I am," Dominic responds, staring Silas down with the fierceness that he's been missing these last few weeks.

Dominic turns his back on Silas and reaches for the doorknob. Before he can open it, Silas speaks in measured tones. "Then hear my threat, boy. If all of you don't come back—including every single one of my people I'm sending with you—I won't stop the crowd next time. I'll let them tear you apart."

Dominic's shoulders tense and he opens the door. Joseph looks at him warily, gun aimed at his chest.

"Let them pass."

Dominic pushes past Joseph and the other guards and waits for all of us to file out. Looking back, he takes one last prolonged stare at Silas as the door shuts itself. Jonah is already leaning over, whispering urgently in his ear.

"Elliot, we are going to walk them back to their living quarters and then we are going to go to my room and plan for the trip. We should all lay low for the time being."

We walk down the long hallway. It's crucial we stay away from the mob scene in the Mess Hall, at least until Silas has time to spread the message that no harm is to come to us. Though, can one man have that effect on the entire compound?

Allison, trying to relieve some of the pressure on one of her arms, rotates Josie and she lets out a weak noise in reaction.

Dominic extends his hands toward Allison. "Let me."

I had thought nothing he would do at this point could surprise me, but, once again, my brother proves me wrong.

With a quick, guilty glance toward Jess, she places her daughter in his outstretched arms. A little awkwardly, he pulls her closer to his chest and keeps walking.

Both Jess and I pause as we take in this scene. Why is Dominic pretending to care?

Allison stretches her arms, mumbles gratitude, and walks evenly with Dominic. While his strides are long, Allison is well over a foot shorter than him and takes quick steps to keep up.

"What the hell?" I whisper.

We continue walking, keeping about ten yards between us.

"Is there something going on between them?" Jess asks. She may be trying to block me out right now, but there is a small twinge of betrayal in her tone—as there should be.

Allison and Dominic turn at the corner, temporarily out of our view.

"You spend more time with her than I do. The two of you share a suite," I say.

She glances at me, her eyebrows furrowed in thought. "Even if there were something going on, I can't imagine she would come to me to talk about it."

I rub my hand through my hair. It's getting longer. I'm going to need to get it cut soon.

"I'm sure there's nothing but a friendship developing between them. Not after Matt being gone so soon and everything..." I take a deep breath and finish. "And everything he did to you."

Her walking slows even more, and she surprises me by maintaining eye contact, scanning my face. I don't say anything else, not knowing what else to say. It's not her fault she was in the situation, but it happened. We can't walk on eggshells around it forever.

"Elliot—" Jess begins.

Allison's gasp and Dominic's raised voice cut her off. "Step back now."

Instinctively, Jess and I run past the corner. Nathan and Peter, who I played football with, come out of one of the classrooms and are carrying a matching pair of knives, waving them threateningly toward Dominic and Allison.

Nathan and Peter are distracted temporarily by the sound of our footsteps rushing toward them when we pass another door to get closer.

Still holding Josie, Dominic takes advantage of their distraction and uses his other hand to push Allison behind him.

Adam and Abe come out of the room we just passed to trap us between them. The two have the same kind of knives in their hands. Now that I'm closer, I recognize them. They took them from the kitchen.

Following Dominic's lead, I position myself so my body is a shield for Jess. Her uneven breathing hits my ears. Lightly, she touches my shoulder. We're in this together.

Even though we're in severe danger, yet again, her touch is a reassurance—if we can get ourselves out of this situation.

"Did you think we'd forgot about you?" Nathan sneers, rubbing the handle of his blade.

Next to me, Abe says, "As far as we're concerned, you're all filth and dangerous."

"Do you think I would ever let my son sleep in the same building as a genetically modified mutant?" Adam asks. Out of everyone there, he's the most painful to see here. He and his wife had struck up a friendship with Allison. Jeremiah and Josie were supposed to play together this evening. How can he forget that so easily?

Dominic turns slightly, keeping his body between Allison and the others, and hands her Josie. Allison takes her greedily.

Amazingly, Dominic smiles, though it does not reach his eyes. "Gentlemen, you understand that I am, how did you put it? Oh yes, a 'genetically modified mutant.' That means I had my genes carefully controlled and selected to produce a stronger, smarter version of your much weaker selves."

Compared to Dominic, I may seem small, but I still have a couple of inches on the men threatening us.

"Watch your mouth," Nathan calls out, spotting his group's hesitation.

Dominic eyes me and nods.

At the same time, the two of us rush toward our attackers, taking them by surprise. Adam gasps in disbelief and lunges at me with his right arm. I duck to the side, Jess's touch on my back telling me she does the same thing, and slam down hard on his extended arm.

In reaction, he drops his knife. Ever so quickly, Jess leans down and picks it up, her forearm muscles tense in expectation.

As strong and prepared as we are against the Letum, fighting real people is different. I'm not confident we can win.

Adam, holding his arm, makes a lunge toward Jess. Using all of my weight, I slam into him, knocking both of us down. Out of the corner of my eye, I see Abe slowly circling Jess, preparing his move.

Confident that she will be able to hold her own against him, I punch Adam square in the jaw. There's a satisfying crunch as he cries out in pain. He tries to hit me back, but his uncontrolled tears hinder his eyesight and he misses. I strike another punch and break his nose. Blood gushes out. His hands, forgetting their attack on my body, cover his nose.

I pull my hand back, prepared to strike him again, but stop. He's so pathetic. He's no warrior; he's a scared father.

"Stay," I instruct and get back to my feet, ready to take on the next attacker.

Jess is still warily watching Abe's uncertain movements around her as he tries to determine her weak spot. Eyeing my movement, he notices my bloodied fist and his injured companion on the floor and drops his knife. Without a word, he runs down the hallway.

Adam continues to moan and writhe in pain.

Now I'm able to spare attention toward my brother. With Allison hiding behind him in a fierce, protective stance over Josie, Dominic is still squaring off against Nathan and Peter.

Dominic's eyes are alert, calculating their every move.

If they try and openly engage him in a fight, even though Dominic is outnumbered, he's still going to be able to overpower them. If he takes the offensive, he'll leave Allison exposed. They're at a standstill.

I pick up the abandoned knife.

"It's already over," Dominic says as we make eye contact. "Your cowardly companions are no use to you."

Peter breaks his focus from Dominic toward Jess and me. Using this opportunity, Dominic dives forward and takes Peter by surprise. There is a quick gasp of pain as he overtakes him.

Nathan watches me close in on him, eyes Dominic fighting Peter, and spits out, "Disgusting mutated monster." He turns his back on me.

"Allison!" Jess calls out, but her warning is too late.

Before I can stop Nathan, he lunges forward and a high-pitched wail echoes throughout the hall as he slashes his knife at Josie. Allison, who was watching Dominic, doesn't move in time.

No... Not Josie. I can't allow that to happen.

Without another thought, I plunge my knife through the back of Nathan's throat. Missing his spine, it slides in easily. He turns around in confusion, knife sticking out from his neck, and coughs blood down his chin.

Nathan falls to the ground.

There's a moment of shocked silence, the only other noise Dominic's ruthless attack on Peter and Nathan's terrible gurgling as he chokes on his own blood. Then, Allison lets out a scream.

Jess jumps over Nathan and closes her arms around Josie's wailing body.

"Give me your shirt, Elliot," Jess demands, pulling my attention away from Nathan's collapsed body.

I automatically rush forward to comply. She rips a section off of my shirt and blots it at Josie's arm, trying to stench the flow of blood.

Dominic finally stops hitting Peter. There's a stream of blood falling down his right arm.

"I shouldn't have left you exposed, Allison. What did I do?" he cries out.

"Stop talking and move out from my light. I need to see," Jess instructs. "I don't think it hit an artery or anything significant."

Dominic steps back as he anxiously watches Josie.

"Is she going to be okay?" Allison asks.

Jess continues placing the pressure on Josie's arm. "I think so..." She sneaks a peek under her makeshift bandage. The flow has already slowed down significantly. "I know it's hard, but I need you to hold her still."

I step closer to help still the frantic infant. Even though my ears are ringing, I take it as a good sign that Josie is able to scream this loudly. If she were dying, surely she wouldn't be able to cry out with such strength.

"We need to get her over to the infirmary," Jess says. "Elliot, I know you're trying to help. You're only making it harder."

I take a step back. I can't do anything to fix this.

"Allison, do you see where my hand is? I need you to apply steady pressure on it. Once we start walking, it's going to be hard for me to do this."

With her hand shaking, Allison places her hand where Jess's is. When Jess lets go, a small spill of blood leaks through my shirt.

"Harder, Allison," Jess's steady voice instructs, and the two of them quickly walk down the hallway without another thought.

Allison adjusts her pressure, and the bleeding slows down again.

Dominic walks toward Adam and kicks him in the side. "Is there anyone else trying to ambush us?"

Sobbing through his pain, Adam shakes his head.

"Follow them and make sure they get there okay. I'll deal with this mess," Dominic tells me.

With the adrenaline leaving my system, I look down. Nathan is dead. His eyes bulge, staring into nothingness. I did that. I killed him.

"Dominic—" I start. I'm horrified at myself.

He puts his hands on my shoulders and waits for me to look up at him. "It had to be done."

Even though I don't agree with him, I nod. He lets go of my shoulders, and I run down the hallway, escaping the horror I committed.

CHAPTER NINETEEN

With her daughter's blood on her hands, Allison walks out of the patient room. They didn't let Jess treat her as she was deemed too close to the situation and therefore, emotionally unstable.

"She's going to be okay," she announces.

Jess and I breathe a huge, simultaneous sigh of relief.

"What did they say?" I ask.

"They're putting in eight stitches and are going to give her an antibiotic shot to help prevent infection."

Jess asks, "They will release her soon then, right?"

Allison nods and, suddenly, bursts out crying. I instinctively pull her in for a hug. Her body shakes as the emotion floods her system.

"I thought I was going to lose her," she says through her tears. "She's all I have left of Matt."

Jess tentatively places a hand on her back. "She's going to be fine."

Allison takes a deep breath. "I'm going to go back to be with her. I wanted to give you a quick update."

"We'll be right here," Jess says.

Without another word, Allison pushes through the double doors to rejoin Josie.

Jess takes a seat on one of the waiting room chairs. Leaving an open seat between us, I sit down with her.

I put my head in my hands and rub my forehead.

I killed a man. Not one of the Letum, but a healthy, young man who still had years of potential to do good. The worst part is I did it without a second thought—it happened instinctively. The knife slid so easily into the weak skin at his neck.

What would my mother say if she saw what I've become? Back when we first left Potentia, two men tried to steal our vehicle and possibly harm us. My brother, acting now on what I realize was impulse, killed both of them without a second thought. My mother was horrified and disgusted with him.

"It had to be done," his voice echoes through my memory.

I now understand why he killed those two men. Does that mean I'm turning into the one person I swore I'd never be?

Jess's voice breaks through my thoughts. "What do you think Silas is going to do? He already doesn't want us here."

I shrug. "There's no telling. We have to trust that Dominic will somehow be able to talk us out of this one."

"Because trusting Dominic has worked out so well for us..." Jess mutters.

"What choice do we have?" I ask and stare back down at my hands—the hands that murdered.

Who am I becoming? Suddenly, I can't stay in this room anymore. I need to get away.

I stand up quickly, and Jess eyes me in surprise.

"I'll be back," I mutter as I escape the confinement of the small room.

I don't wait for her to respond and push through the door. When I get out of the room, my thoughts follow me, so I start jogging. I pass a lot of alarmed expressions, but not one person stops me.

Of course they should look at me that way. I'm a killer now.

When I pass the next corner, I break into a sprint. Unsure of where I'm going, I only know I need to get away.

"Eli, wait up," Leah calls out to me.

I stop, putting my hands over my head to regain my breath.

"What happened to your shirt?" she asks once she gets closer.

Her question takes me by surprise. I can't believe I forgot I've been shirtless this entire time. There was a time in my life where I took giant pains to hide the scar my brother gave me on my chest after our father left us. Now, it doesn't even matter.

I turn to face her with some of Nathan's blood on my chest.

"What happened?" she breathes.

She's the one who was the catalyst for all of this. Without her, none of this would have happened and our futures wouldn't be, yet again, threatened needlessly.

I'm not sure what she sees in my eyes—the eyes of a murderer. She takes a step back and looks at me in fear...the way people have looked at my brother.

I close my eyes and take a deep breath. Even though it's easy to blame her, it's not all her fault. When I reopen my eyes, I soften my gaze.

"We were attacked by the group at the lunch table next to us," I say.

Her eyes widen even further. "By Nathan and his friends?"

Too exhausted to elaborate, I nod.

"Is everyone okay?" Leah asks, not accepting my simple answer.

I chuckle bitterly. How could everyone be okay right now? Josie's right arm has eight stitches running down it, Dominic and Jess could turn at any time, and I've become a monster.

Instead of saying this, I respond, "Josie got injured, but she'll be fine. Nathan didn't survive the fight." I can't bring myself to admit what I did...who I've become.

I take another deep breath and continue my walk down the hallway. I want to take a shower and get his blood off of me.

"I'm so sorry, Eli. I wasn't thinking and opened my big mouth again," she whispers behind me, not moving to keep up with me.

The ugly part of me is thankful she feels so guilty. She should. I have to force that part down. The guilt she's feeling can be appeased; mine can't. If I can take some of hers away, I need to. I wish someone could do it for me.

I backtrack so I can make easy eye contact with her. Her eyes are tearing up, making her face blotchy. She's so young.

"Leah, you had a right to be scared earlier. For your entire life, you were brainwashed to believe that the Planned are dangerous."

I pause as I consider what to say. My whole life I was told the complete opposite.

Tears fall down her face. She's begging me to forgive her, to make her feel better. I try my best to offer that comfort.

"With recent events, it's understandable why you reacted that way."

With the sleeve of her shirt, she wipes her face, confusion overriding her guilt. "Do you not think they're dangerous?"

I've seen my Planned brother murder people, and now I've done that, too. According to my education, the territories were attacked and their people killed by the outside groups that didn't agree with the genetic engineering. However, if you ask the people here, they've grown up with the understanding the territories went on the offensive and attacked them. There's probably a ring of truth in both.

I've always imagined there had to be a place that would be better, where I could truly be happy. I thought there would be a place where people could be decent to one another. Now, I'm not even sure a place like that can exist.

I place my right hand on her shoulder and gently squeeze.

"Leah, it doesn't matter if you're Planned or Unplanned. The violent nature is in all of us, waiting to come out."

I remove my hand and try, once again, to get away from everyone. I hold my breath, hoping she doesn't call out again.

When I turn the corner, I let that breath out and quicken my stride. I need to get away from everyone.

Not knowing anywhere else to go, I retreat to my living suite and lock the door behind me without turning the lights on.

Trying to escape the haunting thoughts, I lie on my bed and fight my way into an uneasy sleep, not caring about the blood spreading onto my sheets.

In my dreams, Nathan's bulging eyes stare at me in accusation as he dies. Unable to speak due to his ruined throat, his mouth gapes as fresh blood pours down his neck.

A knock brings me back to consciousness. Disoriented from sleep, I panic, thinking it's Nathan here to punish me for what I've done.

The second time the person knocks, it's more impatient. I toss my legs over the bed. Of course it's not Nathan; he's dead. I made sure he'll never be able to knock on anyone's door again.

A quick look at the clock tells me it's only 2 a.m.

Even louder than the last, the person knocks for a third time. There's no use in delaying the inevitable. There's nowhere I can go at any rate.

I walk to the door and unlock the dead bolt. Dominic pushes the door open and lets himself in, giving me a small sense of relief that it's not anyone else.

"It's late. What—" I start, voice still slurred from sleep.

He sits down on the floor, leaning against the wall. "I need to talk to you."

"It can't wait?" I ask.

I want to be alone. No one should be near me after what I've done, after who I've become.

He studies my expression. "I don't think it should, Elliot."

Still not used to hearing him use my actual name instead of the cruel nickname I grew up with, the hairs on the back of my neck rise. What terrible news does he have for me?

"What happened? What did Silas say?" I ask, fearing the worst.

He shrugs. "It took a lot of convincing to assure him that we were under attack, but in the end, he believed me enough to view the video footage. They have an old system in place that only captures black-and-white grainy footage—not even any sound—but it was obvious even to them that they attacked us."

"What are they going to do?"

He lets out a deep breath. He's clearly exhausted. If this is all good news, why does he feel the need to share it with me now?

"Peter, Adam, and Abe will be exiled tomorrow morning in front of the whole population here—even the children."

"Abe ran. He didn't do any harm," I say.

"Those are their rules, Elliot. If he lets one exception through, the whole compound will fall. There must be order here…now more than ever."

In my mind, I hear Jonah's voice reciting the laws of Veritas when we first got here. I didn't realize that they weren't more than lip service.

"What about us? We fought back. We responded to their violence with even more violence. And I…" I taper off, letting the words hang in the air. I can't even admit it out loud to my brother—a person who has killed five people that I know of and probably others through the genetic testing he conducted back at Potentia.

"It was self-defense. Plain and simple. We did not initiate anything. They came to us with the intention to kill every single one of us, even Josie. They deserve everything coming to them."

I'm not sure if I agree with that statement. They acted out in fear of something they didn't understand. They should be punished for what they did, but there has to be another option besides banishing them. How long can they survive on their own?

I stare down at my hands—the hands that thrust the knife into a man's throat.

"Out of everyone, your face has always been the easiest for me to read, little brother," Dominic starts, interrupting me from my thoughts.

If someone had told me yesterday before lunch that I would kill a man and have my brother look at me with concern, not pity, I'm not sure which one I would have believed less.

I bark a humorless laugh. "And what's my face telling you right now?"

"That I was right to come talk to you now instead of in the morning," Dominic whispers back. He breaks eye contact and stares across at the opposite wall.

I don't respond. Instead, I fall back into my thoughts of the horror of what I did today. Killing was so easy. Getting rid of the Letum is one thing because they're so far disconnected from being an actual person, but this is completely different.

I wish that I hadn't looked into Nathan's eyes after the knife went into the delicate flesh in his throat. He was so surprised.

So was I.

How long did it take before his body told his mind that he was dying? Was it when he couldn't get any breath because the blood from his slashed throat was choking him? Or, did he lose consciousness in hopes that this was all a dream? That he would be okay?

Finally breaking the silence, Dominic's voice is so quiet I have to strain to hear him. "I wish I had been the one to kill Nathan."

I scoff. "Why? So you could be the hero you've always imagined yourself to be?"

"So you wouldn't have had to." He lets out a deep breath. "As you know, I've killed people before. Some deserved it, some didn't."

Chris and Andrew didn't deserve anything that happened to them. I'm surprised to hear Dominic admit it.

"I thought you said their deaths were necessary for the good of society as a whole."

"I have learned how to justify all of the deaths of the people I have killed. If I had been the one to slide the knife through Nathan's neck, I would have understood it was for protection. That man tried to kill Josie and even succeeded in leaving her with a scar that she is, thankfully, never going to remember how she got."

He's finally revealed the reason why he's here. He wanted to brag about another thing he's better at than me: murder.

"I'm not going to sit here and argue with you on who is the better killer," I say. "Quite frankly, it's late and I'm too tired to listen to you boast about yet one other area where you feel superior."

I stand back up and motion for him to leave. If he wants to be the better bad guy, he can win. All I want to do is forget what I've done.

"Dammit, Elliot. You're so difficult sometimes. It's infuriating," he says, letting anger overshadow his concern. "Stop talking and let me finish."

"Why should I listen to anything you have to say right now?"

"Because you're my brother and I'm trying to help," he responds.

His apparent sincerity keeps me quiet. It doesn't sound like he's playing a game or trying to trick me.

Instead, I sit back down on the hard concrete next to him.

"Until we left Potentia, I truly saw you as weak," he says.

"Thanks," I mutter. He's off to a great start.

"Let me finish," he says through his teeth. Taking a deep breath, he regains composure and keeps talking. "The perceived value I could add to the society was so much higher than yours. Besides the genetics we shared, you were insignificant to me. You were the reason why Father left us and Mother spent all of her time and attention away from me."

The fingers on his right hand twitch on his thigh. "Outside of the bubble at Potentia, our roles have been reversed. I do not think I have ever struggled with anything as much as this. My whole world and self-worth have been flipped upside down."

Taking another deep breath, he stills his trembling fingers. "It does not make you weak that you do not want to be violent, and you are horrified that you killed a man—even though it was in self-defense. It takes a certain amount of strength to understand the value in everyone's life." He pauses and considers his next words. "Not the value they can add to science, but the value they add as a person. You see people's humanity. No matter how hard I try, I cannot always do that."

I remain still, trying to take in his words. I can't even look at him. I'm too confused about what he's saying.

Out of the corner of my eye, Dominic shrugs. "We are different, Elliot. That does not make you less than me—it means you have a different kind of strength."

"Why are you telling me all of this?" I breathe.

"Because I do not want you to lose that about you. You see the good in every person, even when they give you no cause to believe so. Our whole lives, I have used that against you, making you believe that I would be good then using you to gain what I wanted." He hesitates. "But now, I think that might be the best part about you. You cannot lose that."

"What do I do now?"

Dominic stares at his own hands. "You learn to live with it."

I ache for Jess to be here with me instead. If she were, I could listen to her more than I can absorb anything coming from my brother. While fate loves forcing me to rely on him, I can't bring myself to trust him. He's done too much.

"Like how you get through every day, even knowing what you did to Jess?" I spit out.

"What do you want me to say? That I wish I could take it all back? Will that make it any better for you?" He runs his hands through his hair.

Nothing's going to make it better for Jess or me. It won't take away the sharp wedge he drove between us. Even knowing that, I still need to know.

"Do you at least feel guilty?" I ask.

Dominic lets out a deep breath. "Every day."

Though I want to, I don't believe him.

CHAPTER TWENTY

The entire population of the compound has gathered in an outdoor amphitheater. Luckily, we're located in the center of all of the buildings, so there's no risk of the Letum getting to us. I can't imagine the panic that would cause.

At least it would prove to Silas that we were right.

The tension radiating through the Mess Hall is now subdued but still here, bubbling under the surface waiting for an opportunity to come back out.

Leah is the only person comfortable enough to stand next to us, which is ironic since she's the reason we're all standing here. Though space is limited, there's a three-foot gap between our group and the next person, who is Thomas. His attention keeps darting between Leah, me, and where he is standing. We're completely isolated from the group.

In unspoken agreement, our group stands together for the first time since we all arrived here. Josie, freshly bandaged and on light pain medication, snoozes in her mother's shielding arms.

Silas steps on the stage and raises his hand, silencing everyone instantly—once again an eerie reminder of Potentia's late Territory Leader.

"As I'm sure many of you have heard, yesterday afternoon there was a violent attack that ended with a member of our compound dead. The laws that my grandfather created when he founded Veritas are explicitly clear: anyone who incites violence upon another member of our compound will be banished. If any of them attempt to come back or make contact with anyone here, that is cause for execution. This is God's will."

No one makes a sound throughout Silas's speech except a bird chirping happily in the distance. How nice it must be to be so obliviously content, thinking everything is normal.

"As we exile three members of our compound, remember this as a warning as of what happens when you go against our laws. We can't be safe whenever there is a single threat made against another person. And sometimes, these threats can come from within." He pauses to let the words sink in. "Jonah, please bring out the sinners."

Jonah mutters into his communicator and the door opens, revealing guards pushing Peter, Adam, and Abe throughout the crowd.

Peter and Adam are severely beaten, both of them cringing in pain at every movement. Abe's eyes are wild. He tries to call out, but the gag in his mouth prevents any comprehensible words from reaching the audience.

Time slows down uncomfortably as the doomed men make their way down the steps to the outdoor amphitheater.

"This feels wrong," I whisper.

Dominic stares at our previous attackers with open contempt. "They deserve it."

I'm not sure if anyone deserves this. Yesterday, the mob that wanted violence so badly is now getting their chance. I doubt this will be the end of it. Things are never that simple anymore.

Jonah takes command over the first person, Adam. He pushes him toward the center of the stage.

"Adam, you have been found guilty of an attack against other members of our compound. Per the rules we all agreed to, you'll now be exiled with a week's worth of supplies. Do you have any last words?" Silas asks.

Jonah roughly takes out his gag.

Even though Adam is forced to squint due to the swelling caused by my fist, he still manages to stare at Jonah in pure hatred, eyes narrowed and jaw clenched.

Voice hoarse, he calls out, "Everyone here knows this is bullshit. We tried to eliminate the risk of a mutated beast turning. Silas calls me a sinner, but I'm not the one who went against God's nature and altered genetics. One of the real sinners killed one of us, but where are they now? They're watching me as I'm about to be banished for the crime they committed. They don't care about—"

Jonah slams the gag back into Adam's mouth, forcing his head backward. Adam's muted coughing fills the air. He can no longer make any further remarks.

The silence that stifled the group dissipates. Angry voices call out again, the mob mentality returning. I shift, fearing an attack from behind.

Silas eyes this change in dynamics, expressionless. Jonah looks toward his leader for instruction and receives it with a tight nod. He shoves a small bag into Adam's arms and pushes him toward the exit. When they get to the small doors, Jonah unties him and takes the gag back out, gesturing toward his gun to discourage him from speaking. With one last peek over his shoulder, Adam makes eye contact with Catherine. From behind her, I don't see her expression, only the nodding of her head.

Then with one more push from Jonah, Adam leaves Veritas.

Silas holds up his arms, quieting the crowd again. "Let me be clear about one thing; Adam and the others incited the violence. Yes, one of them was killed, but it was out of self-defense. I viewed the footage myself. As I discussed in my sermon this morning, there's no need to fear the genetically mutated unless they show signs of the stomach flu. We must remain faithful as Satan tempts us." He licks his lips. "Violence will not be tolerated here at Veritas."

A movement catches my attention. With his arm around his sobbing sister, Isaac, who so enthusiastically helped us when we got here and quickly became a friend, stares at me, his eyes crinkled slits. He was one of the few people who I didn't believe had hate in him.

But we all do, don't we?

Without thinking, I take a step forward. I want to explain how we were attacked and how I never wanted any of this to happen.

Jess grabs my arm, freezing me instantly. "Don't go in the middle of them. Silas is losing what control he has left."

She lets go, leaving a trail of fire where her hand was.

"We'll now continue with the exiles so you all can get back to your workstations. Jonah, bring the next sinner."

When it's Peter and Abe's turn, they don't get an opportunity to say any last words.

"Let's get out of here," Dominic says.

About half the people are staring right at us. The isolated circle we're in makes it easy for everyone to spot us. While most of the expressions are apprehensive, some of them are angry. No matter what Silas told them, they don't believe that justice was truly served.

I'm not sure if I do either.

Dominic takes the first step and we all follow him closely, with me bringing up the rear. The moment we leave the amphitheater, chatter begins, like our presence was keeping them quiet.

"Keep your guard up today," Dominic warns us all. "Their wounds are going to be fresh, and many of them will blame us. While the fear of the consequences if they do act will be high, don't go anywhere alone."

"Surely no one would…" Leah drifts off, eyes darting behind her.

"I'll walk Jess and Allison back to their room before I head over to work," I say. "I don't want either of you reporting to your assignments today."

The door opens up behind us, revealing Isaac, fear and anger seeping off of him in waves.

"Go before more people come in from outside," Dominic says as he turns to go in a different direction.

"I'll come with you, Eli. We're going to end up in the same place anyway," Leah mumbles as she follows us to their living suite. She speeds up and walks beside Allison.

"I don't need you to walk with me," Jess says to me, though there isn't any real emotion behind it.

"Please. Let me. It'll make me feel better knowing you're safe."

She studies my expression. "After everything?"

I open my mouth to respond but am cut off before I can.

"Dominic is exaggerating what everyone here is capable of, but it's always nice to have a bit of company, right?" Leah calls back as she squeezes herself between Jess and me. Allison raises an eyebrow at her movement but keeps walking forward.

Jess smiles down at her but doesn't respond. The rest of the brief walk passes in silence. Jess and Leah don't know how to talk to one another, and I'm too busy trying to read into her question. Was there hope or only curiosity in that?

When we get to their door, Allison gives me a brief smile before going inside. Jess hesitates outside the doorway. She's pale and a little uneasy on her feet. I want to comfort her, but I'm not sure what support she'll allow me to give.

I say, "I'll see you after my work shift."

"I'll be here," Jess says and closes the door.

I stay, focused on her door. I'm unable to get rid of the dread that something is going to go wrong.

"Come on, Eli," Leah mutters as she grabs my arm to pull me away from the door.

We walk away, though everything in my gut is screaming at me to stay with her. The farther away from her that we get, the easier it is to push the anxiety down. It's probably a reaction to everything that's happened these last twenty-four hours and my attempt to seek her comfort.

It's not until we get to our workstation that I notice Leah is uncharacteristically quiet.

She's not as scared or apprehensive as I would expect. Instead, there's an aching sadness in her eyes.

I open the door for her and the two of us go into the mindless room.

My thoughts drift off as I fulfill the repetitive task of moving the boxes over to the appropriate shelf. While it's necessary work, as the compound goes through a lot of food in a day, it doesn't take much brainpower to sort through the different items.

"Eli..." Leah starts.

I grunt as I move the box full of canned fruit. "Yes?"

"You love her, don't you?" she asks, causing me to stop, midmotion.

I set the box down and turn to face her. "Yes."

"Jess hasn't given you the time of day since you've been here. The two of you have a history, but that's what it is—the past." The rhythm of her speaking speeds up. "Don't be so focused on what the two of you had that it keeps you from having it again with someone else."

Knowing the pain that my words are going to cause her, I still need to say them. "I don't want anyone else."

She shakes her head, blinks away her emotion, and continues her sorting.

I pick my box back up.

"The sooner we finish this, the sooner we can go do something else," she says to change the subject and reaches back into the box for more food.

I try to ignore the anxiety bubbling in my chest.

"Do you think we should follow the expiration dates on cans?" Leah asks, reminding me of an earlier conversation I had with Jess when she voiced the same question.

I look around at the large, cluttered room and wonder what I'm doing here. "I'm going to take today off," I say. "With everything that's going on..."

"You're worried about her, aren't you?" she asks, tilting her chin up.

"I can't help it."

"Then go. I'll cover for you."

"Thanks, Leah," I say as I walk out the door, not needing to be told again.

Through the endless maze of hallways, I quickly walk back to Jess and Allison's room.

A loud scream pierces through the hallway, and I freeze in confusion. It's coming from the direction of the Mess Hall.

I eye that direction anxiously. I left Allison and Jess safely in their room not thirty minutes ago. If there's some struggle going on in there, it's not my problem. Today of all days, I should stay out of it.

The sounds of violence get louder and more pronounced. There's another loud, piercing scream.

Suddenly unable to breathe, my lungs cease working. I fall to one knee as I struggle to gulp in air.

I recognize that scream.

Breath hitching, I force myself back up. My footsteps echo through the hallways while I push myself toward the noises of struggle. The yells get more distinct with every passing second.

I slam through the doors leading into the Mess Hall and run into a mob.

"Kill her!" the little lady next to me screams.

I fight my way to get closer to the source of the agony, ignoring the faces of the people around me.

A voice to my left contributes. "She's a danger to all of us."

"We should have never let them stay with us," another person yells out.

I ignore all the angry glares and push people out of my way. Luckily, because everyone's attention is so focused on the danger in front of them, I'm able to take them by surprise and make it to the front to find Jess as the source of the angry group's outrage.

I call out her name, but she doesn't hear me. Tears flow down her face as she attempts to rationalize with everyone. Her pleas are drowned out by the hateful shouts that have overtaken the room. Callie is the only one by Jess's side and she growls menacingly at anyone who tries to approach her.

I rush forward, wanting to join her, but someone grabs my shoulder and spins me around. Dominic's fist finds contact with my chin and I fall to the ground. I lie on the ground while my eyesight blurs. He roughly gets me back on my feet, keeping a firm grip on me, and says, "There isn't anything you can do. Don't go down with her."

I refocus in time to see two men rush forward toward Jess. One of them kicks Callie away, and she whines and falls to the ground. Eyes flashing, Jess raises her hands in preparation for their arrival.

I struggle to escape Dominic's firm grip. He's relentless. "It's already over," he says.

I scream out, "Don't hurt—" Dominic roughly shoves one of his hands over my mouth, tilting my head back. My eyes water with the pain of the pressure on my neck. I continue screaming, despite Dominic's hand, to no avail. Every movement I make forces him to place even more pressure on my head.

"She's gone," Dominic whispers in my ear. "Stop fighting it."

From the corner of my vision, I see them come at her from two different sides. Punches come from both of them and in the end, there's nothing she can do to protect herself. She's outnumbered.

I take a deep breath and slam my entire body weight back. Dominic falls back with me. There is a quick relief when the pressure is gone from my neck when his hand falls back to catch himself.

I elbow Dominic sharply and he exhales, pushing me down. I scramble to my feet and yell out in a hoarse, gravelly voice, "I'm coming, Jess. Don't—"

Dominic slams in behind me, pinning me facedown to the hard floor, leaving me gasping for air. There's a crack followed by a sharp pain as my nose breaks. Blood pools down, and unable to move my head, I cough as I start choking on it.

Not able to see what's happening anymore, I try to focus on what I can hear, but everyone else is so loud I can't make anything out beyond my own labored breathing.

"Enough," Silas says, and his authority over the group silences everyone. Dominic relaxes his grip slightly so I can turn my head, peer through the blood, and watch. The men have ended their attack and backed off. Jess lies motionless on the ground next to Callie.

I take advantage of the quiet to make myself heard. "What the hell are you doing?" Dominic cuts me off from saying more by placing his hand over my mouth as he pulls me back to my feet.

I try to slam my body back again. Dominic is prepared this time and maintains his steely grip on me.

Silas follows the source of my outburst and studies Dominic and me with an expressionless glance. I use the only form of communication that's allowed to me and glare at him.

"The noise of this exchange has drawn a large number of you to our Mess Hall despite it not being a meal time. It's regrettable that so many of you are here because of your curiosity." Silas looks around the room like he's addressing every member of our community. "Nonetheless, it's time to explain what's going on. Catherine, please tell me what you witnessed."

The recently separated wife nervously scans the room before saying, "I was coming in here to get some water when I heard the sound of someone throwing up. Of course, I instantly became concerned. You told us that's one of the warning signs of the infection."

Jess slowly rolls over and reaches out toward Callie. Her dog whines weakly but is at least alive.

"I'm glad you took those words seriously," Silas says. "Tell us all, who was vomiting?"

"It was her," Catherine says and points toward Jess. My shoulders sag in defeat. This has been one of my greatest fears since I found out what caused the infection.

I'm not ready for this. We didn't have enough time together.

Silas addresses Jess. "Do you deny this?"

Satisfied that Callie is alive and not too seriously hurt, Jess says, "I'm not turning into one of the Letum."

While Jess's voice is panicked and full of desperation, Silas's is completely calm. "That isn't what I asked. Did you throw up?"

"Yes, but—" Jess starts to defend herself, but is cut off.

"And did you come from a territory that's known for genetic manipulation?"

"I'm not infected," Jess says.

Silas's questioning is unforgiving. "Answer the question."

Silas is pretending he doesn't know she's Planned to protect himself. In hatred, I bite down as hard as I can on Dominic's hand. He flinches but doesn't move to allow me to scream out.

She puts her hands up in the air and wipes the blood off her face. "Yes, I am. Everyone knows this, but I'm healthy."

"Your mouth says one thing and your body—something different." Silas looks grimly toward her and then readdresses the crowd. "She's not a risk we can take in our fragile state. We can only assume she was one of the genetically mutated who have threatened to destroy everything we are."

Calls of outrage overtake the room again. "All I did was throw up!" Jess screams out. Callie has regained some of her strength and struggles to her feet.

Silas's voice rises enough to be heard. "All in favor of immediate eradication of this infection?"

All around me, noises of approval scream out. How could everyone suddenly be so heartless? We've been living here for weeks alongside them, and now they're acting like she's not even human.

I push and kick to try to get away from Dominic. He's stronger than me and won't let go. "She's done, Elliot. Let her go."

This can't be happening.

I twist and tug, trying anything to get away from him. All I succeed in doing is prompting Dominic to tighten his grasp even further, threatening my air supply.

Jess eyes the approaching mob and fresh tears fall. Callie growls and Silas takes out his gun. "For the greater good," he says and aims toward Jess.

Jess cries out one more time. "I'm not turning."

I can't breathe fully. I start to see stars as my world fades.

"That isn't a risk I'm willing to take," Silas says, and his finger hovers around the trigger.

With the last of my strength, I slam my body back again. Dominic doesn't relent. I push away from his unyielding, viselike grip, but he's so much stronger than I am. I scream against Dominic's hand, trying to get Jess's attention one last time. She needs to know that I'm here.

I want her to know I still love her, and I always will. That we should have had more time. That I'm still here.

She lowers her head.

"It's morning sickness," Jess says, voice breaking as she throws her hands up again.

The shock of her words quiets everyone.

Dominic's grip finally relaxes, and I take a massive gulp of air. What's she saying? Why is she prolonging this?

Catherine shifts her own child in her arm and scoffs. "She's trying to save herself."

"No, it's true," Jess says between sobs. "I'm pregnant. I was coming in here to get some crackers to settle my stomach."

Silas's weapon lowers marginally. Dominic lets me go, whispering in my ear. "Claim the child."

Now that I'm no longer restrained, I rush forward to her. I tie my fate and put myself between the gun and Jess.

"Elliot, remove yourself from this situation," Silas says. Jonah moves in anticipation of a fight.

"The baby is mine," I say hoarsely and remain in the same position.

Silas tilts his head and focuses all of his attention on me. There's a tentative touch on the back of my left shoulder. The sound of my heart beating in my chest, her desperate sobs, and Jess's touch are the only things pinning me to the present. Finally, he says, "If the child is yours, then why do you appear surprised?"

One misstep here and the two of us could get killed. I race through different responses in my head until Dominic breaks the silence. "How would you appear if you found out you were going to be a father?"

I break away eye contact with Silas to see Dominic, keeping my expression as even as possible. Allison has joined him in the front, holding her daughter. Dominic whispers in her ear.

To my surprise, my brother joins my protective barrier and acts as another shield for Jess. She retreats even further into herself and holds on to Callie. Allison stays where she is, holding Josie, eyes darting across the room.

Now it's Silas's turn to look startled. "You want to know what I think?" He pauses before answering his rhetorical question. "I think she's infected and smartly thought a fake pregnancy would buy her some time." He motions toward me. "And your brother has some innate desire to protect her, so he's claiming the child. What I don't understand, however, is why Dominic joined us all."

Dominic responds, "Before we came here, we were all at a genetic testing site back in my territory. During this time, we ran tests on Jess and discovered she was pregnant. She had previously been intimate with my brother."

Jess raises her head before she hides it once again in Callie's fur.

Silas lowers the gun another notch. "If you knew for all this time, why didn't you tell Elliot that his ex-lover was pregnant?"

Why would he go out of his way to prolong the inevitable? This doesn't benefit him in any way. It's actually the opposite.

Dominic shrugs. "It was not my place to say anything. I was going to leave that up to Jess as to when she wanted to share this information."

Clearly undecided, Silas stares down at all three of us. Without a warning, he calls out and yells, "Jonah!"

Jonah immediately straightens and says, "Yes, sir?"

Silas keeps his razor-focused attention on me while he addresses Jonah. "You're to escort Jess back to her chambers and watch her take a pregnancy test. If that test is negative, you must eliminate the problem without hesitation."

"Yes, sir." He marches forward toward Jess, and she recoils away.

Dominic and I both automatically shift so he can't get to her. "Don't touch her," I say. Once I'm sure that Dominic is going to stay in his position to block Jonah's path, I lean down toward Jess and say so only she can hear me, "I'm going to help you get back to your room."

Then, for the first time since the genetic testing facility, Jess opens her arms and lets me touch her. I cradle her to my chest as she wraps her arms around my neck. Her sobs echo through my body. I close my eyes and appreciate the feeling of her in my arms again.

I reopen my eyes with fresh determination. I need to protect her. I stand back on my feet and call for Callie to follow me. She limps along while we exit the Mess Hall. From Jess's announcement and Silas's command, everyone is too confused to react.

A couple sets of footsteps follow us, but I focus on what's ahead. We'll need to overpower Jonah and somehow escape. They tore our vehicle apart when we got here, but surely their trucks can't be that hard to learn how to operate. We'll need to race back to the territories as quickly as possible to give Jess the most amount of time. If we can get her back before she fully turns, Dominic should be able to help give her more time than even Andrew got.

My shirt feels damp from Jess's tears, but I welcome them. She's finally letting me comfort her. I shift to hold her tighter. No matter what happens, at least we're going to end this together.

CHAPTER TWENTY-ONE

I turn another corner and sneak a glance behind me. Dominic follows closely behind with his eyes glazed over, hiding his thoughts. Jonah and Allison take the rear. Josie is oblivious to the situation and lies peacefully in her mother's arms.

I return my attention to what's ahead and shift some of Jess's weight in my arms.

"We're almost there," I say to her.

The end of the hallway appears and I take the last turn to reach Allison and Jess's suite. I push the door open and we enter.

Even though my arms ache from the stress of holding Jess, I don't set her down. I take a seat and keep her in my lap. Dominic stands next to us. His tense body language sets me on edge. Why is he suddenly pretending to be protective?

Allison hurries ahead and immediately enters her room with Josie.

Jonah says, "You must go into the bathroom and take the test." He holds out a small package.

I need to buy more time. Every one of my heartbeats reminds me that the truth is ticking closer. The amount of time she has left is directly related to how long she has until she takes the test and exposes her lie. "Can you give us a couple of minutes? She was attacked."

"I have my orders. If she does not take it now, it'll be considered a failed test." His voice echoes across the room.

I take a deep breath in preparation for a rebuttal, but Jess stops me by letting go of my neck. "It's okay. I'll take it."

She stands up and takes the package from his hand.

Does she not realize how important it is to stall right now? Is she that willing to die? Callie follows her to the bathroom as her faithful bodyguard.

Allison returns to the living area. "I put Josie in her crib," she says needlessly. She hands me a couple of Josie's wipes.

"She's taking the test right now," I say as I accept them and clean the blood off my face. I cringe when I touch my nose.

I try to convey nonverbally to Allison that we need to be prepared to escape if we want to be able to save Jess. Even if we can get out of the compound safely, it's only a matter of time until she turns.

Allison bites her nails, her eyes wide as she stares down Dominic. He purses his lips and takes a step closer toward Jonah.

Always observant, Jonah says, "If the test comes back negative and I follow through on my orders, it would be unwise of any of you to fight back."

Allison's attention remains on Dominic's stance while she says, "It's not going to come back negative." Her eyes then connect with mine, and I see the truth behind her words.

It doesn't make any sense. We took precautions to make sure this wouldn't happen. She must be wrong or a better liar than I imagined.

The bathroom door creaks open and Jess wordlessly hands the test over to Jonah. His eyebrows shoot up.

"I appreciate your cooperation," Jonah says. "Congratulations."

He walks out of the room, presumably to report the results to Silas, and leaves a blanket of silence behind.

Dominic runs his hands through his hair. He looks at Jess and drops his gaze. Without saying anything, my brother exits the room and leaves the three of us alone.

I slink down on the floor, mind numbing. Sensing my distress, Callie comes closer and licks my hand. I automatically pet her, not even fully realizing I'm doing it.

I absentmindedly follow the motion of Allison hugging Jess and whispering something in her ear, with Jess listening intently. Allison takes a step back and studies her expression. Slowly, Jess nods.

I drop my head down and stare at my lap. Even though a part of me suspected the worst all along, it was too horrible for me to truly accept it as a possibility. I couldn't bring myself to believe that even Dominic would stoop so low as to rape her.

I'm not ready for this conversation. I want to leave the room, like Dominic.

Josie cries out. Allison's head shifts between Jess and her room. Without saying anything, she moves toward Josie and closes the door behind her.

Jess comes closer and says, "There are some things I should have told you a long time ago. I don't want to keep secrets from you anymore."

The memories of us together are now tainted, forced into an unwelcome darkness. How could Dominic take them away from me? I let out a deep breath, trying to get rid of the disgust that this revelation is causing. No matter how hard I try, I can't push it down. He did the unimaginable.

"Elliot, please look at me," she begs, her voice breaking.

She breaks my trance, and I force myself to make eye contact despite wanting to avoid her confirmation. A fresh bruise is forming across her cheekbone, and her face is blotchy from her tears. Despite this, her eyes convey a small sense of strength that I haven't seen from her in a long time.

Her eyebrows are furrowed and there's fear in her expression, as if she's afraid of what I'm going to say.

I can't turn away from her. She needs my support. How can I deny her?

She's still Jess. I can't lose her.

I reach out and take her hand. "Come back to me," I say, voice cracking.

She pulls her hand away and drops her head. "I'm not good enough for you. I owe you the truth."

A strand of hair has fallen in front of her face, so I gently cup her chin and move it back behind her ear. "Do you want to be with me?"

She hiccups. "It's not that simple."

"Answer the question."

Her jaw clenches and her shoulders tense as if she's trying to find some internal strength. She stares down at her hands. "You don't understand what happened. I owe you the truth."

I take a deep breath and close my eyes. "I don't need you to tell me what happened because you think you owe me some type of explanation. I thought for a long time that I needed to know, but I don't. All I need to know is that you want to be with me. That's all the truth

I need." I open my eyes. She doesn't need to say it. I don't want her to. I want the small element of possibility that the worst hasn't happened.

"I've been absolutely horrible to you. Why would you even want to be with me?" Jess asks.

"Because I love you. No matter what, you're the person I want to share all the good and bad things that've happened to me. I wish more than anything that the whole episode at the genetic facility hadn't happened, but it doesn't make me think any less of you. You're so strong and worth all the love in the world."

She blinks as a tear escapes. Her voice cracks as she says, "There were some personal battles that I had to go through that I couldn't share with you. I was at a dark place for a long time. I would go to bed every night crying and wake up every morning wanting to be anyone else." Her eyes are unguarded now.

All of my fears and suspicions about what could have happened between her and my brother don't matter as much. All I care about is moving forward together. "Let me in," I say.

She pauses and considers my request. I hold my breath in anticipation. Slowly, she nods.

I flash a small smile and lean in to gently kiss her. The moment our lips touch, balance restores itself to my life. The pain and confusion from the last couple of months are less significant.

I feel her grin as she pulls away slowly. I angle my forehead in to touch with hers. She doesn't resist my touch. I focus on the promise of what this means.

"I love you so much," I say.

She runs her hands through my hair, looking deeply into my eyes. "As I love you."

Josie's wails from the other room bring us back to reality.

Jess's large shirt still hides any evidence of her pregnancy.

She notices where my attention is. "I'm not holding you to any sort of expectations with the child." She takes a deep breath and continues. "You said you didn't need to know, but I want to tell you. When we were held prisoner back in Potentia, there were things that happened."

I hold my breath.

"Dominic...he...well, he..." Her voice breaks again. She gazes down at her stomach. "He's probably the father. That's why I'm offering you an out. We aren't your responsibility."

I let out a breath at her confirming this news. She is so vulnerable, and I want to be the man she needs right now, but I'm not sure if I have the strength to be. I say the words I suspect she wants to hear, though I struggle saying them.

"I'm all in, Jess. I'm going to be everything I can. You're my family. Not the one I was born with, but the one I choose."

Instead of replying, she tentatively takes hold of my hand and places it on her stomach. I stare at it in wonder, struggling through the conflicting emotions. On one hand, the child is a part of Jess, so how could I not care about it? But the baby is also evidence of Dominic's sexual assault, not an act of love like it was for Josie. It will always be a reminder of the wedge he forced between us.

Even if I can't guarantee I'll be able to truly treat the child like my own, I can at least promise to be with Jess and support her. That's the most I can offer at this time.

"No running. Even when it gets hard. We're in this as a team," I say.

"Together," she agrees.

A fierce sense of protection almost overwhelms me, but it's only toward Jess.

Allison comes out of the room. She spots our position and smiles. "I'm going to go check on Dominic and make sure he doesn't do anything rash. I'm leaving Josie in her crib."

Once the door closes, a fresh awkwardness spreads through the room. I've spent the last couple of months struggling to break my way into her heart again. Now that I have, I don't know what to do.

We exchange a glance and Jess chuckles lightly. "Come sit down with me on the couch, Elliot," she says. "It'll be more comfortable than the floor."

I stand back up and move to sit on the couch in the living area. Tentatively, not fully convinced of what happened, I place my arm around her shoulder. I breathe out a sigh of relief when she leans into my body. Her steady pressure is the reassurance I've been searching for ever since we were last in Potentia. This feels so right. Maybe it can end up okay.

Callie limps over to us and lies down on the floor, head resting on Jess's feet.

"Have you thought about any names?" I ask, trying to be supportive like she needs.

Jess exhales a breath of air. "What?"

"For the baby…for our child," I say, with only a slight hesitation. I hope she doesn't notice.

She places her right hand on her stomach. Even though she's had some time to adjust to the fact that she's pregnant, she still appears shocked that there's a life growing inside of her.

"I haven't put much thought into it. It's been something I've been trying to ignore. It's a reminder of…" she trails off.

I cradle her face in my hands. "Jess, I'll protect you from him. He's never going to touch you again."

I kiss her on the forehead. I start to pull back, but she holds my face so our lips can meet. It's a timid touch.

She pulls back, our foreheads still touching, and says, "I guess if it's a boy, I would like to name him after my brother."

"You've never told me your brother's name before, Jess," I whisper back.

Her breathing hitches. "His name was Bryant, and he was the most wonderful person."

I gently kiss her again. "Then I couldn't think of a better name."

"What if it's a girl?" she asks.

"Honestly, I've never considered the idea of having kids. With all the attention given to genetic engineering, it never made sense that anyone would want to ever be with me, let alone have kids with me."

She's not actually having a child with me but with my genetically pure brother. I shake my head to dispel that thought. If I'm going to protect Jess, I'm going to need to continue the ruse of being the father. Otherwise, people will fear that the child could turn.

I freeze. What if the child does turn? If it happens before its brain is fully developed, at least according to Dominic, then he or she would die unexpectedly. If it happens after…

"Where we're at isn't necessarily better, but I'm glad we're out of the territories," Jess begins, snapping my attention back to her. "They discriminated so heavily against Unplanned for nothing more than how they were born. The three people I've cared most about—you, Allison, and my brother, were all Unplanned. What a terrible belief system."

"I wish we could get away from everything. I want to get away from all of the societies out there and live in a protected bubble with you," I say.

She smirks and leans back into my shoulder. "Wouldn't that be nice…"

I rest my head on hers, blowing some of her hair out from my mouth. "It would be perfect."

The two of us comfort each other, letting the months of separation float away.

"What about after your mother?" Jess asks, breaking the silence.

"Annalise is a good name," I say, emotion causing my voice to break. I'm not sure if I would want the result of Dominic's rape to be named after my mother.

I let out another deep breath as I internally struggle between being the man I know I should be and the weaker one who's fighting to the surface.

CHAPTER TWENTY-TWO

After spending all day together, only breaking for a quick dinner, I left to sleep in my own bed. She didn't ask me to, but I felt like it was the right thing to do. I don't want to push her too quickly.

Right after waking this morning, I rushed over to Jess's to walk her and Allison to breakfast.

"By the way, when did you find out you were pregnant?" I ask as we walk down the hallway to the Mess Hall.

Her step hitches, but she keeps walking. "I suspected right before we left Matt's parents' vacation home."

"Ahh," I mutter as another piece clicks into place. I clear my throat. "That's why you changed your mind and left with us—even though you wanted to stay."

"Yes," she admits. "I needed Allison."

Allison smiles and squeezes her free hand.

I swallow down the pain that she didn't need me then, even though I wanted her so badly. None of that matters now, however.

At least, that's what I keep telling myself.

When we enter the room, everyone stares at us. While there was the anger yesterday, there is no shame in what they almost did. Holding her hand, I guide her through the line to get our food.

No one says anything to us, and we sit at a table in the corner with Allison.

Even though it makes eating the eggs and toast a little awkward, I keep my left arm around Jess's waist in a fiercely protective gesture. Allison sits on her other side with Josie happily mumbling incomprehensible chatter.

Jess warily eyes each person as they pass, but the message must have spread that she's pregnant and not turning. Some people even stop by and mutter half-hearted congratulations. It's amazing how quickly people are willing to forget their bloodlust and cast it away. It's not easy to accept your own terrible nature.

Leah eventually joins us. She sighs before forcing a tight smile.

"That's great news about the baby. The two of you are going to make wonderful parents." Her eyes rest on my arm holding Jess.

"Thank you, Leah," Jess says, smiling a lot more warmly at her than when they first met.

"It's going to be an adventure, that's for sure," I say.

"How far along—" Leah starts.

Dominic, uncharacteristically unkempt and desperate, cuts her off. "I need to talk to you," he says pointedly to Jess.

Jess turns her head away from him and looks at me, eyes wide and desperate.

"Not now," I answer for her.

He ignores me and addresses Jess again. "I need to talk to you."

Allison, probably recognizing the ticking time bomb that he is, leans forward to touch his arm. "Dominic, what—"

"Now," Dominic says, shrugging her off. His jaw is clenched in determination.

After what he did, how could he have the audacity to want to be alone with her? I take a deep breath and try to remain calm.

Jess opens her mouth, but I cut her off by whispering in her ear, "Let me handle this."

She nods in permission, her shoulders tight.

I remove my hand from her waist and stand up, trying to ignore the six inches of height he has over me.

"Let's take a walk."

He shakes his head, causing sweat to fly from his brow. "No, I need to talk to Jess."

I lean in and speak in his ear. "You're making a scene right now. We can go talk, the two of us, away from here. People are starting to stare."

His eyes sweep around us, finally recognizing the number of people gaping at him in fear. Without a word, he slumps his shoulders and walks toward the exit.

I exhale. Now that the tension is dispelled, everyone quickly loses interest and returns to their conversations. I follow Dominic silently through the room.

Once I go through the doorway, Dominic motions for me to join him in an empty space. Gathering my emotional fortitude for what's about to happen, I confidently step into the room. Nothing he can say will change that Jess is mine and we're back together.

"Elliot..." he starts. "I need to talk to Jess."

I clench my fist and punch him square in the jaw. There's a sharp pain in my right hand, but the satisfaction at seeing him fall back is much stronger. All along, I was wrong. The fact that we're brothers doesn't make it acceptable that he's a terrible person. There's no redemption for him—no good inside waiting for the right opportunity to come out. Pretending otherwise is idiotic.

Slowly getting back to his feet, he runs his hands through his hair and I look him in the eye. The person staring at me isn't the twenty-eight-year-old man who can control any situation. He's a scared boy.

"No, you don't," I say, my tone remaining firm. I don't care how anxious he is; his train of thought needs to stop now.

His panicked eyes, the exact same color as our father's, stare into mine. I force myself to maintain the eye contact.

"Elliot, I was up all night thinking about it. I need to talk to her," he repeats.

"You don't," I repeat.

He runs his hands through his hair again as tears threaten to spill from eyes.

"You don't understand!" he exclaims in pain. "I lied about the test revealing she was pregnant when we were doing the testing. I was trying to protect her. I have to talk to her."

He makes a move toward the door. I block his exit. I'm not letting him go anywhere near her when he's in this state. If I don't nip this in the bud now, it's going to be a lot worse for all of us. The boundaries need to be set.

"The baby isn't yours," I say. I don't want to leave any room for misinterpretation. I tilt my chin up and take advantage of my full height. Even though he's still towering over me, he shrinks down.

His eyes widen in a childlike dread. He's never been so out of control before.

"Elliot—"

"I don't care what you think. Assaulting Jess doesn't give you any right whatsoever to be a parent. If you don't step down, I'll make you," I threaten.

Both of his hands thrum uselessly on his thighs as he stares across the room to avoid my steady gaze. A bruise is already appearing on his jaw.

"My genetics..." he mutters. "My child."

I clench my fist, causing fresh pain. I step closer to Dominic, prepared to strike again. "If you try to lay any sort of claim on the child, I promise you'll regret it."

Not trusting myself to keep from true violence, I walk out of the room, hands shaking in anger, and leave Dominic to stew in his own personal hell.

I'm not able to abandon Dominic, however, because once I leave the room, Jonah is standing there, waiting for us to come out.

"Let me guess: Silas wants to see us again?"

Jonah, smirking at my tone, merely nods.

"I know the way," I say and push past him.

From behind me, I hear him talk to Dominic and their subsequent footsteps. I don't acknowledge them.

Not entirely sure what to expect, I slam open the door to Silas's office. Silas is sitting, with near-perfect posture, in his office chair. With the lights on much brighter than they were when we were last in the office, many more details of the room stand out. While there aren't many decorations, what's in the room is well thought out and precisely placed.

The cabinets behind his desk each have one small token of the past on them. One of them has a fishing reel that might predate even the ones my grandfather collected. On the other is an old knife that, while it appears well-kept, has a small stain on the handle that could be blood.

"Take a seat," Silas instructs.

Without saying a word, Dominic sits down and raises his eyes to meet Silas's. Whatever Silas sees in his expression causes his eyebrows to furrow in shock. He quickly recovers and gestures to the seat next to Dominic.

"Elliot, you may sit as well."

"I'd rather stand."

Silas opens his mouth and then closes it. The two of us stare at each other, waiting on the other to make the first move.

"Congratulations are in order, Elliot. Jess is indeed pregnant," Silas starts.

"That's all you have to say?" I ask.

"Yesterday's events were..." Silas pauses as he considers his statement. "Unfortunate."

I scoff. "That's putting it lightly. You almost murdered Jess in front of everyone."

He puts his hands up in placation. "I wanted to call you and your brother in here to speak, man-to-man, to make sure there are no hard feelings." His attention lingers on Dominic's slumped figure in the overstuffed chair.

The bruise forming on his jaw almost makes me regret hitting him because Silas must be able to easily spot it. Even knowing that, I can't get rid of the satisfaction. He deserves so much worse.

My chest tightens. "You think because you call a situation unfortunate, I'll forget that you almost killed Jess and my child?"

Silas's eyes don't leave Dominic.

"Your child?"

"Yes," I say with enough force that he finally looks away from Dominic. "My child."

I keep my expression guarded to hide how my stomach drops at the thought of having to raise my brother's baby—after everything he's done—and pretend it's mine.

Silas studies me as if he's seeking a weak spot—or a lie.

"Anything to add, Dominic? You're uncharacteristically quiet today."

Dominic is hunched over in his chair, hair wild, lips tightly pursed. Dominic doesn't have to say anything verbally right now; his body language is speaking volumes.

"Elliot's the father," Dominic mutters. At least he's saying the right thing. No matter what state he's in right now, he knows that if he tries to lay any claim on the child, it will doom both Jess and the child.

Silas tilts his head toward me in acknowledgment. "Very well, it's your child, Elliot. Though, in our society here, children born out of wedlock are severely discouraged, though they're still considered blessings, of course."

"Of course..." I mutter, wondering where he's taking this.

"As such, the two of you should be married before God. I don't want any negative influences on the young here because of your sinning."

My eyebrows shoot up at his nerve. "That's not something I'm willing to discuss."

I turn to leave the room.

"Wait," Silas calls out sharply.

I freeze and turn back to face him. What does he want from me now?

"I need to know that you or your brother aren't going to retaliate against anyone here."

My cheeks flush in anger. "And what reason could we possibly have for that?"

Silas stands up from his chair. I don't back down.

"I have you in my office, and I need to decide whether to let the two of you leave. Right now, Elliot, you're so angry that I'm thankful you're unarmed. Dominic, on the other hand, seems like he could snap at any moment. What reason do I have for not locking the two of you up until you calm down?"

His raised voice causes Jonah to poke his head through the door.

"Is everything all right?" Jonah asks, eyeing our stance warily. His hand automatically falls to the holster holding his gun at his side—his favorite toy to play with.

Silas takes a deep breath and smiles tightly.

"Yes. You can stay outside. If I need you, I'll call you directly," Silas says.

"You should leave," I add.

Jonah's entire body tenses at my dismissal. He's grown accustomed to hearing it from Silas but not me. He slams the door, his words of anger still breaking through the doorway.

Silas laughs quietly. "I'm here telling you that I worry I can't allow you to rejoin the rest of the compound because the two of you are so unstable, and what do you do? You anger the man with the gun."

"What do you want?" I ask through my clenched teeth.

He taps his fingers on his desk. "What do you want?" He repeats back to me.

I let out a breath at his unexpected response. What do I want? I break eye contact with Silas and stare out at the sun shining through his window. I don't want to be in the room with him. I want to be away from it all.

"You shouldn't let us stay here," Dominic mutters and breaks my attention away from outside.

"Why?" Silas asks.

Dominic shrugs. "The longer we stay, the more likely events of violence will break out due to their fear." He licks his lips. "To everyone here, I'm tainted and dangerous."

We can't stay here. We've already had two dangerous times where some of us almost got killed. Luckily, Dominic has been able to talk us out of each of them, but one quick glance is enough to convince me that we can't rely on him anymore.

"We're all going to leave the compound as soon as we're able. It isn't safe if we stay," I announce.

Silas blinks. "Why would you want to leave Veritas? With the culture we have here and protection we offer from the outside, it doesn't make sense. You're not thinking clearly. Your group needs to focus more on fitting in."

The sad part is, he's sincere in his confusion and belief that his compound is so much better than anything offered anywhere else. How can the two of us interpret the same thing so differently?

"We're not the reason why we don't fit into your culture here. We're not the problem. It's the environment," I say. "I need to watch out for my family."

Silas clicks his tongue in thought. "You want to protect your family? I'll give you two options. Either you go into protective custody until I deem you safe to reenter society, or you continue with our original plan of leading the mission to Potentia to bring back the technology for us."

"Did you not listen to what I said?" I ask. "We don't want anything to do with this compound anymore. We're done."

"I'm not letting you leave," Silas says.

"What? You can't—" I start.

"We had an agreement, boy. I let Dominic and Jess survive, even with their disgusting genetic mutations," he spits out.

Dominic tenses up...and amazingly doesn't say anything.

Silas continues. "If I wanted to, I could have Jonah dispatch a group of men to kill Jess, Allison, and the child. They could make it an accident. No one here would question it too much. I'll tell them it was God's will. They believe what I want them to believe."

I shouldn't have left Jess's side. I can't protect her if we're separated.

"Is this the type of leader you want to be? You want to rule out of fear and oppression—by twisting your religion to suit your needs?

From what I've heard about your grandfather, this isn't the type of community he would want," I say in a frustrated whisper.

His eyes dart to the knife as he responds, "My grandfather would want Veritas to remain strong. I'm doing everything I can to further that vision and provide a safe home for everyone who lives here."

Dominic sits up straighter in his chair. "I'll agree to lead the mission for you. We'll go to Potentia to gather the equipment, and I will bring it back and personally set it up and train your team how to operate it to its fullest capacity," he says, voice lower.

I'm not letting us get separated again. There's no guarantee that all of us will come back together again.

"The rest of our group will be coming with us. We're not leaving them behind in the hopes that you'll maintain your word and protect them. You've already proven that you can't do that," I say.

Silas turns his chair to look out the window. Almost absentmindedly, he grabs his knife off one of the cabinets. He rubs the handle where the blood spot is and tests the blade. A small red line appears on his finger where he cuts himself.

Slowly, he rotates the chair back around, still playing with his knife.

"They may travel with you, along with my own men to ensure you don't attempt to run away without upholding your end of the bargain. You leave tomorrow morning."

I breathe a sigh of relief. We'll all be together.

Silas redirects his attention to my brother. "And Dominic?"

"Yes?" Dominic responds as he stands up from his chair, sensing the end of our impromptu meeting.

"You will no longer be leading the mission," Silas says. "Elliot will."

"What? Why?" Dominic asks, uttering the same internal questions I'm having about the change in plan.

I carefully control my facial expression. Can I step up and take on this responsibility? I'd at least do a better job than Dominic or anyone else here.

"You're too unstable right now, Dominic, and not suited to lead. You will go to assist Elliot once you're in Potentia, but I can't place my men under your command as long as you're in this state."

"But—" Dominic starts.

Silas cuts him off with an impatient gesture of his hand. "That's my compromise for allowing the rest of your group to join you. If you don't like my terms, we can see what a few weeks in custody will do to change your mind."

I tug on Dominic's arm. "Let's leave."

He snaps his head around.

"Now isn't the time. It's time to go, Dominic," I say, hoping he won't argue and make our situation worse.

He yanks his arm away and pushes through the door in an angry sulk.

"He's your responsibility now," Silas calls out as I exit his office.

CHAPTER TWENTY-THREE

I follow behind Dominic, keeping my distance. With his head down the entire time, he shuffles back to his room, closing his door.

I knock. When his door doesn't open, I knock again—harder—and wait.

The door slowly creaks open. I grab it and force it open the rest of the way. Angry tears fall down Dominic's face. He's not even trying to hide or wipe them away. The only other time I saw him cry was right before we fled Potentia when the infection started.

"Who am I?" he asks, voice barely audible.

I sit down next to him, feeling a strong sense of déjà vu.

"What are you talking about?"

"My whole life, I've believed that my genetic engineering made me a superior individual, so I could contribute positively to society as much as possible. I was born, predestined to do great things. One day, I knew I would have my own children and their genetics would push them to be even better. I was supposed to be a leader of our society." He laughs bitterly. "Now, who am I?" He repeats his earlier question. "None of that's relevant anymore."

"Life hasn't exactly worked out the way either of us planned, has it?" I ask, hating him even more for forcing me to comfort him. His instability threatens all of us.

"This infection and destruction of society have worked out a lot better for you, little brother," he mutters.

I rub my forehead and try to figure out what to say. For the most part, I've benefited substantially from the collapse of the social hierarchy. How do I comfort someone who pushed me down my entire life and is now so upset that he's lost his presumed superiority? Does someone like him even deserve to be comforted?

The desperation in his eyes reminds me of a hurt, wild animal. You can't safely help a wild animal. It won't understand what you're doing and could end up lashing out. Sometimes, it's best to put them out of their misery.

If Mother were here, she would be so disappointed in me. No matter what Dominic had done in the past, she always wanted us to act like true brothers. After what he did to Jess, I can't do that.

I let out a deep breath and squeeze Dominic's shoulder, pretending to care. Whether I like it or not, he's coming back with us to Potentia, and if he remains so unhinged, someone is going to get hurt—maybe even killed.

"Your life isn't over yet, Dominic. There's still plenty of time for you to discover your true purpose. Not the one you think you were born or predestined for, but the one that you choose."

His wide eyes scan my face. "Do you think that?"

"I do," I say, omitting the fact that I think his actions have damned him. There's no forgiving him anymore—no coming back from the atrocities he's committed.

Dominic continues to search my expression intently. I maintain his gaze, hoping I'm not as much of an open book anymore.

He lets out a deep breath.

"We're leaving tomorrow morning, and I need you to be well prepared and rested," I continue. "I don't know who all Silas is sending with us, but I suspect we'll be going with his most loyal followers. If we're going to stay a step ahead of them, you're going to need to be at your best."

"Is that an order?"

My tone softens. "No, Dominic. It's a request."

"I'll be ready in the morning. I won't get into any trouble until then. You can go."

I leave my brother, and without thinking of where I'm going, I walk to the other side of the compound. Even though there's a lot to do, I need to tell Jess what's going on.

I knock lightly on their door, hoping she's in there.

When she opens it, I enter the living area and close the door behind me. Keeping my voice low, I say, "We're leaving tomorrow morning to go back to Potentia to retrieve the technology."

"You're leaving so soon?"

"Jess, we're leaving tomorrow. All of us are going on the mission."

Her body relaxes slightly. "Even Allison and Josie?"

"I'm not letting us get separated."

Though she seemed relieved that I'm not leaving her tomorrow, there is still this film of tension radiating off of her. I want to ease her mind and help her relax. There's no reason why both of us should worry so much.

I grab her hand and squeeze. "It'll all work out. We'll get them the technology and Dominic will show them how to use it. Once we're done with that, we don't have to stay anymore. We can go away."

She laughs humorlessly. "Where would we go?"

I let out a deep breath and shrug. "We have time to figure that out."

"Do you think we should give them that technology? Do you trust them?" Her eyes skim my face, reading my expression.

"Not at all," I say.

She lets go of my hand and sits down on the couch. "Then why would you give it to them?" she asks in a frustrated whisper. "Haven't you seen what they're capable of?"

I sit next to her, placing one hand on the top of her thigh. "We don't have a choice, Jess."

"There's always a choice," she fires back.

I look away for a moment. "Not one I was willing to accept."

She lightly places her hand on my chin and turns me to face her. "What did they threaten?"

I shake my head, not wanting to worry her anymore.

She narrows her eyes.

"Who did they threaten?"

Whatever she sees in my expression is answer enough for her. She drops her hand and stares angrily at the floor. I remove my hand from her thigh.

"Why is everybody so terrible? How come every place we go, people are trying to harm us? It doesn't make sense. We're all wired the same, yet you don't see me running around attacking anyone who is different."

There's no benefit from this chain of thought. We can't do anything to change human nature.

"I need to go gather up supplies and the crew. Please stay safe today."

"You be careful, too. I can't wait to get out of here," she says and lets out a deep breath. "If you can, please come say good night before you go to bed."

After a long day of getting everything ready for tomorrow, I walk through the dark, quiet hallways. Everyone has long gone to sleep and I want to do the same. There's only one last thing to do.

Careful not to wake Josie, I lightly knock on Allison and Jess's door.

"Who's there?" Jess asks in a sleepy voice.

"It's me, Elliot."

The dead bolt clicks back out and she opens the door. Her hair is up in a messy bun, but she's still alert as she scans my face.

"What took you so long?" she asks as she gestures for me to come into their suite.

"I wanted to say good night." Suddenly, I feel guilty for waking her so I could see her face again, even though she requested it. "I'm sorry to wake you."

She covers her mouth as she tries to hide her yawn. When she recovers, she chuckles lightly. "That's fine. I'm glad you did. I asked you to."

"You should go back to bed. Silas has instructed his men to get all of the supplies ready by morning, but we still have a long day tomorrow." I pause. "We're going to have a lot of long days coming up."

Wordlessly, she nods.

I kiss her forehead and stand up from the couch. My hand is reaching for the door when her voice stops me.

"It's late. You don't have to go tonight."

I slowly turn back around. "Are you sure? It's only a short walk back."

Instead of replying, she opens the door to her room and gestures for me to join her.

I hesitate and stay by the front door.

"Are you coming?" she asks.

I walk across the living area and peek into her room. Her bed isn't as big as the one we shared at Matt's parents' vacation home, but the two of us will fit if we're close enough. I smile, but the grin leaves at the thought of what Dominic did to her.

Jess stares at me in her doorway, indecision covering her features.

"I can leave, Jess," I say. "I don't want you to do anything that makes you uncomfortable."

She lets out a deep breath and relaxes her expression. "I want you to stay."

I remain in the doorway.

"Please," she whispers.

Making up my mind, I close the door and walk over to her. She smiles tenderly and rubs my chin.

Her guard is down and she lets me in. Past the fear and apprehension, desire fights its way to the surface. I pause, waiting to follow her lead.

She bites her lip and raises her eyebrows in invitation.

I turn off the lights and take it. Our lips touch tentatively, both of us trying to navigate this new change in our relationship. We're resetting the boundaries, testing to see if we can get past my brother's abuse.

Jess lets out a small moan and rubs one of her hands through my hair, with the other resting firmly against my chest.

I push her back against the wall and take off my shirt. I pull hers up and she leans back to let me finish. The AC chills my skin initially, but the heat of her body quickly warms me back up.

My hands wander down her back, marveling at how amazing she feels. I pick her up and lay her on the bed. Staying on top of her, I nudge her head back and kiss her neck.

Her entire body tenses.

"What ha—" I back off and sit next to her.

"I'm sorry, Elliot," Jess cries out. "I can't."

She sits up and throws her head in her hands as she shakes with suppressed sobbing.

Tentatively, I rub her bare back. She freezes.

I curse myself for moving too quickly. Just because I'm ready for something doesn't mean she is.

"It's okay. We don't have to do anything. I'll be happy to lie here with you and hold you."

In the darkness, I can't see anything but the basic motions of her body.

"I'm sorry," she repeats.

"You have absolutely nothing to apologize for."

Continuing to face me, she lies back down. I place one hand on her cheek and use my thumb to gently wipe her tears away.

"It's not that I don't want to, Elliot. I promise I do. It's..." She hiccups. "I'm not here with you anymore. I'm back with him. It's not you touching me. It's him."

He should have no place in our relationship, yet here he is again, slinking back in.

"I'll be right back," I say.

I get out of bed and walk toward the door.

"Where are—"

I flip the light switch and the darkness evaporates from the room. Callie startles on the floor and moans as she readjusts to go back to sleep.

"It's worse in the dark, isn't it?" I ask as I get back into bed.

Jess nods, her face blotchy from her recent tears.

"We can keep the light on all night if it makes it better for you."

"How are we going to sleep?" she asks.

"We'll close our eyes. And if you wake up, you'll be able to see that I'm here with you. You won't wake up wondering."

"You don't mind?"

I push an escaped strand of long, curly hair behind her ear. "As long as I'm with you, I couldn't care less about the light."

She holds my hand and squeezes it.

"I still don't know if I can yet," she mutters.

"Come here, Jess," I say.

She scoots closer, and I bring her to my chest, breathing in the scent of her.

I hold her and promise, "Everything is going to be okay."

Her hand rests across my back, keeping me close to her. As time passes, her body relaxes and becomes a steady warmth against mine. Without her shirt to hide her stomach, it protrudes slightly more than it used to.

I stare down at it, wondering what kind of future I can promise the child.

Even though I should go to sleep soon, I fight to stay awake. I've wanted to hold her like this for so long, and I finally can. I'm not entirely sure what the future holds for us. We're going to be traveling with a large group, and there's no guarantee of any sort of privacy. I'll gladly sacrifice sleep for this.

Though her breathing has been slowing down, it suddenly picks back up. Her heart beats quickly against my chest.

I blink at the attack of the light.

"Jess?"

She lets out a quick intake of breath. "I need this. I need you."

Jess places my hand on her heart, a reminder of our first night together when she did the same thing. "Why?"

"I need to remember what it's like when it's a good thing."

I shift back, dangerously close to the edge of the bed.

"It doesn't have to be tonight," I respond.

She smiles ruefully. "You can't promise there will be another opportunity. We're going back into dangerous territory. If anything happens—"

"Nothing's going to happen," I automatically say.

"Please," she whispers and grabs my hand.

As always, she overrides any objections I have. If there's anything I can do for her, I'm going to do it.

I stare into her eyes, waiting for her to confirm this is what she wants. She nods and I rotate over her and cup her face.

Right before our lips touch, she says, "I think..."

I pull back. "What do you need from me?"

"Let me control the pace. Is that okay?" She bites her lip again in apprehension.

"Whatever you need from me, I'll do it. If you want to stop, we'll stop. If you want to keep going, that's in your control."

She lets out another deep breath and pushes me back so I'm on my back. Leaning over, she lets her hair down and it tickles my chest.

"I love you," she says.

I tuck her hair behind her ear to see her face clearly. "I know you do."

"Be gentle."

"Jess, I'll be anything you want me to be. Talk to me and let me know how it is for you, okay? We can stop at any time. You don't have to do anything you don't want to. You're in absolute, complete control."

She closes the gap between us.

A knock breaks through my sleep and brings me back to reality.

"It's time to wake up," Allison calls out as the door opens.

Jess is a steady pressure in my arms, both of us facing the wall opposite the door.

I turn my head to find Allison smirking with Josie in her arms, staring happily down at us.

Jess moans and rubs her face. "What time is it?"

"Late night?" she asks, still unable to get rid of the knowing smile on her face.

Keeping the sheets above her chest, Jess asks again, "What time is it?"

"It's a bit after six. Dominic's already been here to make sure we were awake."

I jerk upward, exposing my scar. Is he in the living room?

"I didn't know you were here, Elliot, so he's off trying to find you," Allison answers my unspoken question.

Beside me, Jess loosens her firm grip on the sheets and I lie back down.

"All of us need to finish packing up the necessities. Dominic said we're expected to leave by eight."

"Uh..." I mutter and gesture toward the blanket that's keeping us decent.

Allison laughs and closes the door behind her.

I start to get out of the bed, but Jess's hand on my chest stops me.

"I never thought I would willingly go back to Potentia," she says so quietly I almost miss it.

I face her, trying to figure out what the best response is. I don't want to promise her something I can't follow through on. At the same time, I can't downplay the danger of what we're getting into. She'll see right through the lie.

Her hand rubs down my chest.

"I know we have to go soon, but do you think we have time..."

Jess's hand goes lower, and I jerk in surprise as it passes my stomach. "Jess?"

"I don't know when we'll get another chance." She drops her eyes. "I want this with you again. When we get back there, I want to have as many memories with you as possible to help overshadow all the rest."

I focus all my energy on thinking coherently.

"Is this what you want? Not something you think you should do, but something you want?" I ask.

"Yes."

"Then I'm all yours."

CHAPTER TWENTY-FOUR

Wanting to get one last moment of peace before whatever the future will bring, we go to the roof to watch the sun rise.

Jess walks over to the edge and leans forward to rest against the boundary. The breeze flirts with her hair and moves it gently in the wind.

I place my arm around her. She shifts her weight and leans into my body, her head resting against my chest. As we watch the sun rise, she lightly hums under her breath. The light overcomes some of night's shadows.

No matter what the future holds, we'll face our demons together. I don't need a religious ceremony to confirm what I already know.

"Are you ready?" she asks.

I let out a deep breath. All of the pressure of trying to fit in here goes out. When I breathe in, the space that's left behind is taken up with the responsibility of leading the group back to Potentia.

"Yes," I say. "Let's go get one last good meal."

My stomach rumbles in reaction. She playfully pokes my side. "Sounds like you need one."

I smile at her, amazed at how quickly we fit back together. I can make it alone and I'm strong enough to do it—and she's able to as well—but we're so much better together.

We rejoin the rest of the compound, though their stares don't bother me as much anymore. I'll be leaving them all soon. When we first got here, Isaac said this place wasn't for everyone and he was right. I'm not ashamed that I don't fit in here.

Once the fog lifted and I saw this place for what it truly is, I had no reason to want to stay anymore. It's another offspring of the territories with some different characteristics, though deep down, the motive is still the same: power.

In line, I request pancakes as a reminder of my first meal here. Jess gets the same, and we go to our table in the corner of the room.

We eat in silence, my thoughts on what's coming—what it means to go back to Potentia. When I'm almost done with my meal, there's a tentative tap on my shoulder. I turn away from my breakfast to find Leah staring at me in a panic.

"You're leaving?"

Swallowing my bite, I nod.

"When?"

"In about twenty minutes," I say.

She sits down to my left, fighting back emotion. I pretend not to notice it.

"Why didn't you tell me sooner?"

I pat her hand. "We haven't had much time," I say, neglecting the real reasons why I didn't ask her to come.

"We'll be back," Jess offers from my other side.

"I can come with you. You know I'm reliable and could help," Leah says, her watery eyes wide with hope.

I want to agree and let her come with us. No matter what she's done, I can trust her to have our backs if the time comes and we have to make our move.

I sigh. It's not fair to bring her into danger. I can't make another innocent person a casualty of my battles, especially one who has feelings for me I can't return.

"No, Leah, you need to stay here," I say. "It's not safe for you to come with us."

She puffs her chin out. "But you're bringing her, aren't you?" She gestures toward Jess sharply.

Jess's hand freezes as she's about to take another bite of her meal. Slowly, she puts her fork down and gives Leah all of her attention.

"It's not safe for her here. You know that," I whisper, trying to keep anyone else from hearing me. We've had enough incidents in the Mess Hall already. No need to add another one to that list.

Tears well up again. "I don't want you to leave. This is all my fault for opening my big mouth. That's what started all of this, isn't it?"

I open and close my mouth as I struggle to find the right words. While she was the catalyst, she isn't necessarily what caused this situation. There's an infection that courses through the population of Veritas's humanity. It cuts deeper than the virus that turned countless people into the Letum. How do I articulate that to her?

"This was going to happen regardless," Jess answers for me. "Our secret wasn't going to keep forever."

"You don't blame me?" she asks, nearly begging for forgiveness.

"No, I don't. Eventually, the truth was going to get out about how some of us are Planned. It was only a matter of time," I say.

She wipes an escaped tear away. "I wish I could come and help."

"You can still help, Leah," I mutter, once again keeping my voice down to avoid the prying ears.

"How?" she asks, sitting up straighter.

"It's not stable here, and I'm worried about how much things are going to change when we come back," I say.

She leans closer and whispers, "What do you want me to do?"

"I need you to be my eyes and ears here while I'm gone. Watch Silas and whoever he trusts and speaks with the most."

Jess tilts her head at my words but gives no other indication that she's listening.

Leah, with the rebellious glint again, asks, "What are you going to do?"

I exhale a sharp breath and keep my voice low. "When we come back, I'm going to need your help to change the status quo—it's not sustainable."

"I'll do my best. I promise. They never gave you a chance. That's not right," she says as she peeks around to make sure no one else is listening.

"I'll be back," I assure her.

Almost knocking over the rest of my milk, she pulls me into a fierce hug. Before I can react, she leaves without another word, wiping her eyes as she goes.

I watch her walk away, feeling guilty for leaving her, especially since I'm taking Thomas with me. She'll have to be fine without us.

"Ready?" Jess asks, breaking my attention away from Leah's exit.

I smile at Jess, place one arm around her shoulder, and kiss her forehead. "As long as you're with me."

I open the door and take in a deep breath of the fresh air. About a hundred yards ahead of us, the rest of the group is waiting by the rusted trucks. I close my arms together to fight off some of the morning's chill. It won't be long now before this mild autumn turns into winter.

All of the trees are preparing for the shift in seasons, turning their leaves a beautiful array of oranges and yellows, soon to turn the same monotonous brown when they die.

I let out a sigh and take a step forward. When there's no movement behind me, I ask, "You coming?"

There's a small hesitation before her footsteps follow behind me. I wait for her to catch up so we can walk alongside each other.

"You didn't want Leah to come with us because she cares deeply about you, right?" Jess asks, voice even and controlled.

My step hitches, but I keep walking forward. "There's that." I rub my thumb on my freshly shaven chin. "More importantly, she's also the only one I can trust who won't lie to me here."

Jess's eyebrow flicks upward.

Feeling like I have to elaborate, I keep talking. "I know she has a big mouth sometimes, but she means well and wouldn't intentionally do anything to harm us." I shake my head. "I don't trust anyone else at this place."

I smile weakly at her and hasten my steps. We're still about fifty yards away, and Dominic is waving at us impatiently.

"You've changed, Elliot," Jess responds quietly.

I slowly turn to face her, afraid of what I might see in her expression. She pushes her escaped hair behind her ear, and there's a sad smile on her lips.

"You've come a long way from when I first met you," she says.

I'm unable to maintain eye contact. "I've watched almost everyone I've cared about die, and I've killed a man."

Jess steps closer and brushes my hair across my forehead, waiting for me to look at her again. When I finally do, she says, "That's not what I'm talking about."

"What do you mean then?" I ask.

Her eyes search my face. I'm not sure what she's looking for.

"You've found the strength to get through it all." She bites her bottom lip in thought. "I think you've found yourself. Don't forget who you are."

She places her hand on my chest to get me to stop moving. Almost tentatively, she stands up on her tiptoes and waits for me to kiss her. I pull her in and take what comfort she can offer me.

When our lips break apart, she leans her forehead to mine and whispers, "Thank for you waiting for me to come back."

I squeeze her hand and let out a deep breath at the sound of Dominic calling us over to him. Without saying anything else, the two of us walk—hand in hand—toward the starting location of our next journey together.

"Took your time this morning," Dominic mutters, though there is no real malice in his voice.

"We've a strict schedule that I expect everyone to follow. There's no need for us to be away from our families longer than necessary," an unwelcome voice calls out.

I stifle an internal groan at the sight of Jonah's fake smile.

"You're coming, too?" I ask in a higher pitch that gives away my surprise. I can't believe Silas would let him leave his side.

"Of course. I'm the only person Silas can trust to supervise the mission to make sure it goes smoothly and doesn't take any detours," Jonah replies. He puffs out his small chest in self-importance. "I'm in charge of this trip. Don't forget that."

He pats my shoulder. "Are you?" Jonah turns his back and addresses the group. "This is probably the most important trip we've gone on in our lifetime. If this goes well, we'll bring back the technology to ensure the protection of Veritas and our people."

At the sound of his voice, Josie lets out a loud cry in protest. Allison hunches over and tries to silence her.

"If this trip is so important, why are we bringing them?" Isaac asks, clearly not wanting to be here, but I requested it. I want to make things right with him. That's only going to happen if I can get him out of the compound and open his eyes to how things really are.

Dominic glares at Isaac, but it doesn't contain any of his previous menace. Isaac, noticing this, smiles at my brother and raises his eyebrow in an open invitation to say something.

"Enough," I say in warning. No matter how lost Dominic may be, I know my purpose. I glare at Isaac, thankful that I'm taller and stronger than he is.

Callie, sensing the change in atmosphere, lays her ears back and steps closer to Jess.

Isaac places his hands in the air in a placating manner. "It's a fair question. Bringing a baby, a new mother, and a pregnant woman isn't exactly an ideal situation for an important mission."

"We all know about the territories from living there, not from some skewed lesson in school," I say, appreciating the irony that that's how we first learned about Veritas, though we called it something different.

"Give it a rest, Isaac," Leah calls out. "It's not his fault your brother-in-law attacked him."

Leah struts toward us, dressed in the same casual pants and shirt as everyone else. She's carrying a small bag, as if she thinks she's coming with us. Her lips are in a tight smirk, eyes lit up in that same mischievous glint I've seen so many times before. This time, however, I don't find it amusing.

I ask, "What are you doing here?"

She drops her gaze.

Jonah answers for her. "She requested to join us and I saw no reason to deny her. Can you?"

He smirks and winks, waiting on my response.

I bite my tongue and gesture to the trucks, wanting to dispel some of the tension and move on. The sooner we get going, the sooner we'll be done.

"Let's load up," I say.

The trucks are older with rust covering the hoods. They were made without solar power and run on gasoline, like the car Andrew and Chris's parents drove when they died.

In the bed of the trucks, all of our supplies are smashed together. We have enough food and water to last us all around a month. What takes up most of the space, however, is all the extra fuel. It makes sense—there's not going to be another refueling point as we travel to and from Potentia.

The four of us, with Allison holding her daughter, make our way to the closest truck.

"No, your group will not all ride together," Jonah's voice calls out from behind.

Allison snaps around. "Why not?"

"It's an order from Silas," Jonah says.

"He doesn't trust us," Jess whispers. "He wants us separated."

Instinctively, I put my arm around Jess's waist. I'm not letting that happen. Leah watches this with a slight frown.

"I'll go with Allison and Josie and you and Jess can go in the other truck," Dominic mutters.

Jonah rubs his gun and winks at me. I sigh. Silas must've given that instruction because he was worried we would try to overtake one of the trucks if we were all together.

That's not where we would be a threat, however. None of us ever learned how to drive a car manually. Even at my grandparents' cabin, the mode of transportation they relied on most was solar powered.

Jess leans in and mutters in my ear. "Let it go. This isn't where we make our stand."

I nod tensely. "Very well. Let's head out."

Leah eyes me expectantly and gestures toward our truck. Being stuck in a small space with the two of them is a horrible idea.

I shake my head and turn my back on her, but not before watching her get into the truck with Allison and Dominic, her shoulders slumped.

"Come on, Callie," Jess calls and the dog jumps into the truck full of excitement.

Thomas, another one of my recruits, chuckles at Callie's joy. "Has she ever ridden in a truck before?"

"None of us have," Jess responds, her dry tone silencing Thomas.

Once we're all loaded, Thomas puts his key in the ignition and it roars to life, much louder than the solar-powered vehicles the territories produced.

I put my hand on Jess's thigh and she leans her head against my shoulder. I close my eyes in disbelief at how much everything has changed—yet again. When I open them, the compound is fading in the distance as we head toward Potentia.

We're going back.

ABOUT THE AUTHOR

Originally from Plano, Texas, Robin is a graduate of Kansas State University and currently lives in Tulsa, Oklahoma with her dog, Juno, cat, Cat, and plenty of bottles of wine. Dispersion is the second novel in a three-part series that explores the provocative and divisive theory of genetic planning.

For more information on Robin and her upcoming projects, visit her website at www.robinberkstresser.com.

www.ingramcontent.com/pod-product-compliance
Lightning Source LLC
Chambersburg PA
CBHW060920250626
47159CB00008B/3091